AIDAN TRUHEN

SEVEN DEMONS

Aidan Truhen lives in London. He worked in commodities of one sort or another until he was thirty, which is an age when a man wants his positive achievements to outnumber his acquittals. He's trying to reinvent himself as a writer. We'll see how it goes.

Also by Aidan Truhen

The Price You Pay

SEVEN DEMONS

SEVEN DEMONS

Aidan Truhen

Vintage Crime/Black Lizard

Vintage Books

A Division of Penguin Random House LLC

New York

FIRST VINTAGE CRIME / BLACK LIZARD EDITION, MAY 2021

Library of Congress Cataloging-in-Publication Data
Names: Truhen, Aidan, author.
Title: Seven demons / Aidan Truhen.
Description: First Vintage Crime / Black Lizard edition. |
New York : Vintage Crime / Black Lizard, 2021.
Identifiers: LCCN 2020045429 (print) | LCCN 2020045430 (ebook) |
ISBN 9780593311622 (paperback) | ISBN 9780593311639 (ebook)
Subjects: LCSH: Criminals—Fiction. | Bank robberies—Fiction. |
GSAFD: Suspense fiction.
Classification: LCC PR6120.R84 S48 2021 (print) |
LCC PR6120.R84 (ebook) | DDC 823/.92—dc23
LC record available at https://lccn.loc.gov/2020045429
LC ebook record available at https://lccn.loc.gov/2020045430

**Vintage Crime / Black Lizard Trade Paperback
ISBN: 978-0-593-31162-2
eBook ISBN: 978-0-593-31163-9**

www.vintagebooks.com

Printed in the United States of America
10 9 8 7 6 5 4 3 2 1

When I was young, I believed in three things: Marxism, the redemptive power of cinema, and dynamite. Now I just believe in dynamite.

—Sergio Leone

This book is dedicated to everyone who still believes in more than that. You people are idiots, and if we didn't have you, we'd all be even more screwed than we are.

SEVEN DEMONS

THE FIRST I KNEW IT WAS ALL GOING WRONG was when Evil Hansel came running out of a pastry shop and stabbed me in the leg, and that was really just the best thing that happened that day. If you do not get stabbed in the leg by a nine-year-old once every so often, then that is nice for you. Hi I'm Jack hi and this story is about me and I am the kind of person who has enemies who know nine-year-olds who will run out of a pastry shop and stab you in the leg, not because they think it is a game but because they are commercially minded fucking psychopaths and that is the world.

Hi.

I did not know that Evil Hansel was called Evil Hansel at that point and indeed it is not his actual name. Evil Hansel was a little *Sound of Music*–looking motherfucker in actual lederhosen and a white frilly shirt and he came out of the pastry shop like he was about to break into song and then he stuck an oyster knife into my thigh so close to the femoral artery that I can still feel it in my sphincter. If someone cuts your wrists, you have quite a long time before the problem is irretrievable. The femoral is like if you are a balloon animal.

Sploosh.

And that's it.

Happily, Evil Hansel is left-handed and I carry my billfold in my right-hand pocket so what the little fuckhead actually stabbed was about a thousand Swiss francs in twenties and fifties, which is totally appropriate because money is your sword and shield here, although I guess in that case Evil Hansel should have stabbed me with a hundred and he did not. He used an oyster knife. I did not have quite enough money in quite the right denominations so the knife did absolutely pierce me in a tender region and I was very unhappy.

Doc said: "Do not touch the knife."

I did not touch the knife because I am not a fucking idiot.

I said: "What the fuck ow you little what the fuck?"

Evil Hansel did not respond to this question. Instead he tried to twist the knife and Volodya the sniper threw him under a car, and I do mean under because Evil Hansel just hunkered down and the chassis went right above him and he ran away.

I said: "What the fuck is wrong with you man, you couldn't aim for the fucking wheels?"

Volodya said Evil Hansel was lighter than he thought he would be.

I said I did not care about if Evil Hansel was lighter than Volodya thought he would be because right now I had about a thousand Swiss francs nailed to my leg with an oyster knife.

Like he just realized he'd left the oven on, Volodya said: "Ah shit, Price."

"What, man?"

"I told you we should not come."

Then I fell over because that is what happens when you leak a bunch of red stuff out of your body onto foreign currency.

I fucking hate Switzerland.

ONE

DOC WHO IS MY NOT-GIRLFRIEND and a global science felon has a dog. The dog is called Tycho and looking at Tycho you would not think he was named for the guy who lost the middle part of his nose in a duel with swords. Tycho is a saluki and that is a tall skinny expensive dog like if Gaultier styled a greyhound for Miley Cyrus. Looking at Tycho you would assume he was gentle and shy and that is true insofar as it is mostly true and things that are mostly true are not true at all. Tycho is gentle and shy but he is also a dog and he will therefore attempt fornication with anything at all. The animal has no discretion and no sense of boundaries. Beneath the elegant exterior of a dog bred for generations by emirs and sheikhs there lurks the heart of a dissolute sex pest, and despite what is undeniable—that Tycho is a sight hound and can see the hairs on a gnat's ass at a hundred paces—it is clear that love or at least savage and inappropriate lust is blind. If he thinks an object is even moderately suited to receiving his organ he will absolutely positively fuck it until one or the other of them is incapable. I have seen Tycho initiate coitus with a salt-baked sea bass and that will be in my head forever.

For. Ever.

It is therefore something of a surprise that Tycho recently refused his affections to the lady dog belonging to a rich old Dutch party called Mrs. Van der Zee but that is what he did and there is no accounting for taste. Looking at Mrs. Van der Zee's dog I would have said there was nothing to object to.

Certainly Marta—this being the name of the lady dog—is a more obvious friend with benefits than two kilos of Michelin-starred fish on a bed of shaved black radish but I am not judgy. Tycho and Marta did not make it and that is that but it is not that for Mrs. Van der Zee. Mrs. Van der Zee takes a dim view. She sees the absence of dog fornication as a slight upon Marta, and any slight upon Marta is a slight upon Mrs. Van der Zee, and one does not slight Mrs. Van der Zee. As a result of the nonfucking by Tycho of Marta there had to be an owner-to-owner meeting in a truth and reconciliation mode at which I was present purely as mediator and it was not a good meeting at all. Mrs. Van der Zee lives in a big place by the sea, and it has gardens and tennis courts and two heated pools and thousands and thousands of deluxe ultra-premium rare tulips.

In fact the whole place smells of sickly tulip stink because Mrs. Van Der Zee chooses to wear a customized perfume made by a guy named Jort. Jort is present at this exciting gathering in a sort of Roman short shorts playsuit. He is from Den Haag and has no body hair whatsoever and I am fairly sure Mrs. Van der Zee keeps him as some sort of quasi-sexual pet. I do not want to know what she does with him and I do not think Jort wishes to talk about it. He works with both ancient wisdom and sophisticated modern techniques to create a unique signature scent experience using whatever you give him, which in this case of course is ultra-premium deluxe rare tulips. I am not a perfume guy but when I was the cardinal of coffee I developed a sensitive nose because if you cannot tell when someone is trying to sell you basic sawdust arabica for Hacienda La Esmeralda, you will get fucked in the civet hole, and this perfume smelled like someone had done that with violet to a perfectly innocent vetiver and then shaken the whole thing with turpentine. It is dis-fucking-gusting and it is all over everything in the house, and when she shakes your hand it goes on you like she's a plague vector and it will not come off your clothes, so I may not have been entirely at the top of my game during this encounter and it did not go ideally well.

Over the salad course, by way of peacemaking, Doc ventured the opinion that the absence of sex between the canine companions may be owed to the fact that their antibodies were not sufficiently complementary, which seemed like a good no-fault explanation to me, but Mrs. Van der Zee recorded around a mouthful of lollo rosso the alternative view that Tycho is a hate-filled canine Communist. Doc said he was not hate filled nor indeed did he, being a dog, possess the necessary cognitive architecture to form political opinions of this kind, and Mrs. Van der Zee audibly concluded that Doc was One Of Those. When Doc requested clarification of what sort of Those this might be, I was unable to prevent Mrs. Van der Zee from explaining that Doc—as evidenced by her lack of belief in dog politics—was a DOINO, or dog owner in name only, or she would know that our furry friends understand more than we think. Doc noted that she might could arrange for Mrs. Van der Zee and her damn dog both to get a virulent and fast-progressing hemorrhagic fever, and I said shush because that is a thing that Doc has done in her life, and ixnay on the lowing-bay ouryay overcay, and Doc said I should ticksay tiay puay ymay sasay, and it was at this tense moment that Tycho chose to initiate vigorous and vocal sex with a Semper Augustus. A Semper Augustus is a kind of tulip whose petals look like marbled steak and which costs ten thousand dollars a bulb.

Also, when a saluki fucks one, it makes a noise like cleaning a window with a squeegee.

———

It was to distract Doc from some kind of precipitate overreaction vis à vis Mrs. Van der Zee that I went to Sharkey and said to find us a project.

"Hi Sharkey it's me Jack!"

"Holy FUCK—"

"Sharkey! Wash your mouth out with your bad language."

"Fuck, Jack, you scared the shit out of me no one is supposed to be in here right now."

"Sharkey. We are professional men. Let us profess as men do."

". . . Jesus fuck okay sit the fuck down."

I sit.

Sharkey says: "(Fuck.)"

Sharkey is a middleman. Globally speaking, Sharkey is The Middleman. He is an unprepossessing sort of asshole with a girlfriend called Crystal, which is pronounced like the champagne, although I know for a fact that her real name is Isabel and she comes from a town on the riviera with only one cow. I like Crystal. She is just trying to get along is what. I do not like Sharkey he is a dick. I would much prefer to deal with Crystal but that is business for you, quite often you have to deal with the dick rather than the Crystal.

Sharkey is not a small guy and in the heat he smells strongly of folded male groin. Heat is all you get in southern Europe in the summertime anymore because: have you heard? There is a climate crisis. Right now this means not only is the world dying but also too there's a lot of ambient groin up in my olfactory. So fuck you very much to the petrochemical industry once for the planet and once for that.

I say: "The Demons are open for business give us business."

Sharkey says: "Jack no one is looking for your kind of trouble right now."

"That is why they pay you the big bucks Sharkey you got instincts you got what they say you got a nose—"

(He cannot possibly have an actual nose, he would die of himself.)

"Jack I got a nose I don't got like Vulcan telepathy force powers I cannot—"

"O shit Charlie would kill you right here Sharkey."

"What?"

"Vulcan force powers?"

"What?"

"Never mind I will not explain it to you Sharkey the only possible way for you to learn is if someone kills you with a cruet. Proceed."

"You got weird people Jack. Dangerous and weird."

"They are individuals Sharkey and exemplary professionals in their own fields."

"That's your problem. Fred was dull and people like that in contractors Jack. It makes them happy."

"You are saying no one wants international assassins to be fun at parties."

"They do not want them to come to their parties in the first place. Not even their families really want that, in case they get in a disagreement and someone has to be buried under a patio."

". . . I would not do that it is fucking suburban."

"But they don't know that! Like if you were Fred I would know the cruet thing was a gag man but with you with your Demons I am not sure."

Actually I am sympathetic to this position because I also am just a person who is trying to get along in the world, but regrettably last year there was a kind of a what you would call a misunderstanding, except that there was no actual misunderstanding per se, more like assumptions of questionable value were made by certain parties, and the consequences of those assumptions were really surprising to actually just about everyone involved, and several of those people did not come by their surprise in positive or sustainable ways. We shall call those people the bad guys and they are not alive anymore.

The way it happened was I was conducting my business and getting on with being a citizen, and then Sean Harper— hereinafter known as item 22 for reasons which will become clear—but anyway Sean got all up in my face about a murder that he went and committed in my building. He thereby kicked off this whole convoluted shebang we already know about, and I'm not going to go through the details except to say that it became ultimately a perceptual issue, which flat out had to be addressed for everyone's sake, because that kind of thing just hangs around forever if you don't get in there and deal.

In consequence of the measured and necessary steps I had to take to secure my ongoing well-being during that difficult time, I am no longer the owner-operator of a bespoke commodity concern distributing and selling the branded and locally sourced cocaine which was once known as the Pale Peruvian Stallion. That is a tragedy for everyone's leisure time but there you go. I have a new role as CEO of a global criminal enterprise with deep roots in the community and a justified reputation for unparalleled savagery. I manage five deeply alarming people who are my team, including the Doc, who basically is walking science with whom I am in a Nietzschean and highly charged sexual relationship; Volodya, who is himself a former boss of this same outfit but who had retired and was living off the fat of the land or possibly the fat of his neighbors, we do not ask, in a romantic little shack somewhere up above the

Arctic Circle; Rex, whose brother I accidentally got killed and who is largely focused on exploding things and believes we are a deep-cover spy team operating to save democracy from someone I have never identified but Rex probably assumes is either an alien or a lizard or French; Charlie, who is a digital artist and has only ever murdered one person but really seems down with the whole lifestyle; and Lucille, who is a large guy wearing a suit made of sharp edges whose ability to process the world in a rational fashion I irretrievably compromised with a psychotropic drug overdose in order to turn him into a human booby trap for a barbecue-obsessed illegal fight champion. Presently I also hold the voting proxy of my predecessor, Fred the Head, although Fred is exploring a new career as an actual head on a stick or more properly a bleached skull and therefore does not talk much or have opinions except insofar as sometimes when you look at him you can see that he really does not think much of his present situation and I am fine with that.

Fred was an asshole.

So I am sympathetic and above all I am a professional so I say:

"Well okay that is legit I guess Sharkey but that is my point is that our next job will go off in total silence." Which I absolutely intend that it will. And Sharkey says:

"Silence?"

"Total silence. No one will ever know we were there."

"How silent are we talking?"

"Silent silent."

"Yeah but there is silent like a silencer, which is kind of a whoop whoop noise, and there is silent like silent, like—"

"Silent silent. Like below the thermocline."

"The—thermo—what—Jack I don't know what that is."

"Like a submarine for fuck's sake Sharkey did you never watch *Das Boot*?"

"I'm claustrophobic Jack I don't watch movies except Westerns and not even those if they spend too much time in the saloon. Mostly I watch those nature shows."

"I did not know that."

"We all got our crosses man."

"Yeah I guess. Okay well we're going to do our next thing in total silence like a gliding majestic whale."

"Whales make a surprising amount of noise Jack like they go WHOOMMMNAAAARP to one another right and that is—"

"Sharkey would you get on board with this please? We are going to do this like a real quiet whale, maybe shy maybe even mute."

"That would be a serious fucking evolutionary problem for an animal that navigates by sonar Jack."

"So this will be a short-lived metaphorical whale, man, but the silence will be forever."

"I dunno Jack—"

"They are bored Sharkey."

". . . Bored?"

"Yes Sharkey the Demons are bored."

I let him consider that in its fullness. Corporate boredom is just what happens and that is fine when your coworkers are typists or software engineers or even sheep herders but it is not fine when their skill sets revolve around germ war and artisanal murderings and making things explode. Then it is not a good thing for anyone.

"All right Jack I will look into it."

"That is fine Sharkey. Do your thing and we will do ours. If we crime it, they will come."

And I am right.

Incoming call, Poltergeist Secure VoIP: accept? y/n

(Poltergeist is this whole electronic thing that happens in Iceland it is like a concierge service for the digitally liberated societal and legal nonconformist, which is to say criminals of all stripes but also revolutionaries and freedom fighters and so. It is like the spy equivalent of the Apple Store or Google if they were based in nuclear-proof cells hollowed out of the Arctic ice and staffed by ice kobolds with computer science magic coming out of their ass. They are obsessed with client privacy and digital hygge and some variation of Scandawooj libertarian communism I do not comprehend because I do not have husky semen in my blood. Helluva nice people do not under any circumstances piss them off.)

Accept y/n?

y

(Ping and the little light goes green.)

"Hi it's Jack."

"Jack Price."

"Yes that is me hello."

"I wish you to rob a bank."

"I would LOVE to rob a bank. I have not done that it is a classic."

". . . Mr. Sharkey suggests that we speak."

"We are in fact doing that now."

"I should like to meet in person. I will wear a gray suit Mr. Price. I am of ordinary height. I am told I appear intense."

"That's nice for you I guess, are you—I mean do you also put that on Tinder because—"

"Mr. Price. You should now tell me how I will recognize you."

"We are in touch Mr.—"

". . ."

"We are in touch Mr. Client we are now talking as men do. I figured I'd book a table and like they would bring you over and I'd do like a cool thing with one hand, 'please do sit Mr. Client,' right, and then we'd just make our deal. But now I sense that is not where you were going with this."

"It is not."

"You're thinking all yellow chalk and Gauloises I guess, and that is fine but I have to tell you sign and countersign for a meeting where you are in phone contact with the principal, that is kind of more obvious than actually just calling out a person's name to the maître is all. Like I could wear a flower and carry a copy of, I don't know, like *Butterfly Sex Quarterly*? There is a place down the street which sells really fucking outré magazines, there is one for people who collect only model trains made in India before partition. Can you believe that is a thing? So I can absolutely do that but if I do that and someone is there, let us say doing a vice bust or whatever, doing something that is in no way like what we are doing, they will pay close fucking attention Mr. Client, and that is not to our advantage at all. And that is before we discuss the other diners Mr. Client, they also might be the kinds of person who watch for that shit who are even a little bit attracted to it that would depend on where we meet. I was going to pick that sports club on the marina. I'm guessing you can do that."

". . . I can."

"Yeah what I thought so—"

"That will be fine. Until then Mr. Price."

". . ."

". . ."

". . ."

"Are you still there Mr. Price?"

". . . Yes?"

"Why?"

"I honestly have no idea it just seemed rude to put down the phone."

(Click.)

What I could have done is I could have traced Mr. Client after the meeting. I did not because if you get caught doing that, people think you are not going to deal square and they become antsy and oftentimes they will do something regrettable like try to kill you or set you up later. They think you want to maybe blackmail them or kill them or in some other way you are seeking power over them, and that is inevitably what people in this situation absolutely do not want. Therefore at a certain point in a for-hire criminal enterprise everyone has to accept everyone else's boundaries. Everyone has to decide they do not want to know stuff the other person does not want them to know because knowing that stuff makes you enemies, and you need to be friends or at least like able to put your hand in your pocket while standing in the same elevator without that other person thinking you are going for a knife no not a shiv that is taxonomically inaccurate plus also fuck you.

So that is what I did.

I respected everyone's boundaries.

Yeah I hear ya but you were not there.

The marina restaurant is one of the places with those seats that look real comfy and when you sit it turns out they are harder than stone so the first thing that happens is you go OOF as your ass bounces on the uncomfortable seat and this happens every time. The food is deceptive as well like the fried fish is cold and the ice cream is hot who fucking does that but: business so la la la. Why do these people meet and eat? Because they are human and humans think that if you share food it makes a bond it is mammal shit evolutionary shit and it is bullshit but that is what they do. Oasis comfort zone. Every man's L'Affable is his castle.

This ain't no L'Affable.

Maître fusses over. Fuss and fuss and la and I stick out my hand. Heavy bill in there because that is how you achieve focus in a place like this. Maître takes it like his paw is a vacuum cleaner like SLURP and gone and now we are old friends.

"Hi I am Pierre-Paul Gondorf I am here to meet that gentleman over there here is my credit card this meal will be on me—"

And la la la please come this way sir. I am not Pierre-Paul Gondorf that is a made-up name: I am a criminal and that is how we do.

I sit at my table until the maître d' brings me someone to talk to.

Mr. Client is a slim fella with deep eyes. I don't mean he has bedroom eyes ooo la la and I don't mean he has skull face like you see sometimes a perfectly ordinary person has skull face like a fucking reminder of mortality.

No this guy has eyes that spend way too much time seeing you. Most people, their eyes see you a little and then they skate. Eyes go someplace else then back then someplace else then back it is polite. Try not doing it sometime you will find it is hard and people start to edge away from you. But this guy: his eyes do not travel they just rest and sometimes he is looking at you and sometimes his eyes have not moved but he's seeing something else. Like the guy has a multiplex in his head and you are only one of the screens and not the best one.

Mr. Client sits down (oof) and he says hi and I say hi and we drink sparkling water with ice. I say the fucking seats in this place and he says yes they are by Emmersen and she is overrated. I say I do not know Emmersen and he says I am very wise.

He takes lemon: two fingers and PLINK. Winces as the glass touches his lips. Mr. Client has lips like a baby's all pure and pale and soft and that right there is what you call a tell because until this morning this guy had a mustache and maybe some bit of a beard but like a real fucking pretentious bit of face fur like you would have if you were real into your villain mojo. Right now the guy has a baby face and he is all tender. Fastidious that is the word he is fastidious to the point that it's a thing with him.

Mojo, by the way, in parts of Spain is a tangy red pepper sauce made with bread but that is not the kind Mr. Client is into.

"Good day sir and what do I call you?"

"Mr. Price I feel I have been clear that I do not wish to be known to you."

Got an accent but so does everyone. That just means he hasn't got my accent but what accent it is I don't know. In the modern world Henry Higgins is fucked. Guy with Dutch parents grows up in Dubai learns English from American movies and a French teacher who studied in Canada and BOOM where are you? You're nowhere and don't pretend. That does not matter I am respecting the guy's boundaries I do not care where he comes from.

"Okay I'll just carry on calling you Mr. Client is that okay?"

"Mr. Client will do fine."

"Great. Have the ajiaco it is excellent."

"I will order some for appearances but in fact I will not be eating, Mr. Price."

"O well that is a relief the food here is terrible—"

"It is, but that is of the nature of such truck stops for the world's elite, they pay for exclusivity not substance. In fact I recently had excellent ajiaco in its native setting. It was delicious but one cannot have it every day. It has an adverse effect on the body mass index."

"Straight on the hips I guess."

". . ."

". . ."

". . ."

"So I'm going to rob a bank for you Mr. Client."

"Yes. If we can come to an agreement."

"So what bank?"

"It is a very particular bank."

"Okay."

"It cannot be robbed."

"Cool."

"I wish you to rob it."

"So you said."

"It is the Kircheisen Festung."

"Which branch?"

"I beg your pardon?"

"Obviously there is only one of those and I am kidding, that is bank felony humor."

"Oh. Is it."

"Yep."

"I will leave that part to you."

". . . Okay."

"I am happy to say I possess physical plans for the Kircheisen Festung Mr. Price."

"O you do?"

"Yes. They are—let us say they are probably accurate but not complete. They are four years old and you know what security people are. They tinker. They tinker endlessly and month by month like hoarder ants until their tunnels are thick with the wax of their obsession."

". . . That is a colorful way of putting it Mr. Client."

"I had not noticed. I will provide you with the plans and I will pay you to provide me with specific items from within the vault. That payment will be substantial Mr. Price although I suspect you will find it is the ancillary aspects from which you derive the most profit."

"And what is this item exactly Mr. Client?"

"Ten metal suitcases weighing approximately thirty-two kilograms each. Three hundred and twenty kilograms in total. For these cases and their contents unharmed I will give you three hundred million euros. But the rest of the vault—I do not care. And Mr. Price the contents will be delightful. All the secrets and treasures of the world. Nonetheless I would not have you concerned as to the profitability of the enterprise so I offer you a share in the value of my part of this. And I very specifically do not want anyone else to have those cases."

"So the cases—"

"Are of uncertain value Mr. Price. In brute terms they approach a notional yield of one billion dollars but there are complications. I say this only for orientation, obviously you would not be so crass as to double-cross me before we have even shaken hands."

"I would not double-cross you at all Mr. Client I just like to know what everyone gets out of the deal. It saves misunderstandings later regarding value given especially if prioritization is necessary during an operation."

". . . That is fair."

Mr. Client's eyes go all dark and thoughtful like Mr. Client is seeing the universe. Figure he's a religious leader some kind of deep Catholic thing and people shake when he touches them and try to walk on broken legs, I'm sure that goes well for everyone.

"Mr. Price these cases contain conflict emeralds totaling one and a half million karats. They are of various sizes but generally with few inclusions, so the legitimate market value would be nearly a billion dollars if they were not also from war zones. As things are, they cannot be sold without a laundering process and in fact it is that process to which I object."

"You do?"

"I object very much indeed. The reintroduction of these stones is being done through a false mining project in Egypt to fund an enterprise of which I greatly disapprove. At one time Egypt was a great producer of emeralds, and so the notion is not preposterous—but the fact is that the entire facility now exists solely to facilitate the appearance of wealth in a particular gentleman with whom I am in competition. Let us say that we have differing dreams for the same future."

"Politics."

"Yes, Mr. Price. Inevitably, politics."

"I do not like politics Mr. Client but at the level of this operation one must simply hold one's nose."

"As in all things Mr. Price so too in our professional lives we must eventually contend with how the world is made, the place it is."

"You would not like us to go and ask this gentleman to dream in some other direction?"

"I am afraid he would be replaced, Mr. Price. But in the event that the funding should dry up, the whole situation will become fluid, and in that moment, I may effect the results I desire. And on that note, Mr. Price, Mr. Sharkey tells me you are eager to demonstrate a deep subtlety in your modus."

"O subtle actually comes out of my modus."

". . . Perhaps a problem in translation."

"But your English is excellent."

"Yes."

". . ."

". . ."

"ANYWAY you were saying—"

"I must ask that you be discreet."

"In practical terms we should talk thresholds and such, so: how discreet?"

"Deaths may be inevitable Mr. Price I accept this. It might be better if the bank were not in a position to admit to the theft, at least initially. Or perhaps if they were not aware, or simply were in such great turmoil for—let us say forty-eight hours— that they could not know for certain what had been taken."

"That is achievable I am sure."

"But noise . . . I do not wish noise. Nothing garish or obvious or loud that would spoil the timing of my own maneuvers."

"I am positively mouselike Mr. Client."

"Then let us drink a toast Mr. Price—to a truly phenomenal amount of cheese."

———

I get the check and I walk away and with each step I take away from the table it is harder and harder to know that I was ever there at all. Ghost money: the Poltergeist in the machine.

Mr. Client takes his baby face and goes back to his yacht or his helicopter or his mansion or whatever the fuck this guy has that he thinks is so all-fired important and I think about robbing banks and my modus out of which I am all the kinds of subtle and shut up yes I actually am and look here is me subtling—

There is one easy way to gain access to any bank. It is the quietest and the most subtle and that is what I am being paid for. Also I am a negotiating sort of guy it is always my preference. Oftentimes you can get more by offering a guy his heart's desire than you ever will the other way. More than that it is professional and appropriate and it is just polite. In any business but in this business most especially politeness is never wasted because you see how disagreements can escalate. You always offer the other guy a parachute.

VoIP call outbound.

Ring ring.

"Hallo Die Festung Kircheisen?"

"Hi there my name is Olembert Hecht."

Obviously my name is not Olembert Hecht that is a lie although you know philosophically if I call myself Olembert Hecht and I perform Olembert Hecht I mean aren't we all in the end just the intersection of our own created no I'm fucking with you it's a lie.

I figure Olembert Hecht is a transactional sort of person he is Australian with diffusely north European ancestry. Olembert is not a made-up name but it sounds almost like it might be. It could come from almost anywhere like the name of a new Asian deluxe-brand executive saloon. By the same token no one knows exactly what it says about its owner. Olembert is himself and nothing else and right now he is the voice of modern economics. He is capitalism walking.

"Hallo Mr. Hecht how can I help you today?"

"I wish to buy you."

Reception guy does not get that Olembert is a fucking structural imperative and a deep premise of our civilization, so he says:

"I will pass you to client care."

"No you misunderstand I do not wish to be a client I wish to buy your company. Entirely."

"We are not for sale."

"Everything that is commercial is for sale the question is only whether the price is right and I am always right. Are you the primary stockholder?"

"No that is Mr. Eiger."

(Like Eye-gher.)

"Then I need to speak to Mr. Eiger this is a time-limited offer."

"I—"

"Eiger. I do not wish to be rude but you understand this is a serious offer and given that you answered the phone you cannot possibly also answer the question. This is not your problem you should kick it upstairs."

". . . Yes very well sir."

Click bloop clicky bloop.

"I am Hans Eiger. Who are you?"

"This is Olembert Hecht I wish to buy you."

"We are not—"

"Why does everyone always say that of course you are. The

market value of your company is assessed at one hundred and seventy million euros. I will give you one hundred seventy-five million euros today consider the extra like a personal tip."

"No this is absurd. Absolutely absurd. No one does business in this—"

"Two hundred and twenty-five million."

What?

"I have increased my offer by fifty million euros I am in a hurry. Also I am a little freaked-out by how inexpensive banks are they should be way more expensive than this that is just common sense. But I looked on the Internet and everything there is true. Yes or no will be fine ideally yes everyone will be happier."

"I do not—you are rude."

"I am energetic."

"You are rude."

"I am just in a hurry I wish to spare you some upset and tribulation is all. Take the money it'll be great."

"I do not want it."

"That is not relevant this is capitalism Mr. Eiger it is the apotheosis of the system of the world. It is the precise statement of your country's ferocious ethos of independence and business. This is your moment sir you can do anything from here. Found a new company in competition with your old one if you wish there will be no prohibition on such behavior. Go white water rafting with a trio of exotic dancers and fall asleep under Mexican stars. Buy an island I know of a very nice one I was thinking it would be ideal for me but for you Mr. Eiger I will step back. The world is your oyster sir it is the overpriced delicacy of your choice. It is your foie gras your caviar your fermented snake."

"Who eats—no that is not important—"

"Mexican stars Mr. Eiger,"

"This also I do not want I am nearly seventy I am respectable—"

"That in my experience is not a bar but you know—"

"Mr. Hecht!"

"Mr. Eiger—"

"MR. HECHT—"

"Mr. Eiger no. I am speaking now. I will listen in a moment."

". . . Very well. Proceed."

"I am interested in your company for reasons. By this time in one month you will no longer have it. You can sell it to me or it will cease to exist as a functional entity, that is not a threat it is simply business. I have a priority the priority requires that I have control of your company, if I cannot have it as part of a willing trade for money I must take it that is all sir it is a matter between entities and you and I are just talking heads on sticks. You sound like nice people you got all kinds of upright and spine and so but that—that does not change things between us Mr. Eiger I reiterate just take the money and everyone will be happier."

"You sound almost regretful Mr. Hecht. Why is that?"

"I'm a person getting along in the world Mr. Eiger and sometimes I feel the urge to do something nice for someone I have never met. I despise vandals Mr. Eiger and you have made something beautiful there. I do not wish to break it for no good reason that is the act of a barbarian sir."

"That is helpful thank you."

"Oh good so shall we do the deal and go eat?"

"Mr. Hecht I will speak clearly because I see this line is secure. You will not have my company and if you try to take it I will make you sorry you were born."

"Oh okay."

"I am glad that you understand."

"It is the wrong answer."

"It is not."

"Have your people do a little research. My company is the AAA Aarhus Holding Company it is not the school of architecture it is a business registered in Panama but you would not believe how pissy those architects can be."

"That is the Danish Mr. Hecht they have a strong sense of self and their own importance you do not want to deal with those people."

"Indeed not Mr. Eiger I am dealing with you. I feel that we are right now bonding over the obduracy of Danes."

"Mr. Hecht there will be no deal."

"Look me up."

"It would make no difference if I did."

"I feel confident that it would."

"Your confidence is as in other areas misplaced. I also despise vandals Mr. Hecht and I feel that you are one such."

"Well now that is just personally hurtful sir I am a man in the system of the world is all."

"Then let the wheels of that system carry you away from what is mine. That would be best."

"I counsel you strongly to consider it Mr. Eiger. I will leave the offer on the table until tomorrow."

"I advise you not to pursue this Mr. Hecht."

"I was going to make you massively rich Mr. Eiger."

"I am rich Mr. Hecht."

"No sir. You are merely vested with money at this time and that is not the same. Your wealth is contingent on many factors."

"Such as?"

"Such as me Mr. Eiger. Such as me."

I wait and I wait and in the meantime I go online and read Mr. Eiger's website and his brochure. I am just full of respect for everything he has achieved I mean this guy. French Foreign Legion in all kinds of hot situations such as the DijonAir hijacking before I was even out of school, comes home and you can see right off he believes more than anything in stability. He believes in stability so much that he builds himself a business that is all about making a hard foundation in the world. He literally carves out a place for himself I mean that is fucking poetic. There are pictures of him looking patrician and hard-ass in the brochure with all the big doors of his bank like big round space doors in big round door frames set into the rock. He has on a blue suit with a little blue flower in the lapel and he is hella good-looking for a guy his age. The Kircheisen Festung is a statement of permanence and I can completely see how he would not want to give it up but but BUT sentiment has no place in business. Business is not your identity anymore, that is some twentieth century you are carrying around right there. Business is process now and who you are is a whole other thing that you do.

Even so I give him the full twenty-four hours because of the respect. Eiger does not call. On the one hand you got to respect that kind of stubborn. On the other, stubborn in the end is just a way of saying you don't take the world the way it really is.

Some people I guess just do not like it when they touch the real.

I go to tell everyone the good news and Volodya says: "No."

TWO

SOME DAYS YOU JUST DON'T KNOW WHERE TO LOOK I mean you just don't. Here is this guy Volodya whom I love like a—I guess a real scary uncle who lives much of the time in a log cabin at an undisclosed location above the Arctic Circle and who may or may not eat ham made of people and we do not discuss it because he's sensitive. He's big and bristle-faced and he has hard hands from the moose wrestling and such and he smells of turpentine and old cotton. He does not wear a ridiculous merchant seaman's hat but you know he kind of should. I lay it all out for them like BAM here is this classic job and we will do it. The world's most unrobabble bank and here it is—

Identification Information Access Execution Departure. IIAED. These are the components of any bank robbery project. I call them The Vowels despite that there is one consonant and Doc calls them Homer because of *The Iliad*, which is a Greek poem in dactylic hexameter about sneaking into a heavily guarded fortress and killing the shit out of it.

Yeah Doc's name is better I guess.

So you first got to identify your target; then you do your homework about it; then you get into it; then you rob it; and then you leave. All parts are coequally important like there is no point doing a crime if you are then still standing in it when the Bolivian Army arrives, but it all begins with the information. If your information is not good you will drill through the wall of a barbershop looking for the hydraulic closure on the vault and you will instead hit a gas main and you and your oxyacetylene and your so many millions that you will now not spend will be the first bank robbery ever to go to space.

We have the fucking plans to the vault. We were given them. But of course we do not trust those plans at all at all because as Mr. Client said security people are like hoarders like weekend engineers they cannot leave it the fuck alone and so now Charlie and Rex build Die Festung all over again. They get hold of every architectural prospectus every brochure every tourist shot and publicity release and they go through them by hand and—

No I'm kidding seriously of course not there's an app for that.

A Poltergeist app made by anarchy ice kobolds and it's not actually an app it's a sophisticated machine-learning-space-management-and-allocation algo intended for reconstructing cities wrecked by civil wars because Mr. Friday does not like civil wars at all.

But it turns out it's just great for planning a bank robbery too.

So now we have archive footage. Something for the Murnau set, all grainy silver nitrate Bolex joy. This must have been some old-school archivist because even back then they had goddamn color they had Betamax.

On the screen, a giant-ass metal spider on the side of a mountain that is THAT mountain, fast motion and slow motion and scratches on celluloid . . . a crane and huge counterweights. Fucking—I swear—fucking COWS and they are pulling ropes alongside the diesels. Fucking indomitable Swiss know-how. You can see a Japanese guy here in the foreground and on his shirt there's SUMITOMO-GERTSCH AG because there is shared mining history there that is the world. Japanese guy grins and his Swiss partner nods and gives a thumbs-up and they—

Mother. Fuck.

Seriously you have not seen insane until you have seen this.

They put the whole inner vault into the castle in a single piece, like force-feeding a PEZ dispenser. And they lock it in place with a set of giant evil doors made of battleship steel.

Like a whole battleship. Like meters thick.

And that is just the start. Inside of the big evil doors on the front at just about every junction that matters there are baby evil doors that see you and do not like that you are there trying to open them. The Kircheisen X8 fully autonomous secure closure is like if a common or garden steel plate door such as you would see in contemporary crime drama fucked the Hulk and they had evil spawn.

To be clear: you do not come at an X8 with your damn tiny plasma cutter. No indeed you do not. Other vaults may have a victim mentality. If you get all up in the grille of a Rubicon 3 or a Holdfast AH1, then sure enough they will phone a friend and wait for rescue. That is not the X8's jam. The X8 cannot even and it will not phone a friend because it does not need a friend to tell it that you can go screw yourself. The X8 is insulted by the very idea that you would think a plasma cutter or a diamond drill or old-fashioned C-4 are even relevant to this conversation and it will straight-out autonomously fuck your shit up.

Frame by frame Charlie and Rex break down the corridors by the direction of the light fittings and the numbers on the fire control stations. They know each door by location. They give them names. Doc watches. I can see her remembering everything. By the time we land Doc will not need the map.

My people. They are perfect for this. Doc because she is a

genius, Charlie because computers, and Rex because construction. Rex is actually in demolition technically but he knows also how things go up. That is where he got his start.

With his brother—now deceased—long story very sad there was shooting not by me. But it was kind of about me, all the same.

Rex puts his finger on the screen.

"These fucking doors," Rex says.

Doc says, "Amen," and everyone looks at her because Doc does not do religious language even for effect but yeah she is right. Amen.

In the shop floor model the X8 is electrified and the frame features nozzles for aerosolized drug dispersal and six asymmetrically mounted recessed shotguns, but the brochure is keen to emphasize that clients often like to commission their own modular accessories and the Kircheisen company is real happy to accommodate such requests. Bioweapons are of course illegal and so Kircheisen cannot supply such things and advises against them but will on the other hand make deployment modules to your confidential design and leave you to introduce your ammunition so long as you assure the company that you will not equip any for example not that you would of course pathogens.

No no, no no no.

There is a social contract in all bank robberies since Dillinger and it is very simple: the robber is stealing from the insurance company, not the account holders and not the bank. There is therefore a tacit understanding between robber and cashier that while this is not a normal transaction it is also not really that objectionable. So long as everyone is calm and professional, there need be no downside.

The X8 is the face of actuarial disapproval at this cozy little alliance and it bears a message for the would-be thief: if you mess with us, the only question for the police when they arrive will be how to get that thin layer of criminal sludge off their shoes.

Every single one of the rooms in Die Festung is secured with an X8.

Except the last, which is something called an X9 and requires Eiger's personal presence. If he dies or is compromised, some wearable tech on or possibly in his body will send a signal, the entire mountain will lock down until the designated alternate arrives. No one knows who that is or how they are contacted that is Eiger's personal secret.

This vault man. This is why we came this vault is PERFECT.

A castle.

On a mountain.

Battleship steel.

Water.

Magnets.

Biological weapons.

And hyperviolent armored robot doors.

That is so entirely my jam.

I want to do things to this vault. Things that it will not like except that it absolutely will. They are what it was made for. They are things that it has always dreamed about and feels guilty about and—

"Price for fuck's sake—"

"Sorry Doc did I—"

"Yes out loud yes."

"I want to have sex with this vault is what I'm saying."

"Yes thank you for making the metaphor quite clear."

"Wait metaphor?"

And then Volodya—this guy—my business partner, my friend—today of all days—he is just not coming from yes.

Volodya says no.

I say: "Kircheisen!"

Volodya says: "Price we should not go to Switzerland."

"But why not?"

"Is bad idea."

"The nature of this badness being unclear is what I'm saying."

"Were you ever at Swiss party on National Day?"

"I don't even know what that is man."

"Is what it sounds like."

"Okay."

"On National Day one time I am in little place called Grindelwald yes Price like in fucking *Harry Potter* is real place. And opposite like a hundred meters away is big chalet filled with people from the Swiss postal service. They are nice like what my mother calls Borrow Milk people. So Federal Day round six my place we are drunk and we are bored and we figure to invade Swiss postal service for fun. Is diplomatic mission from before I am in Demons. We go round there, leave ultimatum. We give them until nine then we figure to go over and ravish their gingerbread houses and eat their women. Consensually because we are serious diplomats now. Then we sit on balcony, drink schnapps made from fruit, pee in snow from great height. At eight fifty-nine we are on this balcony still peeing in snow from great height and the Swiss explode the world."

"They—"

"Here is what these fucking postal clerks have done okay? They have gone down to basement where there is nuclear bunker—"

"There is what?"

"Is Swiss thing. They go to bunker, get alpine camo suits. They sneak up to our house and when they are like five feet away they fire about ten thousand bottle rockets from empty schnapps bottles right at our diplomatic residence. And they are so drunk they completely miss our fucking house and they blow up house next door, which is fucking fortunate because of the peeing in the snow and otherwise I personally would have my dick on fire. When they realize this all these postal workers men and women they are laughing so hard they cannot walk, but also they are very concerned they have maybe exploded neutral third party so they go over there to apologize. Guy comes out and he is local magistrate and so we think: aha now we will get some diplomatic! They explain shit to the magistrate and he looks at us on our balcony and you can see that he totally grasps the situation and he goes inside and he comes out with his own fucking rockets! And now they surround our house with rockets and demand that we surrender our Russian bear asses and let them ravish our gingerbreads all night long."

"Shiiiit . . ."

"Yeah Price, nowhere is that how people do. Not Laos not Afghanistan not Mexico. Those places they can do like constant war they can get violent sure but they are not crazy in the Appenzellers. That is unreal. Nowhere in the world is like that except that I know two demographics where that is normal: Switzerland is one."

"And the other?"

"Is you Price."

"Me?"

"That whole fucking country is made from you."

" . . ."

". . . Oh crap, should maybe not have put it that way—"

". . . Yeah now we're definitely going."

We get in the jet and we go.

I say our jet like we have one jet but I'm pretty sure there are lots. When you really have a jet—rather than a jet has you—then you do not need to know how many jets you have. You possess the quality of jetness and that is all. The quality of jetness is not only about physical jetness it is about your modus again or in fact the world's modus in dealing with you. When you just travel by air there are forms and customs and such but when you possess the quality of jetness there are not. There is just a guy on the runway in Canada called Barton.

"Hi I'm Barton I'm your excise liaison for the Platinum Traveler Global Program how can I help you today?"

"Hi Barton my name is Jack Price I possess the quality of jetness I wish to land in Switzerland with my jet here is money."

"Yes Mr. Price one thing I see on the manifest here we have items seven and twenty-two and I wonder if maybe you are doing a little joshing."

"There is no josh Barton."

"Thing is sir those are what we call red-ticket items sir they're kinda not okay."

"Well let's take them one by one Barton and see what we can do."

"Well okay Mr. Price so item seven is a human head on a stick?"

"It is completely okay really."

"It is sir?"

"Yes Barton it is that would be Fred. He is a really interesting piece by the artist Banjo Telemark which I'm proud to own. We've got him in Perspex here and he's all cased up for transport but he comes with me everywhere you see like a kind of personal good-luck piece."

"I don't know of Mr. Telemark sir."

"No he is a very exclusive sort of artist Barton like a kind of secret brand for the haute concept set is what. It's like you know the Turner Prize in London where they give money to some really fucked-up piece like a cow cut in half right?"

"I do sir yes I guess."

"Well Banjo Telemark pisses on the Turner Prize Barton. He would not accept the Turner Prize if they offered it to him because it is selling out. Banjo is like the unknown god of art in the twenty-first century and he is completely uncompromising. He does not explain or mediate his work and he does not supply provenances for his items so I have no paperwork on Fred."

"That's kinda your problem right there sir."

"I am very rich Barton."

"Yes sir."

"I am super-giant-fucking-jet rich. My friends here are also individually super-giant-jet-rich this means that we are like exponentially rich although mathematically that is not true of course but functionally in the real universe and world it is true. We are singularity rich if you like, Barton do you know what that means?"

"Yes sir."

"If I wanted paperwork for Fred I could have someone make it for me. I could procure it illegitimately. But I don't because respect Barton I respect the law and I respect Banjo Telemark's art and part of that art is the creation of concern, watchfulness and uncertainty Barton. He wants you to have this experience. He wants me to have this experience. When I bought Fred it was part of the conditions of sale that I would take him with me on cross-border travel. This, what is happening right now between us, this is Banjo's art. Not the head. The head is the pretext for the creation of spontaneous situational ambiguity, Barton. Do you see?"

"Uh—"

"He's heavily influenced by Warhol."

"Oh is he?"

"Yes."

"Uh, okay, I guess, I'll talk to the guys about that and see what we can do there sir but we really do have to discuss item twenty-two."

"It seems entirely self-explanatory to me Barton."

"Item twenty-two is an adult male human in a box sir."

"Alive, Barton."

"Yes sir I noticed that."

"That's Sean, Barton."

"Okay."

"This is a friend of mine. He accompanies me wherever I go."

"Sir."

"He never leaves that box. Hi in there!"

"Gnar-fnarr-gnabbit-fnee!"

"He wears a gag Barton so he can't really communicate. But look at his eyes. What do they express to you?"

"I think he's real unhappy sir."

"Yes yes he is. More than anything else he wants you to notice him. He's a narcissist but that's not why he wants you to notice him. He wants you to notice him because every time we enter a new country he thinks maybe he will have a chance at escaping from that box. Do you know who my friend there is Barton?"

"No sir—wait is it Banjo Telemark? Like himself in person? Is this more of his art sir? Or are you—wait that's it, isn't it, you're Banjo Telemark? This is all a whole thing that you're doing."

". . . Wow."

"That's right isn't it sir and I'm going to be part of your next show like *Amazed Man* or something and there'll be a picture and so on?"

"Holy shit Barton."

"Sir?"

"No, Barton, but that is a totally awesome idea you have there and I really have to commend your creativity. I was gonna go with some other crap I have been working on but— wow dude that is just golden. Doc did you hear this guy?"

"Yes Price it is a terrible idea."

"No man no it's like—no it's perfect is what it is I love it."

"No."

"Yes Doc yes. There is an actual art fair where we are going and it is like tomorrow and it is perfect everything is perfect."

"Banjo Telemark. I think I have died."

"No Doc it will be amazing. Okay. Barton?"

"Yes sir?"

"Barton look I'm gonna level with you because we should be friends after that—like—that absolutely astounding thing that just fell out of your face like fucking Pallas Athena into the—never mind that now here's what it is. You see that fucker over there with the Russian-looking smile and the pool cue?"

"Yes sir I see the gentleman but he is not smiling."

"Oh yes Barton yes he is. He is a smiling-on-the-inside person Barton."

"Uh okay sir."

"That is Volodya the sniper. He is a total international bastard. He's wanted in so many places we don't even bother to check anymore. I think the only place he's not wanted is Belize don't ask me why not it's like maybe a filing oversight or something."

"Uh right."

"Basically we're all just horrible bastards Barton is what it is. That guy in the box there did a bad thing and pissed me off and now I'm keeping him like that basically forever. It was a straightforwardly bad thing okay I'm not kidding and it wasn't what you call it morally ambiguous but it was a shit ton less bad than the stuff we do on a regular basis so I'm not gonna try to tell you I'm some kind of avenging angel or whatever. Avenging asshole maybe you could say only maybe don't because—yeah okay anyway. Head on a stick, guy in a box. Bad people. I will give you fifteen million American dollars, untraceable, to write that the noted artist Banjo Telemark who is heavily influenced by Warhol came through here with one of his freaky art stunts and his magically hot manager lady and some alarming art flunkies and consultants and bodyguards and what all and you will nod this whole collection through as massively significant modern art and you will never hear about it again. Or you can go confer with your friends in the office and I will offer them the same money and they will take it because I will also explain to them that if they don't take it Volodya will one day come to their house and kill them and their family and friends and anyone they happen to live near and so on in a kind of biblical propagating extinction wave that will end in the death of I don't know some really nice old lady in Kamchatka or something like in that game and she will die saying what the actual fuck and I will tell her before she goes that it was all your fault but you will not care because when I go and talk to your friends and colleagues in there the manifest will have item thirty-one Another Human Head Still Wet okay Barton so let's just take the low road today my Canadian friend. This is where you say oh yah I guess."

"Oh—"

"Come on Barton it's okay this is the best day of your life man you're rich and you're alive."

"Oh—oh my—oh yah I guess sir."

"Yes Mr. Telemark Barton."

"Oh yah yes Mr. Telemark."

"You know the weird thing Barton is that in my own way I am an artist and this has exposed a deep and profound truth not just to the world but to me, which makes you I suppose some sort of muse or possibly I am your art right now, which is like heavy shit."

"Oh wow sir."

"Cool now let's get this stuff in the car. You got your account number?"

"Uh yes sir."

"You thought I was kidding about the fifteen mil I guess."

"I—"

"You're rich Barton. It's really gonna be okay."

". . . Fuck!"

"There we are."

"Go team sir!"

"Go team Barton. Go team."

And that's it we are on our way.

———

I stare out of the window into jetworld. Up is dark blue, down is cloud and that is all there is in the universe. After a while I eat Chinese food because Chinese food is good at altitude.

Doc says: "What's in the box?"

"Firecracker chicken and rice. Rex and Lucille have the pork noodles, and Charlie and Volodya stole the crispy duck. The Russian is a sucker for those little pancakes I guess."

"Give me the chicken."

"But then I will have no chicken."

"That is crime Price someone always gets no chicken."

And then we arrive.

This is Bern it is eight hundred years old and has some people in it we will say a half a million if you count the whole sprawl, which is not a sprawl more like a kind of lotus or zazen. It is also is the capital of Switzerland and nothing un-Swiss is allowed to happen here and if it does they have actual bears in actual pits that they can feed it to I am not even slightly kidding. They do not do this of course because it would be bad for the bears but motherfucker the implication is right there on the cantonal flag: it is only because we are so fucking civilized that we care about the gastric comfort of bears that we are not going with the traditional option.

The actual technical city is small and pretty and ancient and there's this clock and a river and you should totally go it will make you glad. It is the headquarters of the International Peace Bureau and the International Climbing and Mountaineering Federation and the United International Bureaux for the Protection of Intellectual Property and the World Jewellery Confederation and that actually tells you pretty much everything except that Volodya says that also it is typical of all places filled with rich highly educated respectable people who stay in shape and wear nice clothes in that it is like Babylon. They cannot stop with the erotic sexual boning. Volodya says Bern is spring break for museum curators.

Museum curators some of whom are evidently rich as oil barons because there are quite a few giant fucking jets here.

One of which completely parks me in.

Like parks in my giant fucking jet so I cannot put it in the shady spot which I wanted.

Seriously who does that?

This is not a pretty plane it is horrible. There are aesthetics in aircraft design as well as like you know the basic constraints of aerodynamics and there is shit that is not done and this thing does all of them it is green.

It is green I mean not like branding not like gemstones like oxidized copper like fucking rust. It has rust running down it and it smells like jet fuel from someplace that also sells moonshine liquor and babies in that order. It has giant rivets on the outside and these rivets hold on green rusted metal plates and it has chunky engine thingamabobs on the wings that look less jet-y and more like you are supposed to get out and push. There are actual horses in the fucking horsepower it is a horseshit plane.

I do not like it at all and it is in my space that is the space I reserved on Volodya's advice like from before we took off and that is a giant fucking jet thing that you can do and this thing is in.

My. Space.

Bonk bonk bonk "Hi it is Jack hello?"

No answer.

BONK BONK BONK "HI IT IS JACK I AM VERY RICH ALSO I KNOW YOU ARE IN THERE THEY HAVE TOLD ME YOUR STINKPLANE IS IN MY WAY."

The cockpit has metal plates over the window like a fucking tennis family minivan like sunshades like it is an old fucked-up RV. Little rivety screw thing turns and the plate opens. Lady voice says:

"Hi Jack fuck off bye."

BONK BONK "HEY—"

"Fuck. Off."

BONK BONKY RATATATA BONK BONKABONK—

"Are we gonna have a PROBLEM here Jack is that what this is?"

"Yeah lady we are having one right now your plane is in my space."

"Yeah well it's a relief plane asshole like a starving-villages drought-stricken parachute-drop humanitarian plane we get to park where the fuck we like. Be gone in half a day park someplace else they have given you a number for your penis plane no doubt."

"It is not my penis plane."

"You borrowed someone else's penis?"

"No he is dead also too I—"

"It's a dead guy's penis? You are flying around the globe in a dead guy's penis you are fucked-up."

". . . You are not much like any charity-relief fly person I have ever known."

"Yeah I am and you would only say that if you had never met any of us you capitalist prick."

". . . Actually that's fair."

"Fuck off fancy boy I am listening to my music in here."

"O rly what music would that be?"

"The fucking 'Largo al factotum della città.' Like FIGARO FIGARO FIGARO like that."

"O Mozart—"

"No asshole that is *The Marriage of Figaro* this is Rossini I swear if I had a franc—"

". . . Okay this has been great move your damn plane."

"This is not just any plane it is a lady plane like a duchess or whatever."

"Your duchess looks like a dildo with wings and not a nice one one of those weird ones the tattooed kids use in their nasty interporns."

"This plane—my plane that you are right now—go fuck yourself—seriously though fuck you—it is—no not it she: she is a LADY—this LADY is a modified Xi'an Y-20 military cargo plane with prototype gimbal-mounted quad WS-20s in a VTOL configuration. You do not ask a lady like that to get up and go someplace else so you can manspread your nasty dead man's penis."

". . ."

". . ."

". . . You wanna go again?"

"No but you're right that got weird but even so you do not ask this plane to move."

"Yes I do."

"Nope."

"Yup."

"Nope."

"Yup."

CLANG. (Loud opera.)

RINGADYDINGALING "Hello ground control this is

Jack Price there is a flying turd in my parking space make it go away it is harshing my obscene wealth buzz and I am deciding I do not like your airport in five four three—well thank you that will be fine."

A little truck comes and attaches itself to the wheels of the flying turd and starts to pull it away.

The plate opens and a slender black hand pokes out and flips me the bird.

"Figaro Figaro Jack if you know what I mean."

"Yeah whatever lady take it up with Mozart."

"ROSSINI o whatever asshole whatever."

Bern is also where our lawyer is—that is to say Sharkey has a lawyer here and his name is Reinhard and Reinhard is to facilitate our efforts.

Reinhard says: "Hallo! My name is Reinhard I am pleased to meet you."

Reinhard is tall and slim and wide in the shoulder so that he looks like you could put him on and wear him like a cape. He has silver hair and a surfer tan and real even white teeth. When he smiles he makes me think of Bing Crosby if Bing was stretched upward about a quarter mile. He is obnoxiously healthy I bet he cycles up mountains at the weekend and eats granola. He probably makes his own granola with some sort of heavy stone instrument in a stone-and-wood barn while his equally youthful wife does mindfulness training with the Swiss rifle team. Reinhard makes me feel fat and I am not fat I am in perfectly good shape for someone who does not actually want to appear in a swimsuit commercial. Plus also he is really likable even Charlie is smiling and Charlie will usually sneer at anyone who wears Brioni just because Brioni.

I hate him.

Reinhard is here to introduce me to our crime connections in this country although he would absolutely never say that because it would be rude to talk about these people as if they were in some way part of the same ecosystem as purse snatchers and housebreakers.

"Hi Reinhard I'm Jack."

"Hi Jack welcome to Bern."

"Thank you it is good to be here."

"Well okay that's great can I get you all some drinks maybe? Tea or maybe you would prefer schnapps? What time do you feel it is?"

"Oh well your magnificent clock says that it is breakfast so that is what it is let me introduce everyone I mean Doc you already know but—"

We do intros. Reinhard shakes hands with everyone exactly the same like pow pow pow. Me Doc Charlie Rex like we are all the same we are professional people. Volodya grips his hand and Reinhard grips back and they both make a little grunt and log-cabin motherfucker honor is satisfied. I am quite sure every walnut within a five-mile radius is presently thanking God it was not in the room.

I do not do crushing handshakes in my world they are a dick move but there are cultural norms among men who consider the day poorly spent if they have not actually skinned a large mammal and it is best to let them get on with it. It is real important not to do that with Lucille though because if you macho him he goes for the hug.

Reinhard shakes Lucille's hand solid but absolutely median like he can smell the razorsuit under Lucille's overcoat and maybe he can because he has these really long nostrils.

I do not stare at my lawyer's nostrils that is not professional.

Reinhard does pleasant for a bit longer and then says that we should go.

Our meeting is about to start. Mr. Calvanese is—let us not say he is waiting he does not do that. Let us say that he is presently in the agreed location presiding over other business.

Ottavio Leopold Calvanese is a big old wheel of cheese in a thing called the 'Ndrangheta. This is a sort of a version of the Mafia that they do not make movies about because you do not fuck around with the 'Ndrangheta. The 'Ndrangheta did not get the memo about cooling it off and going corporate they are still very traditional men and they do a whole lot of shit that is on the hot side of criminal. They are quite comfortable duking it out in the street with your Albanians your Ukrainians your Taiwan mob your Irish Republicans your Basque your Islamic Jihad your just about any sombitch got ideas of his own regarding the disposition of nonlegal cash flow in a given region. And yet at the same time in a peculiar sidebar or parallel upper echelon these are the folks who do organized crime over the border here in Switzerland and in that connection they are organized to the max and very dressy. Ottavio Leopold was a knife man in his younger days but now he is fat and velveteen and powdered or manicured and he is quite the best-presented former street thug you will ever know. Fucker has a waxed mustache I shit you not.

We do bullshit:

"Good day Mr. Price I am Ottavio Leopold Calvanese."

"I'm Jack Price hi it is nice to meet you."

"Mr. Price you are welcome in Bern."

"It is great to be in this lovely city."

Ottavio Leopold Calvanese points one finger points at the ceiling like: (wait I was not finished). "Providing always that you are not here to make a fuss."

I guess the bullshit portion is over.

"That is music to my ears Mr. Calvanese because although I was constrained into some fairly extreme negotiating tactics recently I personally have no truck with fuss."

Ottavio Leopold does not know this expression to have no truck but he glances at a flunky and the flunky says something in Italian and Ottavio Leopold smiles.

"That is excellent Mr. Price. I will confess that I had not heard of you until your new appointment and this gave me cause for concern. I do not like to deal with people I do not know."

"Well I respect and understand that Mr. Calvanese but think of it in this instance as a surety. There I was dealing millions of dollars of cocaine in the gaps for years and you never heard anything about that at all and that was my whole deal. No one who didn't need to know knew anything at all."

"Yes quite so. I understand that the Pale Peruvian Stallion was—"

"Do not mention it Mr. Calvanese I beg you I am still mourning its demise."

"A sweet deal?"

"I loved that cocaine Mr. Calvanese. I loved the operational hygiene of it. I loved its invisibility its distributed order and fulfilment infrastructure its all-but-fucking-legality. It was SO sweet."

"Perhaps one day you will have the chance to return to that enterprise. Let us say, with a helpful partnership organization?"

"Yes that might well be an investment opportunity for the future."

Ottavio Leopold laughs because he knows as well as I do that the whole point of the Pale Peruvian Stallion was that I did not have to deal with legacy industry organizations such as his but obviously the fact that I am willing to lie politely is what he wanted to know. Yay I have passed his sophisticated test of character go me.

"Mr. Price forgive me I had to ask. You understand? Here I am embedded deep. In club with ministers I have dinner. With administrators I arrange building permissions for overseas companies there is no bribe no threat just favors one way then the other okay? Maybe someone got a client with bad neighbors in Umbria. They got a daughter in college in Milan her boyfriend is not so nice. You see? But nothing is formal no one has to be concerned. Nobody keep score that is business this—this is just life, like music. I do drawing room. You know this expression?"

"Yes you talk about wine and wear slippers and you talk art maybe."

"Esatto. I wear slippers. Not working boots. But you understand I still got boots."

"Of course."

"This is natural."

"It is natural Mr. Calvanese. I was raised on a farm sir and I know how it goes with slippers if you don't also got boots."

Big laugh like to rattle the Venetian chandelier. Big hand waving. Big big everything and now we are all friends forever.

"Wonderful Mr. Price WONDERFUL so few modern men in our line remember the soil. I am delighted to see the Demons in this city again. And I will be honest Jack I did not find your predecessor convivial. He was—come si dice insipido?"

Flunky steps up and whispers.

"Veramente, is called: bland? It's the right word? Okay bland Jack he was bland. So tell me what can I do for you?"

"I need a guy. Like a guy with certain capabilities that I do not propose to use."

"What capabilities?"

"Gunplay and hitting folk."

"Ay ya ya yai."

"Yeah I see where that would alarm you maybe a little given our conversation but again I gotta point out the negation is the promise sir we don't have that person already on the team. That is not our thing right now hence we recruit. The one thing we do not have is a straight-up guy who goes first through the door."

"I could lend you this."

"With respect sir—"

"No. I also would not accept. You promise me you are going to be quiet?"

"I want to show a certain mood like to reassure my wider clientele at this time. It is just good business I am reviving a very traditional brand of crime here."

"Okay Jack. Okay you go ahead. I am delighted to meet you and I look forward to seeing what you can do. But please don't put me in the way of a . . . noise complaint."

We shake hands. Under the manicure, Ottavio Leopold Calvanese has skin like he builds stone walls for a living without gloves.

"I am pleased you come to me Jack not the other guys."

"I had no idea there were other guys Mr. Calvanese."

"Jack in Europe there are always the other guys. Deep in the woodwork there are always those guys. You know what guys I mean?"

"Those guys?"

"Those guys."

"We're talking about those guys still?"

"Those guys still again Mr. Price. Now more than for some time. They are everywhere."

Doc says: "La sua gente era partigiana," and Ottavio Leopold starts a little, then smiles like a sunrise.

"Dottore," he says, and makes a little bow over his gut, and a nod. Partisans like anti-Fascists, back in the day when that meant the Calabrese equivalent of mujahideen.

I know there are Fascists because there are always Fascists but the idea that there are enough of them that a guy like Ottavio Leopold is talking like they are an actual opposition to his thing—but I guess I watch the news so I should not be surprised.

"Well I do not in general make business decisions on the basis of personal distaste Mr. Calvanese but even if you were less of the kind of person that I like to deal with than you are I still—well gosh how to put this delicately—"

"You do not feel they would be a good fit?"

"Well maybe not but also just to put it nicely and in language appropriate to a working environment and where there might be children and so on: fuck those guys."

Ottavio Leopold stares at me for a moment, and then mirth ripples out of him like dancing. He waves his hands up and up in huge approval.

"Oh yes. Oh yes! Quite so indeed." And then intense as he takes my hand: "I am sure we can find a fellow who will work well with you Mr. Price."

So Ottavio Leopold has arranged at my request a brief recruitment fandango and it is here in this hotel. It is a nice hotel and I do mean nice. It is a luxury hotel in the business district it is totally anonymous and very shiny because it is not for tourists it is for the other kind of people who need a two-story fish tank in the lobby to know that someone somewhere will one day love them. It is opulent and yet not opulent because really opulent is unfettered by good taste and true bad taste is not Swiss. There's good taste involved even in the really terrible decisions around neon ceiling art and Cyber-Casbah chic. They've gone completely overboard in this totally non-ridiculous way. The Swiss are a people who own lots of guns but do not have much gun crime and evidently there is a connection there with interior design.

We take the big conference room, which we do not need but it is big and there is a giant gold squid over the table and I am all about the giant gold squid.

Because you got to have a fucking process.

"Hi Nico so tell us about yourself."

"Hi Jack I am very happy to be here I got my start in the 'Ndrangheta. I have experience with blockade running and interpersonal violence, extortion, high-level governmental corruption. Some criminal-systems analysis, you know, because I am modernizer."

Doc says: "We are looking for someone familiar with small arms and close combat at a commando level ideally I would like to see some krav maga or similar."

"Wait Jack I must ask it would be required to work with this lady?"

"Yeah and Charlie too."

"I have a concern there. It is alien to my culture. Also historically it has not gone well for my people, to share secrets with females."

"I—wait females?"

"Is not the right word?"

"Something of a red flag in terms of nuance there buddy."

"Thank you is better to say girls?"

"Okay thank you for coming in."

"No problem man."

". . ."

". . ."

"Doc did you pat him on the shoulder? Like in a friendly way?"

"Guiding him to the door."

"Doc."

"Price."

"Doc."

"Price."

". . . How long?"

". . . Fever in ten hours, respiratory problems in seventeen, total deliquescence in eighty-one hours give or take."

"Dammit Doc what if he turns out to be the best option?"

"Well he's not now is he?"

". . . no that is true but please do not do that anymore."

"Mmph."

"Doc."

"Mm."

"No melty."

"Mm."

"Hallo m'name is Anthony 'm a foh'mah mimbeh of the Rhodesian Light—"

"Nope thank you nope."

"I'm Susan I was in charge of interrogation at Camp—"

"Adieu."

"Hi I—"

"Nope."

"Price—"

"Dude has a lightning bolt tattoo—"

"We cannot hire on aesthetic principles Price that is irrational—"

"Excuse me hi about this tattoo? Actually it is a caduceus with lightning bolts instead of snakes?"

". . ."

". . ."

"Doc?"

"Mm."

"Comments?"

"Mm-mm."

"I am Colonel—"

"No."

"No?"

"No but we do really like your epaulets man that is a lot of braid."

"It is important to convey authority."

"Disco authority please god please let this—"

"Hi I am Saul—"

"Do you have any obvious fucking personality flaws or stupid body art?"

"No if you wish I will remove my—"

"Please god no you are hired. Trial basis for this job probation five months thereafter no-fault break clause."

"I have a variety of unarmed skills and I am proficient in big guns that go fwoosh and small guns that go bang I do not do sniper work that is kind of not my thing."

"I said you're hired."

"I also like to be the first man through the door in combat situations that is kind of my thing."

"You're—"

"Yes I heard you man I just don't like to stop until I'm good and finished I'm a fucking commando. Respect the skill set."

". . . Okeydokey."

"Also the break clause is mutual and I will under no circumstances shave my head or respond to any of the following names: Skipper, Chuck, Zinger, Flea-Ring, Dumptruck, or Kandahar."

"Why not?"

"Did you just hear me say those names? Those are terrible fucking names for me my name is Saul."

". . . I'm giving you a raise Saul."

"Pleasure to work with you sir."

"And you Saul. My name is Jack."

"Hi Jack."

"Hi Saul. Saul Saul Saul."

"You don't have to keep saying Saul every time Jack."

"I'm just getting myself over the hump I really kinda liked Kandahar."

"Yeah well I thought I did but then I went there."

So that was nice Saul is a perfectly nice person who also will shoot someone in the head for me and he starts in the morning because he has to go say goodbye to his boyfriend who comes from Chur and is a landscape designer. We say ciao to Saul and Saul says ciao to us and we finish the coffee because it is not at all bad and then we go see the mountain we are going to climb.

Figuratively. We are going to rob the bank on top of the mountain we are not climbing the actual mountain because it is huge and cold and none of us has the faintest fucking idea how you climb a mountain. Except Saul probably you look at Saul and you just know he will just bivouac all damn day and night. He probably bivouacs at home in his living room like his partner is making vegan bauernwurst on a science-fiction-looking Swiss stove top and Saul is hanging from the ceiling by two fingers singing along to Dietrich Fischer-Dieskau in his all-spandex briefs.

I have asked Saul about this and he says that is exactly how it is so there.

No one is allowed up onto the plateau until later this week. So we take the tourist bus and look up at the black rock.

Swiss tour lady wears Hermès like it is just overalls.

"Welcome to the Kircheisen this is a UNESCO Heritage site we are twinned with Huascarán in Peru here you will see many remarkable wildlife opportunities including chamois and ibex. We cannot dismount from the car at the summit there are preparations in place for the art fair but we can make a round trip and the view is quite amazing. Before this we will go to the waterfall called the Teufelhammer. This is a very important natural resource here in the valley. There is here hydroelectricity for the whole region and also a tourist attraction here one may see thousands of cubic meters of water passing through the underground cavern every second down the fall pipe from the gipfel that is the peak. It will be very nice."

"Thank you yes I am sure that will be nice."

"So here we will please all put on the wet-weather gear although in the mountain of course the weather is always the same it is wet. You will notice there is no life jacket included do not fall in."

"Okay."

"There is no life jacket because no point. If you fall in you will not drown the water is very mineral heavy not so much like the Dead Sea but still you will float."

"Okay."

"But you will still die because you will be crushed by the force of thousands of cubic meters of falling water descending from a distance of one kilometer also because the shock of the temperature would be fatal within a few minutes if you did not already die from the crushing."

"Yes I see."

"So it is best to not fall. We do not include a life jacket because we do not encourage this experiment."

"No right no."

"Okay then we make the tour."

We make the tour.

It's true that the waterfalls are amazing. Basically the whole mountain is like a hot dog bun wrapped around a giant sausage of pressurized water but that does not tell you how it is at all. Umptybajillion gallons of it filter through cracks in the stone and form a great big gigantic flood, which drives down here with a noise that is like a skull-crushing version of one of those old recordings of water falling they used to give you on channel 7 on transatlantic flights to help you sleep, back when the headphones were just plastic tubes with air in them and the sound was literally piped into your ears through a clear plastic wishbone that looked like a stethoscope. On the tour, you stand on a steel bridge over the cauldron of water and look into it and it is the most powerful thing I have ever seen in my whole life. It is not water like water you have ever seen not even if you are a deep-sea fisherman a long liner a rig diver not any of those things. This is water like a war in the earth like a pit full of people fighting over and over for one scrap of food before dying like they would crawl and fight and die and eat the fallen and still they cannot get less hungry and more are

born out of the sky and more are eaten in every passing heartbeat and it will go on forever.

So of course it is part of the security inside.

I mean you would you just would.

Part of the access corridor to the the vault is flooded. It is
part of the Teufelhammer and so no, you cannot just swim
through. Swim in this and the pressure would not blow out
your eardrums it would smoosh you down into an easily por-
table jelly ball.

So sure you can wear diving armor. That is what used to be
called a JIM suit yes yes of course I know what it was called
because I was a kid in the '80s and it was a thing.

Except that it will not help here unless we can hack the
security system because the flooded section ALSO has an elec-
tromagnetic wall and the only release is on the inside of the
vault. You walk into the flooded section all high and hard in
your mecha suit of diving supervillain macho and OOPS now
you are sucked through a hole by this big magnet. In the brochure it says there is a holding net but I will bet you ten million
Swiss francs right here and now that in real life the holding net
does not deploy and the current takes you.

Down.

And down.

Forever.

Like that.

In the video brochure on the Kircheisen website there is
even a little animated fish called Egli who shows you around.
When the magnet gets switched on he laughs his fishy ass off
at the burglar guy who is wearing a stripy mask under his JIM
suit and carrying a swag bag.

"I find the sound very soothing," the Hermès lady says, and
we all say yes of course it is very soothing of course.

It is not soothing.

If there is a hell anywhere it is here and it is made of the same clear cold stuff you drink in bottles in fancy restaurants and you just look at it and know that it would kill you and it does not care.

Would not notice.

The Teufelhammer is just like the universe.

I do not like when the universe is bigger than me.

We go up in the gondola and I say again: We are not climbing this thing. Not an option. The rock has vertical and even overhanging sides with a plateau where the castle is and above the plateau there is a tower of stone like a single finger telling you to go fuck yourself.

This being Switzerland the mountain is not known locally as the Go Fuck Yourself it is known as the Kuhglocke or cowbell, which is cozier I guess but does not really express the identity of the thing. The castle itself is 711 meters up from the valley floor and is accessed exclusively by the cable car and as you sit in it and think about explosions you remember it is a little metal bubble suspended on a high-tension wire cord rope. Looking up and down you can see that the gondola stations at both ends are heavily fortified. Saul looks at me and I look at Saul and Saul makes a face like he does not immediately know what kind of can opener you use for this we do not have one and if we had one we would right now need a bigger one.

I go over to Rex and I whisper maybe thermite and Rex says maybe. Maybe just a nuke. A small nuke would not be overkill, Rex says, because you'd need an awful lot of thermite.

Rex likes thermite and who doesn't. Thermite is when all the oxygen that is married to iron or copper gets horny and runs off for explosively hot sex with aluminum and their chemical love creates a pillar of fire that burns white and enormous. A detonating thermite grenade will turn steel into soup in a few seconds but gosh.

Most steel.

Maybe not this.

The gondola takes six minutes to go from the ground to the top. As we reach the upper station it's kind of like being swallowed by a whale. A big reinforced concrete whale specified to resist a low-yield nuclear blast of the mid-1960s vintage so you know now just basically a nuclear popgun but still hashtag nuclear so there's that. You can see the battleship doors beyond that, just a glint: defense in depth. Volodya sighs.

Mountains are poetry from the earth, Price.

Yeah still wish this one was smaller.

Nyet. It is as it should be. Big strong mountain. Otherwise why are we here?

True fact I suppose. But still.

The Hermès lady directs our attention to a goat on the cliff. We look at the goat for a while. The goat looks back and then quite deliberately pees off the ledge so that a stream of yellow goat urine falls three quarters of a kilometer to the valley below.

The goat is mocking me.

The bubble gagagagagonks its way through the machinery at the top of its run and goes back down again. In the lobby Volodya gives Doc a spontaneous hug. He lifts her right off the ground.

"Put me down you idiot."

"The mountain is very beautiful. The world is alive Doctor it is joy. So we hug."

"You hug I get lifted in the air you ape put me down."

"Nyet."

"Da."

"Nyet."

"Da or I will scream that I am being abducted by a giant Soviet and they will rouse the militias."

But he won't until she hugs him back.

"Idiot," says Doc.

"Sure," Volodya says all smug, "Sure. I am idiot. But still is beautiful day."

And then we go out into the street and a tiny little *Sound of Music*–looking motherfucker comes out of a pastry shop and stabs me in the leg.

It hurts getting stabbed in the leg. It communicates like few other things communicate that someone would like you to fuck the fuck off.

Doc says: "Do not touch the—"

(ZwinggggSMASH.)

(That is the noise bullets make when they are fired from a long way away.)

(It is one of the few other things that communicates more than being stabbed in the leg communicates that someone would like you to fuck the fuck off.)

(Bang.)

(That is the noise of the shot being fired it comes really late it is quite annoying. Now we are hiding behind a post-box. Swiss postbox. Good iron construction. It is a criminal offense on a pretty massive scale here to interfere with the postal service Volodya said so someone is in big trouble also probably shooting people in a built-up area for just no good reason that is likely to be a no-no also. That and stabbing but Evil Hansel is a minor so probably some sort of really shiny Lego-based rehab for him if I don't catch him first and cut off his pointy little *Sound of Music*–looking motherfucker head with—eheheh—a Swiss Army knife, which I will totally buy for the—)

"DO NOT TOUCH—"

"I am NOT—"

"Do not touch the fucking knife Price for—"

"I am not touching it—"

"You are touching it how are we having this conversation DO NOT TOUCH THE—"

"I AM NOT—"

(ZwingggSMASH.)

"In fact you ARE that is—"

(Bang.)

"Cops will be here any—"

"That may or may not be a good—DO NOT TOUCH—"

"It's in my fucking leg of course I am touching it in that sense it is touching me—"

"I did not mean that, your other hand is—"

"I—oh shit I had no idea I was—"

"Keep your fucking hands away from the—"

"IT IS IN ME I HATE—"

"STOP TOUCHING—"

"I AM NOT IT IS ITCHY IS ALL I—"

"PRICE LEAVE THE—"

"GET THE ITCHY OUT OF ME—"

"NO NO NO NO YOUR DAMN HANDS YOU DAMN—"

(Bonk.)

No one says bonk but it is the noise I hear.

Somewhere Doc says: "Thank you Rex that was very timely. Lucille get that car please I'm afraid we'll have to kill the driver—yes stop screaming madame—I know it's unfortunate but I will make this painless there we are—goodbye I will do my best to take care of your family and so on if you have any—no that's it relax good and five four three two one done. Rex you drive GO. Jesus that's a lot of blood Price you IDIOT Charlie give me your belt now hold this and—for Christ's sake Charlie I do not want to fucking hear it you ALWAYS wear underwear when robbing a bank that is just professional—now TWIST—"

White light and hot cold and sleep now.

"Oh what no Doc I might just sit down—"

"No Price you can't fucking just sit down—"

"But I'm all awake now and I just need a little—"

Volodya says: "Doctor he is lose blood give me the kit."

"We need to stay together—"

"He must lie still and get transfusion. Cannot be in car chase and running or he will tear the artery open and then is fucked-up. I will take him. You make diversion. Meet at Black House. I will take care of it."

"You? What the fuck are you going to—"

"I am universal donor give me the kit."

"Fuck no you cannot just—"

"I can and I will and I am experience. I have done before. Give."

"Jesus fuck no Doc don't give him the kit he makes human ham don't let him give me human ham blood that's just wrong—"

"Shut up Jack."

Big dumb Volodya face all up in my vision tunnel: "Also too Jack it is not human ham we have discussed and I find this continuing hurtful as you know—"

"Yeah sorry big guy I'm a bad man but hey look this mail is real comfy—"

"Doctor. Give me the kit."

"Fuck. I know you're a—Jesus fuck it'll fucking—"

"I know. If not he will maybe die certainly no good for weeks. These are realities. Give me the kit."

". . . Fucking take it then. FUCK!"

"You are good doctor, Doc."

". . . Fuck!"

I wake in the gray place that is the place that you go when you are not unconscious but not also the other thing. The edges of the gray place are brown and when you push too hard into the real world the brown makes you sleep.

Negative universe coffee.

I am lying on sacks of mail and the world is softly in motion. I can feel an engine working GOGA-GOGA-GOG.

I am in a mail truck.

No.

Not a truck a—

Volodya says: "I get off now Price you go on to end of line."

"What? Fuck buddy don't leave me in this shit OW what—"

"I take transfusion kit not good if they find us with it."

"Well OW but also man stay with me we'll—"

"No Price I got stuff to do now. You sleep. Will all be okay, Okay?"

"Fucking human ham blood transfusion so wrong. You're gonna leave me NOW? I'm fucking dying here."

"I don't think so. You got my blood in you now. Very rude to die anyway."

"Where the fuck is everyone?"

"They make diversion. I get you away. Was bad situation."

"But you're leaving me now?"

"Bad situation got consequences."

"More people need to think about me is what I'm saying because I got stabbed."

"You are asshole Jack."

"Yeah buddy I am."

"Yeah you are."

"Yeah I am."

". . ."

". . . You're a good friend I'm sorry."

". . . Hah. Now is truth."

"Well I got your blood in me I guess truth comes with."

"You are good friend Jack you got to make it okay?"

"Don't get all misty on me—"

"I don't get misty asshole I am totally male and Ukrainian."

"Sorry buddy didn't mean to overstep."

"Now sleep. Go on to end of line."

"I don't want to sleep I got—"

"Price."

"Yeah?"

"Sleep."

I sleep.

———

A mail train.

Not a truck because this is the country of the train. Seriously they have the best trains here there are actual armchairs and bars with real beer and a playground even like red and yellow plastic and happy children all on a train. Standard class because civilization is not a luxury. I tell you, this country, man, they make capitalism look a lot like Socialism sometimes.

Not always.

Bright light and blue blue sky and a man do not wake me man I am sleeping MAN pay attention you are waking me with your waking—

The man does not approve not at all. He is stern because I have bled on the mail. Bled a lot he says which you know he likely hasn't seen a lot of bleeding because that stuff spreads super-duper thin and is real dramatic I feel fine.

The man is also pissed because I have traveled in the train without a ticket. That is a fine. Also because the mail van is not certified for human transport it is unsafe I am totally risking injury like whiplash with my shabby leg.

But now he is stern plus extra stern because the blood is a health hazard yes a hazard to public health and that is quite antisocial. It is irresponsible. Am I Swiss? This is un-Swiss.

I tell the man I am not Swiss.

He says good.

He carries me like a child.

"Are you arresting me?"

A noise like one of those toys they sell that you shake that is supposed to sound like a cow.

"Yaaaahhh-uuuuuuuaaaaawh. Later for all this. Now just

get you to a bed. You have lost a lot of blood. I know. It is in my mail."

"Yeah sorry man I honestly got no idea how that happened."

"Yaaaaaah-uuuuuuawh. Of course not."

"No I mean obviously I got stabbed I just got no idea how I ended up in your mail van."

Guy is old like old old how is he carrying me? I am not small. Straight back and strong legs. Smells like pomade. Snorts again like a bull seeing a very small dog.

Tiny dog.

"No of course it is not simple as I say it is obvious that you live an untidy life."

"Untidy. Heh. Yeah I like that."

"I am Martin."

(MAAAHR-tin like tin should apologize for even being there.)

I can't remember what I'm supposed to say my name is right now and it's not like Martin is a damn computer. He doesn't know Jack Price or he'd be handling this different. So I tell him the truth.

"My name's Jack."

Not what it says in my wallet but I don't have my wallet. Don't have my phone got nothing where IS everybody? Where's Doc and Volodya where's Charlie and Lucille and Rex?

Martin goes up some steps fucking skips up like I weigh like a bouquet of flowers it is the ballet up we go.

He says oopla. (Oh-op-lah.) This is a general purpose thing that Swiss people say. It can mean that you have fallen down a crevasse and they are holding you over certain death by one arm or that you have dropped your ice-cream cone. It can mean you are starting a downhill ski race or getting out of a chair. It is extremely scalable I like it.

"Oopla."

At this point we have to talk about Swissness because Martin being a thousand years old and carrying a bleeding stranger up a hill like that is totally normal is a Swissness thing and Swissness will totally keep coming up.

There are countries that have identities and there are countries with civic pride but there is only one Swissness. I will tell you but you will not believe it until you have seen it. So first of all Swiss people are basically immortal and they can bend steel using only their disapproval and that is just normal here. That story where grandma lifts a car off a kid that would not make a Swiss newspaper and if it did people would write in to say that standards are falling because she used both hands. But more than that Swissness is a way of being in the world that is very very Swiss. Like for example: a while back they passed a law here banning minarets because oooo scary Muslims! So right away a Catholic guy builds a minaret in his fucking yard because restricting personal freedom and freedom of religion is un-Swiss. He basically took the whole country out and spanked it and heads were hung in shame. Being un-Swiss is about the worst thing you can say here about someone who actually is Swiss. Foreign people are naturally not Swiss and that's like a tragedy for them on every level but you know with application and study and wealth and focus it's not totally impossible for them to become Swiss or at least Swiss-like even if they never get an actual piece of paper saying they are Swiss because not everyone wants to hold a Swiss passport. That is respectable to a Swiss person: there are three or four other passports in the world that are very almost as good and everyone should be allowed some choice and identity of their own.

Being un-Swiss is something that can really only happen to you if you are Swiss but you do something that has actual negative-energy anti-Swissness like publicly fuck a chicken. It has to be public because fucking a chicken is disgusting and whatever but private chickenfucking is a matter between a person and their poultry and likely one day the poultry will get its shots in because chickens are dinosaurs with those mad little eyes and you fuck them at your personal risk. But while you'd be a fucking degenerate if you were forever fucking one chicken or another you would only be actually un-Swiss if you either sold that chicken for human consumption—because that is a risk to the health of society—or fucked a chicken in public because then everyone else would have to deal with your degenerate chickenfucking. They would have to contemplate a window of reality which actually encompassed the idea that a Swiss person would fuck a chicken. You would have damaged the concept of Swissness and just let everyone down and that is fucking un-Swiss which is like dying only you don't get a headstone.

Martin has a cot in a little wooden house. I'm pretty sure he built the house himself. It has initials carved into the wooden wall by the stove top and the first one is M. There's another set alongside and I figure them for his wife's and that is sad because there's two dates right under.

Martin puts a towel on the bed and then puts me on the towel and says he's going to do some things and not to move.

I tell Martin that I am really good at that right now.

And he laughs.

See Martin thinks I'm funny it's just you assholes.

I go to sleep smelling woodsmoke and snow.

Did you ever do a thing knowing it was a bad idea but you did it anyway because you thought it was what you wanted and it was not and then you did it and wished you did not?

I have never done that.

I wanted this and now I have it and that is all.

But looking out of this window at a gray blizzard with your actual lightning somewhere out there I got to admit—and that lightning is like horizontally far away not vertically—I got to admit that this has not gone in the direction I totally foresaw.

This fucking house is made of wood is that good or bad? Like I mean they make airplanes out of metal so that the lightning goes straight through them because if you insulate them they just explode. Fuck me Martin you better not have just built this place knowing fuck all about the mountains you better not be some wannabe homesteading trader retired and jerking off to his long-held log-cabin motherfucker fantasy—

But yeah Martin does not smell of city poseur he has hands like unfinished pine like this table like this whole house.

Jesus I wonder if he built this house.

Jesus that is a lot of snow. Are we gonna get snowed in?

Jesus I hope there's Internet.

If I had a phone I could check and see if I could use my phone.

I wonder if he has a password on his Wi-Fi.

Or maybe he just locks his pigeon loft.

Fuck.

I fucking hate Switzerland.

Pressed white linen and expensively neutral detergent. Crisp, mid-high thread count, soft as goose feathers. Large ugly Soviet peering down at me is not a plus also I am pretty sure I am imagining him because he has on a chef's hat and an apron.

Unless I am about to be ham.

"Oh hey what time is it? Fuck that I'm getting up—"

(I do not get up. I sort of wiggle a bit. It is very tiring.)

"O for love of Stalin's cock don't be dipshit Price you lost maybe one and half pint you're gonna feel like shit. Lie down stay in bed. I bring you Goulaschsuppe."

"I do not like Goulaschsuppe."

"You got no idea what it is."

"That is true and that also is part of why I do not like it what is it?"

"Meat stew with paprika. Everything in this country is with paprika. Even the catsup is with paprika. Also curry for salad dressing. These people are insane."

"I want a beer."

"Goulaschsuppe."

"Crazy Russian."

"I am Ukrainian. Is different now don't be in my minorities."

"Everything is different now. What are you even doing here where the fuck am I?"

"Bed."

"O fuck off and get the horrible soup."

"Sure Price. I go, you stay. Was my whole point."

"Hey buddy where you going?"

"I am going Price."

"To get soup?"

"Sure."

I sleep and then I open my eyes and Martin is coming through the door.

"Jack? I am home!"

"Hi Martin O Hai you brought a friend I am a little bit almost naked sorry hi."

"Yes this is Hannah."

"Hi Hannah."

Hannah has her hands empty and loose by her sides. It's where seriously dangerous people keep their hands when they don't want you to think they are about to fuck you up. Officer Hannah or Sergeant Hannah or Ranger Hannah: she is five foot four and she has wide shoulders and strong arms like she would change a tire one-handed; swimmer's muscle as if her momma was a dolphin. A sexy Aryan dolphin from maybe from an extremely inappropriate manga cartoon. Short hair like a motorcycle helmet and a wide rose mouth that smiles and she is—fuck she is the negative universe version of Doc. Doc is tall and witchy and you can see her mind in her eyes. She is so smart you are closer to a monkey than you are to what is going on in her head. Hannah is broad and mountain strong and not the same but the eyes are there like she is alive in her own head fully present and real.

Not cop Hannah not officer not sergeant.

Agent Hannah.

My leg hurts and as I look at Hannah I have a boner. I get a fear boner the way rabbits do shortly before they get eaten that is absolutely one hundred percent a thing that happens to rabbits.

O God she's a fed. She's a fed like some sort of appalling Swiss elixir of fedness the way Martin is just an old caretaker who can do field medicine and carry me unconscious up a flight of stairs at altitude. Just like that I know Hannah has competences and skills and ways and means.

O o o o—

O damn it all to fuck.

Hannah the Anti-Doc Hannah says: "Hello Jack I am Hannah Müller and I am here to place you in custody. You have committed offenses under Swiss law. Please keep your arms and legs inside your restraints at all times and do not put your head out of the car or it may be cut off."

Holy shit that voice like Lauren Bacall she's a smoker and a drinker of whisky after midnight that I do know. Learned English somewhere in North America I'm gonna say upstate New York. She's still talking. Also what offenses? I do not know and she has not specified and for obvious reasons I don't want to suggest some that would be counterproductive.

She's still talking.

"Do not flee into the snow. We will catch you but if you escape you have the right to have your toes fall off. You have the right to die of exposure and Martin and his mountain rescue team will retrieve your corpse tomorrow and take photographs for the coroner."

I look at Martin and he shrugs yes.

Hannah says: "Okay Jack we are going down the mountain together. I am certain you are just in the wrong place at the wrong time and this will all be sorted out. Are you going to give me any trouble? If you give me any trouble I will have to give it back. Which will make me sad Jack because you are my kind of trouble I'm QUITE sure."

WINK.

Omigod she—that is SO inappropriate—she is doing a thing at me like hi I'll be your arresting sexy-time secret agent today this is me working my anti-Doc on you and no of course you cannot touch this.

(Synth brass.)

Can't touch this.

Anti-Doc.

Agent Hannah.

She puts my arms in the approved position and cuffs me with the real cuffs with the short metal rod between them which you cannot get out of. She just happened to fucking have these on her? Or she's a fucking neighbor?

Someone has changed the bandage on my leg so Doc's fingerprints are just on my skin Jesus I wonder if Doc's actual fingerprints are anywhere and if they'll think to check.

I have been working on a story I totally have an explanation for all this like you see where I was attacked in the street and bandaged up by a medical professional and then unfortunately I became I guess non-lucid and tore my stitches and wandered off before I could report the whole thing like a good citizen and I am you know the injured party there is no reason to arrest me.

No doubt Agent Hannah will say that is fine but even so formalities you understand—

And then I will say perhaps if I might call a lawyer we could sort all this out—

And she will say I don't need a lawyer because legal legal but then she will—

She will take off her clothes. And mine.

Swimmer's muscle and wide curves. I can see them now. I know them. I know exactly and—

Agent Hannah lets her eyes slide up to my face and. she. grins. at me.

Oh SHIT now I am always a little bit going to want to be caught by her.

But on the other hand she is always a little bit going to want me to get away.

And neither of us is ever going to get what we want.

This woman is my fucking apocalypse. My kryptonite.

Can you lick kryptonite is that a thing that is allowed?

Doc has always been real specific that she will kill anyone I have sex with who is not her because Doc is territorial.

But this woman is the anti-Doc I could have sex with her and it would be fine because Doc is going to kill her so much anyway.

Omigod I can just see it now like electrical germ death versus dolphin commando death and they would crush me like—

Bunny fear boner.

Agent Hannah looks at my thigh and groinal area and then meets my eyes and absolutely does not smirk but I can feel the weight of satisfaction and all of the very much smirking she is not doing.

"Come on felon," she says.

I am going to Swiss jail with a bunnyboner.

I sit in the snow cat all tied up and notably fucked and I look down into the valley. There's plenty of moonlight on a clear night plenty of ghost-white light and there waaaay down there below there it is. Agent Hannah puts me in her giant machine and drives me down the mountain. She talks all the time so I think maybe she wants me to stay awake because even if she is arresting me for being some sort of a hoodlum who fled the scene of a shooting and la la la I am also a guy with a hole in his leg and such and she does not want me to go unconscious where she would have to stop and worry about my possible death. I am just thinking I could take advantage of that to escape when I look out of the window and see it.

It.

The mountain.

The whole damn reason we came.

From here it sticks up from the valley floor like a headstone, so dark it is hard to get a sense of scale until you see the spire of the church at the foot of the cliffs and it is a pin. Less than a pin like a fucking mote.

The Kircheisen Festung sees you and it is not impressed. You cannot rob this bank but thank you for your interest and have a nice go fuck yourself.

Yeah.

That kind of thing just invites a certain sort of attention.

Swiss jail looks like a pine guest house with electronic locks and high-durability airport carpet. By now I have sufficiently got my shit together to do some this is an outrage and some on what charge and Agent Hannah calls me

"Mr. Hecht"

and that is great news because that means I am arrested for the purpose of sorting things out and maybe because I was near where a Swiss lady was carjacked. I say very Teutonic that I am Olembert Hecht and I am respectable to the point of affluent and I must make calls and sue the shit out of Swiss jail and Agent Hannah says sure. That is fine but I have things to be doing and I cannot just hang around waiting for my team to come lawyer me out of here and getting their faces on the security cameras and such like. I make my one phone call to a number I just pulled out of my ass and get a blarp blarp signal that means some sort of nope and I tell everyone it is the busy signal. I ask Agent Hannah if there is something to read while I wait and there is a tourist magazine. I read about kite surfing on the lake of Thun. It looks lovely and we should all go.

The magazine is quite old and when I put it down a lot of the middle pages fall out and I say sorry. I futz around on the floor picking up pages and Agent Hannah leans down to pick up the one near her feet and while she does that I take the two metal staples from the middle of the magazine and twist them together around the pins of the two-prong 220-volt AC plug for the reading lamp and put it back in the socket.

The whole room screams like not the people literally all the wires and appliances scream and all the lights go out. Happily also although the office is super new and shiny it is retrofitted over a much older wiring layout and this layout does not shield the desktop computer very well from fluctuations and power surges so there is a popping sound and a thick nasty smoke goes everywhere and gosh I guess that sort of thing can be trouble for storage media so there's a chance the security footage also is gone.

The smoke triggers the fail-safe on the main door so that we do not all get burned alive—which is again super civilized and responsible—but also the sprinkler system, which is unfortunate because electrical fires do not like that sort of thing. And something else goes bang and starts to spark. Agent Hannah grabs at me in the dark and I totally have to applaud her Jedi senses because she is right on target. I duck my head and feel her nose collide with the top of it and you know that hurts. That is going to bruise like raccoon bruise is what. I am sorry Agent that is my bad.

I go into the street and I can hear the fire trucks coming already and since everyone is running because smoke is pouring out of the police station I can run too, and I do. I run around the corner like I know where I'm going and then I walk like a commuter all the way to the train station but I do not get on a train I walk right through the station and get in a taxi, tell the driver I want to go to Bern.

Driver shrugs. "Take a couple hours," he says and I say that's fine. He's wearing a three-piece and if he was my size I would probably have killed him already but he's like eight inches shorter than I am and wide like a pool table. There's no way that'll fit me. Also I'm gonna guess he's Swiss by way of Istanbul, which is not an uncommon thing, and you if you're gonna pick a fight with a guy driving a car who also happens to maybe come from an ethnicity which has seen some local struggles for social recognition in a community not always noted for acceptance of outsiders you better bring a very big fucking stick and I do not have a stick. He might kill me back in a fair fight and if I bite his ear off, which you know works well for me, then I cannot wear the fucking suit so it is better we are friends. I sigh because both Switzerland and Turkey are cultures which admit of a certain amount of the Romantic spirit. This is ethnic stereotyping but some days you go with what you got especially if what you got is two case-hardened steel bangles plus a stolen soft-shell jacket exactly 311 Swiss francs and a hole in your thigh.

"Yeah my fiancée kicked me out of our hotel man. Turns out she was sleeping with my best man but for some reason I'm the one gotta leave."

Driver pulls a face like: that is totally not okay. I can tell he's judging me for not drawing a hard line.

"Yeah man but you know it turns out they're in love. It's not—I'm not happy about it. I'm all kinds of broken up and angry and of course my parents are coming next week for the wedding but—well I mean—it's love ya know? What is she gonna do marry me anyway? Who's that help?"

The driver shrugs and makes that Swiss noise. Yaaaaaawuh.

"You can't fight love," he says, and turns the key.

Car drops me at the river.

Keep the guy's card because you never know when you might need a guy. Plus I might have to kill him later.

And go to the Black House. He wants to know where in Bern and when I tell him the Black House he laughs and says yeah of course.

The place is really called the Kropotkinhaus but everyone just says Black House because like forever ago in the '90s they painted it black. Black for the Black Flag of anarchism right like obviously. There are actually two anarchist settlements in Bern and one of them is kinda legit. This is the other one which has in it the kind of anarchists who long for the final conflict and in furtherance of that end will you know take a bunch of illegal drugs and get wasted and therefore are the kindsa people who will maybe get a fucking handcuff off you without calling the feds.

Way it is: the Kropotkinhaus declared itself the Free and Independent State of the K in 1979, which was totally not a ketamine reference at all, and the Swiss government did not send in the tanks because like both of them were being repainted plus also Swissness is liberty and you do not want to piss on that so they negotiated.

The ambassador of the K was a hairy nicotine-stinking motherfucker named Ferdi Albrecht. Man o' his time is what because again back then it was all Carlos the Jackal and hijacked planes like all day every day. They called in Albrecht and said: "Okay Arschloch it is like this we have much shit that you will need like access to sewers and electrical power and free movement so you can attend your hairy-ass college classes and maybe one day some of you will get a fucking job but for now we will give you all these things in exchange for a trade treaty under which you pay an amount which will be mysteriously fucking identical to the rate of tax per capita calculated by an accurate statement of the population of your pocket utopia of Mary Jane and hand jobs. And since you wish to remain Swiss you will be a unique autonomous Gemeinde within the Swiss Federation but not within any specific canton because there is no canton, Bern included, that will sit still for your crap. There will be no border posts or any of that and you will not be part of the policing jurisdiction though you will absolutely call us in if someone is for example god forbid actually murdered but in exchange for this restraint we expect to get exactly no fucking backchat from any of you hippies and you will comport yourselves with the closest you can manage to dignity if you venture into our flowered capitalist streets. Does that work for you Ferdi Albrecht or shall we revisit the tank discussion?"

Albrecht was no dumbass and he took the deal, and the Kropotkinhaus has basically been a rolling criminal slumber party ever since.

———

Knock knock.

"Hau ab."

That is to say get lost. I do not get lost.

Knock knock.

"Hau ab, Schlappschwanz."

That is super-duper rude in Swiss. Do not mess around with saying it for a joke they will lock you the fuck up and bring your teeth along in a separate car. I hold up my bangles and say: "Dude I have a season pass open the fucking door."

Door has in it what I would call a speakeasy grille but given the age of the house it is more like maybe a judas port or an arrow slit. Through this hole I can see eyeballs and one of those creases a certain Viking sort of physiology gets above the bridge of the nose and between the eyes. My friend Karenina who is now bio-anonymous slurry in the ocean under a tuna cannery had a crease like that and when she was drunk in bars back home and hoping to get laid with attractive waiters hoping to become movie actors at some time in the future she would put her credit card in it and claim to be a casting agent.

This did not work ever.

Guy behind the door makes a farting noise with his mouth and I hear big locks and the door opens. Big black door in a big black Dracula-looking house. All hope abandon yada yada but in fact I am reasonably sure it will be a broken pair of rigid stainless steel cuffs with custom Swiss-flag-pattern polymer overmold I am abandoning here so you know.

I go inside.

———

"Hi I am Jack hi so No Gods No Masters right viva la you know anyway I have this little problem and I—"

Before I can finish my hilarious riff I feel a hand across my face. Soft, fast hand, across my eyes so smooth like the lights going out. Another tucked into the small of my back and turning and turning. I am bent back and now I am nodding nodding like a toy dog. This way that way this way before I feel the wall on my shoulder blades and the air goes out of me like OOMPF and then there is a pressure on my mouth. Pressure. Fingers. Lips.

She's so fast, the doctor.

So so fast.

And warm.

And now everything will be fine.

She holds me until I cannot breathe and then lets go and she is crying, which is so totally not like her and of course I know why and I have been avoiding it this whole damn time.

The room is big and the wallpaper is peeling and there are things living in the roof. There's a bathtub with a shower and a screen curtain on wheels.

"Hi Doc."

"Hi Price."

"Wash me."

"Yes ma'am."

I wash Doc. It is like church and very sad. She washes me and changes the dressing on my leg. She puts her arms around me and tells me what I already know because I am not a dumbass. I do not cry because I do not.

Yeah. I guess you know it too.

Rewind the tape.

I said: "What the fuck is wrong with you man, you couldn't aim for the fucking wheels?"

Volodya said Evil Hansel was lighter than he thought he would be.

I said I did not care about if Evil Hansel was lighter than Volodya thought he would be because right now I had about a thousand Swiss francs nailed to my leg with an oyster knife.

Volodya said: "I told you we should not come."

bonk

And—

"I get off now Price you go on to end of line."

He got in the train with me and he gave me a transfusion and Doc did not want him to do that because there was a bullet in him and he decided this was what he was going to do and he did it.

And he got out of the train halfway up and then he died somewhere.

He went out into the mountain and he fucking died.

Like in a blizzard or something like an explorer.

Log-cabin motherfucker doing his thing I guess. Doing his log-cabin-motherfucker thing and that is his choice that is what he chose to do.

Doc got everyone else over the border into Italy. She checked the Demons into a hotel there and she hired a kid named Matteo to take the dead lady's stolen car and drive like hell to Naples and set it on fire. Charlie made everyone's IDs disappear, just gone. Thermocline magic. Then Doc walked them all right out the back and around the corner to another hotel where they were other people, and the old other people who they were and are not now are notionally still in the first hotel because Matteo's girlfriend is in suite 501 eating as much room service as she wants and making random calls to Indonesia until Friday when they're both going on a four-week cruise.

When Matteo gets back, he will also be taking a suitcase full of money to a house in St. Gallen where there are two kids who just grew up hard and fast because their mother had a heart attack on a visit with friends in the capital. Dead-lady dues. Doc is nothing if not truthful. And then they came back over the border into Switzerland by train and back to Bern to look for me and they figured if I was not dead and the cops didn't have me, then this was where I would be and they were right and that is nice and now everything will be okay. Business is business and everything will be okay.

"Volodya—"

Doc says that they found him already, that he threw himself into some kind of hoist machinery on a farm and got all cut up so no one could tell he was shot.

After giving me his actual blood.

Charlie already did a thing. Charlie of all people has friends here. She is known in the Black House and the Black House has gray connections because of course it does. That is a good thing although she seems to feel there may be personal friction if we stay for too long. Romance, man, go figure.

Task-management thing. Someone will collect his body for us. Store it.

On ice.

He'd laugh. Volodya would laugh about that he has a horrible sense of humor.

Guy eats corpse ham.

Not really.

Ate corpse ham.

Had a horrible sense of humor.

I don't understand death at all it does not make sense and I have seen a lot of it but the more you peer into it the less you get it. People who die don't go anywhere and there's no mystery about it they just stop talking to you and stop doing anything else and it's really shitty if you like them because there is not them anymore.

I don't get how that works.

He had a horrible sense of humor. Had. Had had had had.

I used to do this at school. Where Jack had had "had," Volodya had had "had had"—

Had had had.

And that's all it's just a part of—you know—it's normal.

It's completely normal.

Turnover is normal it is part of the conventional challenges of human resourcing in a dog-eat-dog sector.

This is what it is.

This is the life.

I'm not upset like personally I am just—

It's professionally upsetting is what I'm saying like it's inappropriate it's—

This is not okay man. This is not okay. I am legitimately unhappy with the loss of a key man—a KEY MAN in my organization. That is a term of art there are contracts with those words insurance policies and shit it is professional to talk about a key man and that is all.

There are consequences in this situation there are bills that come due and there's a—

That's crime Jack. Someone always gets no chicken.
Right?
That's just how it is I'm fine.
I'm fine without my Ukrainian chicken.

I meet some of the anarchists and they are quite nice although they all have these ridiculous names and shticks like I guess—though they would not like this description—they have anti-capitalist personal brands which speak to their personal struggle so for example Loob is a greasy little fucker like an emaciated seal and he does underwater welding as for example you would do on tanker and oil rig maintenance except that Loob is opposed to all such structures which are acts of violation toward Mother Earth and he is her warrior; Rosa is tall and thin and has a face like a kindly camel and she makes cakes for the mass of mankind and I greatly approve of free cakes; Fruit eats only a fungal preparation he makes himself, which he says is the future, and I have tasted the future and it is horrible; Thing has much hair; and we do not ask about Thong.

Ever.

The anarchists are kind and they know we are sad so after some mammal grooming behavior to let us know we are welcome in their space they leave us alone. We eat cheese and bread and we drink beer and we lie down in the bed. I think she drugs me but maybe she does not. Sex can be life-or-death it is both and humans are chemistry and Doc understands that in ways I do not.

I feel her skin against mine as I wake in the dark. My leg does not hurt. I feel as if I am on fire. So does she. We do not speak. She is all over me. She is in my mouth and on my chest. She is behind me and in front of my and everywhere and she is happy and then she is not. I don't know how long it all lasts. It feels like hours but half the time I'm not there.

Then she lies next to me in the dark.

"Doc?"

"Jack."

"Volodya—"

"Yes Jack."

"But I mean—Volodya. I mean there is not Volodya anymore. Not ever."

"Yes Jack."

"I don't understand how that works."

"No."

"Doc do— Never mind."

"No Jack say it."

"Doc do we have a future?"

"We have a present Price that is all anyone has."

"Yeah but they also have a future do we have one of those too?"

"Price of course we have a future."

"We do?"

"Do you want to know how I understand the world Jack?"

"Yes. I guess."

"Every single one of us changes and vanishes second by second and when you wake up tomorrow you'll be someone new and so will I so in a very real sense you and I were born together and we will be together for the rest of our lives. You are the only person I've ever slept with and in this moment between night and morning you are the only person I have ever known or will ever meet."

"Jesus Doc."

"What?"

"That is some nihilistic fucking shit right there."

"It's the truth Price and the truth is all the beauty there is."

"Jesus."

"Price?"

"Yeah."

"Think about it."

"No one exists and no one knows anyone? It's like gazing into the fucking abyss is what."

"Do you know what else it means? It means that death is meaningless. Death only happens to other people."

"I dunno Doc I feel a close kinship with me."

"So do I. Don't worry. See you and I we're a rhythm and a way of doing things and we are a dance. Ripples is what. And for as long as we are who we are we will dance around each other. The moment we're not is the moment we part but that person—that person who does not feel what I feel around you—that person I have no feelings for she can fuck off and so can he. You and me Price we are the Universe."

"Aw Doc!"

"Shut up."

"You made a science pome about me!"

"Not what happened."

"A romantic free verse pome with science."

"I swear to you Price you better do some more sex stuff to me now or I will kill you."

"Yes ma'am."

"Hhhhah ahh uh nnnm. Yes."

"You made a pome."

"The gluteus and quadriceps muscles are among the strongest in the body I will rip your head clean off."

"Yes ma'am."

And then we sleep and then it is morning and Volodya is still dead and I am not fine.

Beyond the obvious there is a problem here like an organizational problem like in terms of information availability and compartmentalization. That is to say that certain facts are privileged within the organization and our close partners in our enterprise and it is worrying very worrying that these facts may have been revealed to third parties in a competitive modality that is to say snipers.

There's a problem.

There's a limited number of people could have made the call to get someone in place. There's us and a limited number.

This wasn't one of us.

In the general run of things you work with criminals you assume some measure of betrayal as kind of ambient. There is ambient treason. But look: Charlie straight up liked the old guy and Lucille is so batshit crazy that it's hard to say if he actually deals with the world in a sufficiently parallel fashion that there's anything he could want that he could get this way. Doc doesn't need to betray anyone because she is totally fucking terrifying and if she wanted us dead we would all die full stop no discussion. And then there's Rex and if you had to say one thing for Rex you would say he is true to his friends.

That and he really likes blowing shit up.

It's true that as a group we are variously and ambiguously involved in the sad death of Rex's brother Big Billy but that was mostly Fred and Fred is now resident on the end of a stick.

If Rex wants to get even with Fred he could have the stick. I have offered it to him and Rex says no that is fine he just likes to look at it from time to time and laugh.

Normally I would look at Saul because Saul is the new guy like the temp hire and although correlation is not causation you can always kill it and burn it with fire and just see what happens. But Saul does not know what we are doing here.

I would look at Calvanese but ditto and plus also if it was Calvanese we'd know by now because something else awful would have happened most likely Saul. While I do not know Saul well I believe it would be pretty awful to have him happen to you.

So there's a limited number.

A limited number and that number is three. In no particular order—

There's Mr. Client. There's Sharkey.

And there is the lawyer.

VoIP outgoing ring ringaling—

"Grüß Gott Herr Reinhard."

"Hi Mr. Reinhard it is me Jack."

"Oh hallo Jack what can I do for you?"

Wow you know what that is—wow. Did not see that coming at all. Reinhard has absolutely no notion I am supposed to be dead and tragically Lucille is in his house right now with you know something of a brief like an instruction and the worst thing is that I can't really change that. I mean I can change that but—

"Mr. Reinhard I—gosh I am just so sorry. I should really have had Doc or Charlie make this call."

"They are very charming Jack but—"

There is a noise that Lucille makes when he hugs. Nothing else makes the noise that that makes. I hear it now and I wish I hadn't. It is not a noise you ever want to hear but somehow I never quite manage to not listen.

Reinhard says something. I hope it was a really amazing thing. Reinhard was kind of chipper but you know he was a professional but once he heard my voice he knew I was alive— well you know, operationally speaking, that can't be allowed at this time.

I mean we could have kidnapped him I guess that would actually have been—

I am so off my game I should really have considered the possibility that it was not him. That is totally on me. Waste of resources but you know I am sad right now.

Well okay what's done is done.

That leaves two.

THREE

LEAVE BEFORE DAWN. SAUL COMES TOO. I like Saul he is like having a really huge scary support animal. We talk about old-time TV, which is to say I talk about old-time TV and Saul says he prefers old-time radio, like apparently *Richard Diamond* is his jam. I say *Peter Gunn* is better and he says no it is not better it is the same stories on TV but with Craig Stevens.

Train to the west and south. Guard has a nose piercing and sits down to talk about Spanish politics. His mother is Spanish Catalan. She is conflicted. Madrid is wrong but so are the separatists. None of it is what matters. What matters is that his brothers cannot find work and people are saluting Franco's bones. I say that only a total asshole would have an ongoing dialogue with the skeleton of a dead monster and the guard says yes I have a clear understanding and Europe right now is full of such assholes.

I say that is very bad and I do not say that Saul has a sawed-off shotgun in his luggage because that sort of thing often offends. Sawed-off like at both ends like pistol short. It's a murder stick not a marksman's tool and it would be a huge disappointment in any sort of gunfight but as a discussion piece like face-to-face it is super persuasive.

When the guard has gone I tell Saul that I one time made a cannon out of pipe and a gas cylinder and Saul says he doesn't have much time for improvised weaponry generally. Saul says that of course all weaponry is improvised in one way or another but he makes yogurt at home and is familiar with the variations of flavor and intensity and texture that come with fluctuations in climate and he does not look for that kind of variation in his professional tool kit. I say that Saul is hooked on the gun crack of the military industrial combine and toxic masculinity and Saul says that we are not in a competition about our genitals so it is okay for me to have a homemade cannon and for him to have a room full of specialized mercenary stuff.

For the record anyone who is male and alive is in a competition about genitals with Saul. The only reason I am not actually destroyed by the mere existence of Saul and Saul's genitals is that he bivouacs with a landscape designer and I am the recognized sex partner of the world's premier psychopathic bioscience researcher. My boy parts may or may not be physically equal to Saul's but they are fucking intrepid. Doc's present erotic jam is an experimental memory drug called Fisahypnozerasol. FHZ is the next thing I will illegally sell if I ever get back into the illegally-selling-things business because it is fucking brilliant. It acts on the brain to blur memory around the point of orgasm so you can remember the fact of having amazing sex but not exactly what was amazing about it or what led up to it, which means you can ask your partner to do something motherfucking weird without fear because both you and they will forget details of the whole thing the following day. On the downside if you do not orgasm you remember everything and therefore it is crucially important to have a backup plan because you do not want to collect a mental library of frustratingly incomplete sexual experiences. But that is fine because you also can do the same amazingly obscene thing over and over and not get bored of it. So Doc and I are having exceptional sex right now and every time it is nervous and new and intimate and totally disgraceful and then we get to do it all again. A month ago I woke up with scratches from my ankles to my ass and words from a Swedish road map written on my junk and I can safely say I will never see the Frösö bridge in the same way again.

I sit and think about the astonishingly obscene things I have done that I cannot remember until we reach the next station.

Cross the border into France. New guard is silent. She drinks coffee. She has a mark on her finger where there used to be a ring. Clips my ticket and we're done.

Like that.

I read half a book and leave it on the table. Monte Carlo station looks like a golden bathroom with trains.

Short walk across town.

I let us in to Sharkey's apartment and we get in the shower. Water comes out hard and hot because billionaires love not paying tax but they still expect good pressure or they start to think they're getting ripped off.

I stand in the shower in my clothes. Saul stands next to me. Saul stands next to me in the shower in his clothes getting soaked and he is okay with that because he is a professional.

"Saul this is super professional I am impressed."

"To be honest Jack I was thinking about porn. This is a kind of a porn scenario here."

"That also makes perfect sense but the point is that I could not possibly have known that if you had not told me. That is professional."

So we stand there being professional and now I'm also thinking about porn. I think about Doc and all the terrible things we have done to each other and about the way she moves and

about the terrible terrible things she will do to Agent Hannah
and—

Professional.

Sharkey gets in the apartment and hears the water and
makes the obvious wrong deduction that his lovely lady Crystal is here and no doubt that in his mind there is also baby
oil because he comes through the door naked and flings open
the shower cubicle and after a minute or so where we all just
look at one another. Because it's there I guess Saul just rests the
emphasis gun right over Sharkey's erection like a cloche on a
cake.

Sharkey passes out on the bath mat.

While I work I am still a little bit unhappy about the sawed-off
situation like I feel I am the boss I should definitely have the
coolest gun but the gas cannon was a very specific moment
in my life and you know what they say you cannot go home
again.

Sharkey wakes up.

Sharkey says: "What the fuck do you think—"

"No Sharkey no. Please not today. Today is a me day I am
taking a me day."

There is something in my voice or Saul's face or maybe just
the emphasis gun because Sharkey listens.

"I am unhappy Sharkey. I wish to converse in honesty and
openness as between professional men. Men of commerce
Sharkey who respect one another and who understand the ebb
and flow of economic totality and who recognize imperatives."

"What fucking imperatives Price for—"

With my free hand I point one finger downward. "Whut

wait whut now," Sharkey says, and looks. Then after a while he says: "What. The. Shit?"

I say: "That is a suicide vest for your scrotum."

Because it is.

The vest is not absolutely a vest because it is more like a snood. I crocheted it out of detcord. It will not actually kill a person outright. Not immediately at least. Having your scrotum explode is not necessarily fatal it is just what you might say a turning point in a life such that there is a time before and a time after. That said, Doc assures me that very few people will voluntarily act in such a way as to cause explosive testicular vaporization. It is psychology plus also even in the event you are not real into scrotal lifestyles—and Sharkey is—having your sac blown into orbit by a detcord snood is no one's idea of rock and roll.

Sharkey gets some clothes on like baggy sweatpants and a sports jacket so now he is real on-trend for the Yacht Club brunch and he says that I have his full attention which I do.

"Here is how we will do this Sharkey are you paying close attention? Say yes Jack."

"Yes Jack."

"I am right now in a mood Sharkey. I am in a pisser of a mood. But I will trade your continuing scrotitude for information freely and unstintingly given."

"Aw come on Jack I cannot—"

"No Sharkey NO. I am TALKING."

". . . Okay Jack."

"I do not want your general business details or your confidential shit. I just want to know about my confidential shit namely who WHO sent a tiny evil *Sound of Music*–looking motherfucker and a dude with a long gun to do me wrong Sharkey WHO?"

"Not me—"

"Of course not you or you would be on a fucking magic hideaway island somewhere hoping I cannot track you like a bloodhound, which I can. From now on always I can."

"You can like forever?"

"Once I have tied detcord around a scrotum Sharkey I can always find it again. Unless I have exploded it then basically it becomes a concept scrotum more like a concept piece than something you could hang."

"Fuck it Jack FUCK IT this is precisely what I was saying with reference to your team being weird that kind of statement is—"

"Sharkey. Say Yes Jack."

"I do not—"

"SHARKEY."

"Yes Jack."

"I am prepared to accept provisionally that you are not enough of a stupid fuck to send a prepubescent to stab me with an oyster knife and leave me alive although also too I am blessed with an exceptional team of persons and it is possible you just messed up your knockout in some way. But seeing as you are going to be super-duper frank with me—and bearing in mind always that there is detcord around your man apples—I am gonna go with the idea that you are not at fault here."

"Okay."

"For now."

"Okay."

"But that then creates a problem Sharkey because then we touch on the tender area of your professional connections."

"O shit."

"Yes. We do."

"O shit Jack."

"Yes Sharkey here is the problem it was you or it was one of mine or it was Mr. Client."

"Okay Jack can I say something?"

"Yes Sharkey."

"I don't wanna disrespect nobody at this point in time Jack but someone has to say this."

"Go ahead man I will be indulgent."

"You gotta be real calm."

"I will be motherfucking papal."

"Did you consider it might be Volodya?"

". . ."

". . ."

". . ."

"Please don't explode my balls."

"What—oh—naw man I was not thinking that."

"Okay."

"That suggestion more than anything Sharkey is reassuring to me that you are really giving this some thought."

"It is?"

"Yes it is because that is an intelligent suggestion and it is left field. You are thinking that he fakes getting shot then slips out of the mail truck while I am unconscious and he dumps some vagrant or what have you into the mill engine and now he is invisible and he is coming for me for whatever fortune and glory or just because he is an evil old fuck?"

"I do not know what any of those things are in the middle but yeah I guess something like that."

"It is a classic and you got to respect your history."

"Yes?"

"Even if that history is largely like eighties movies. But there is a problem with your theory Sharkey."

"There is?"

"Yeah man I saw half of his face in a basket before I left this morning. Brain still somewhat in the factory-standard housing."

". . . Oh."

"Yeah so while I completely respect that you took a risk there and that was very cool of you under the circumstances it does not really get us anywhere. But kudos man that was—"

". . ."

"I was going to say ballsy but it seems in poor taste."

"Yeah okay I hear ya but then Jack you know there's the doctor and Charlie and—"

"Sharkey I see what you're doing here and again I got to respect the attempt man because I get that confidentiality is your all but—"

"Jack—"

"There's no help for it Sharkey you're going to have to tell me who Mr. Client is."

"I—"

"Otherwise I will be subject to a reciprocal negative obligation in regard the aerosolization of your ballsack."

"Balzac?"

"Jesus Christ Sharkey answer the fucking question."

". . . It was a shell Jack I swear."

"Of course it was a fucking shell we are crime people we do not—"

"It was a shell is what I'm saying so I DID NOT KNOW or I would have never—"

"You know now."

"Now I'm putting it the fuck together Jack I know something okay SOMETHING but I don't know how much of it is right and I was honest-to-God wondering whether I should call you today but I—"

"Sharkey."

"Yes?"

"Papal-fucking-indulgence Sharkey. I am pissed with you but so long as we can get through this conversation I consider actually hurting you a waste of resources."

"You do?"

"I do and Sharkey this is also the point I am making to you and the world: I am Jack. Fucking. Price. I am not some cowboy I am a professional I like things to BE CALM. That is my fondest hope and in furtherance of things being motherfucking calm I will trade you your fondest hope, which I assume to be retaining your scrotum in non-aerosol form am I right?"

". . . You actually did shoot a guy with a severed head that time."

"And it was huge fun Sharkey and it made a hellacious mediapathic attention-getting mess but my point is it was appropriate and it was proportional to need, okay? Sadly it did not function as a prelude to sensible discussions but that is because other parties who should have known better became needlessly emotional about the whole situation and I cannot legislate for the behavior of others. However exigent fucking circumstances obtain right now, that is to say I have been shot in the Ukrainian and there are—you know Sharkey there are rules and conventions but above all this one, which is we provide a service and we do so according to the norms established by time-honored criminal practice and, you know, all that shit. Okay? We are a service entity and I just want the information necessary to carry on my business in all the relevant directions."

Sharkey says he does not know like know like something you could use in court, and I have grown as a person in the last few days and months so I do not blow him up by the balls right then. Instead I say: "O RLY?"

And Sharkey says that he thinks it may all have been Hans Eiger all along.

Hans Eiger owns the Kircheisen Festung. Obviously it would be not unheard of for a guy who owns a bank to rob that bank. But I offered him a bunch of money for his bank like waaaay too much. Hans Eiger does not care about money or at least he does not care about money only or money in that way.

I say this to Sharkey and Sharkey says that he is once more thinking about the whole business with whales and the thermocline and Saul says quickly I am not to explode Sharkey's balls so I just frown my ball-exploding frown that I have just made up. Sharkey gets the message because balls.

Why would a man who does not care about money rob his own bank?

Sharkey says Hans Eiger does care about money because Hans Eiger is oh so very broke, but he cannot sell his bank because if he tries he will probably die.

The thing is that Hans Eiger did not create Die Festung because it was a good idea, he created it because he wanted it to be a good idea and honestly it is a terrible idea. But Hans Eiger cares about stability so much that he cannot see that and someone who cannot adjust to reality is not a good person to be running a company. No sir.

The truth is that no one gives a shit for physical storage

these days except a few old folks and Hans Eiger. You care that much about physical stuff and you are that rich, you build your own vault in a volcano—but honestly wealth is vapor now. It is concept more than it ever has been and the hoarding of British Empire diamonds in gold nests like an evil chipmunk is no longer considered a sign of taste and distinction. There's a certain class of person that has shit that needs to be hidden away somewhere like Die Festung and that class is old-money sinners with no future and there are fewer of them every year. When you have a dwindling client pool you got to be the only sensible choice for the evil-chipmunk people and as it turns out Hans Eiger is not. Not only is Swiss law getting less and less amenable to the stashing of secret money and secret stolen stuff but also there is competition for the evil-chipmunk market. There's private islands and there's Hatton Garden and old nuclear bunkers in Dipshit, Milwaukee, and there's museum loans with maintenance grants and a condition that the item not be displayed for twenty years, and a dozen other ways to get the job done that do not require putting your expensive and illegal shit in a bunker with a ROB ME sign on the door.

Eiger built his dream just in time for almost everyone else to realize they didn't need it.

He cannot sell because the moment he does the few remaining customers he has—the legacy mob, your older Chinese and Russian oligarchs with fixations on physical wealth, some real traditional gold-standard believers and yeah likely also some of Those Guys that Ottavio Leopold was talking about—those good friends will feel that he has betrayed a sacred trust. A few of them will probably take steps to prevent any sale. Hans Eiger needed an alternative and that alternative was me.

Oh indeed this was not about running off with the proceeds

of robbing his own bank and balling dancers under Mexican stars. This is about the darkest reaches of the human heart.

I'm talking about advertising.

Sharkey says he figured Eiger was legit intending to rob his own bank and claim the insurance on goods he actually still had. Sharkey is wrong. Sharkey is uninterested in revolutionary change. Sharkey is lumpen.

Hans Eiger was not thinking along those lines. Hans Eiger was looking to make a point. A splash. A revofuckinglution in personal financial security. To demonstrate that his bank was unassailable. That his bank had the largest banking genitals in all the wide swinging world of steel and concrete and holes in the ground.

And for that what he needed—what he needed—

He needed us.

The Demons.

Not to rob the bank.

To try to rob the bank.

And fail.

Because if there is one thing everyone likes it is a hero story and for a good hero story you need a villain because a villain makes a headline.

And with the right headlines he could turn the emptiness of the Kircheisen Festung into a frantic demand for space. His perceptual issue will become word of mouth.

If Hans Eiger kills the Seven Demons as we try to rob his bank, his bank becomes the coolest fucking bank in the universe. The evil-chipmunk community will want his smooth stone corridors and his musty steel vaults more than they want sex or money or power. International dumb people will open accounts with him and keep nothing in their fucking vaults at all, just to say that they got an account with Die Festung before their brother-in-law did. So he called me and he sent some flunky to be Mr. Client ooh la la and romance my larceny and—

I fell for it.

I fell for it.

I.

Fell.

For that.

I cannot believe I fucking—well that Eiger would believe I would fall for that is—

It is fucking offensive is what it is and that offense is in no way mitigated by the fact that he was right that is not the point I should not have and he should not have DREAMED that I would. Not EVER.

It's offensive.

It's offensive and it is also—he is also—he is fucking un-Swiss. Can you believe it? This whole shit is un-Swiss. He caused a hazard to the public in pursuit of profit and he got caught doing it. That is un-Swiss.

But there's more than that there is something that is beyond offensive it is fucking Hegelian in its ingenuity to piss me off is what.

Do you know what is beyond offensive? That is a coffee trick. It is a commodities trick. Here is what you do you—and this is why you never invest in the fucking gold market because those fuckers barely do anything except this—you have a bunch of coffee for sale and you get a letter of intent to buy and then you turn around and show everyone that oh so confidential letter and you create a demand. You fuck the first

buyer and the price goes up and you sell at the top and everyone else is left holding the fucking bag when the price resumes
seasonal levels.

"Sharkey this is all very cogent but I have to ask what made
you look at Eiger in the first place?"

"Well Jack there is a thing about Eiger."

"What thing?"

"There is the thing about his being in the Legion and all."

"He was in the Legion he was this hard-ass we know this."

"Yeah but Jack it didn't matter until now so you didn't
likely look much at his record—"

"Just say it—"

"Okay okay he was a recon scout sniper—"

"FUCK—"

"Jack please do not wave the detonator—"

"Saul I'm not waving the—oh thank you yes I was—"

"That is fine but Mr. Sharkey here has been most helpful
Jack and it's important to be seen to be reasonable under difficult circumstances is that not right Mr. Sharkey?"

"Yes Skipper it absolutely—"

Saul hands me back the detonator and asks Sharkey super-
duper nicely not to call him that.

Yeah haha. Very ha indeed but here is the thing Sharkey is
right. Sharkey is right and—

Hans Eiger.

Hans Eiger has done that with his bank and the first buyer
is me and he has fucked me in my Ukrainian.

All around the world there are a bajillion differing perceptions
of what you owe to your friends and loved ones and what

is appropriate when someone fucks with them. These perceptions range from respecting their caritas and the forgiveness of all mankind to burning cities and putting heads on sticks but the points is there is a spectrum or in fact there is a like a complex three-dimensional space into which all these responses could be placed. What there is not is unanimity and no one gets to tell you what is appropriate to your grief your relationship your private inner knowledge that maybe things were not as they seemed or la la la. Right?

But here this is not that, it is o so much simpler because yes Volodya was on some level my friend. Sure. That is to say I enjoyed his company and god help me his dubiously-sourced-dried-meat hobbyism and his grisly Soviet Industrial murder bullshit. I even loved that he carried his ridiculous out-of-date-ass rifle everywhere and we had to dress it up as a puppet one time whatever. He was an old fart and I liked him and he liked me, so to say he approved of my brand of awful and he liked that I liked his terrible jokes and his dubiously sourced dried meats and yeah maybe just maybe there was some kind of commonality of soul or I don't know what.

I am not a soul kinduva person. I don't really do that stuff so I am not sad right now not like sad sad not like crying. I am totally in touch with my emotions but I am not the crying sort of person and I am not sad. I'm fine. I mean I'll miss him but I am.

Fine.

Commonality of soul yeah sure but that is not relevant all that is data for your 3D grief graph and that graph is not part of my workflow now because yes right yes you heard me I said: workflow.

Volodya worked for me. That was the nature of our relationship. It was professional.

I have people and he was my people and we are—we were—our RELATIONSHIP yes fucker I said it twice don't @ me—our relationship is of a professional and even what you would say like a military nature. We were in a killing business and he would have killed anyone—anyone at all in the universe—if I had said so.

Probably not without some discussion and fartery unless the situation was exigent but still.

And he would have—maybe he did and I do not know but that also is not relevant NOT relevant and certainly it is not emotionally relevant or it would be emotionally relevant IF we our relationship was of the sort where that sort of thing was itself relevant but see above—he would have stepped in front of a bullet for me because he was combat and I was leadership and in the end that is what it is.

And reciprocally there is stuff. My Person stuff. Like debts and obligations and interestingly those obligations are super consistent across cultures.

So when I say this it is not like an irrational response to emotional pain at all it is totally rational it is a professional matter is all.

Completely professional.

Mr. Eiger.

O Mr. Eiger.

I am rethinking my approach to this job sir. I am considering a new vision of our onward relationship with certain stakeholders in the wider community. Certain stakeholders who have taken a negatively aspected route in re our privacy and the confidentiality of our new venture. It is not likely Mr. Eiger I am afraid it is not likely at all that everyone will retain their present employment status in the new iteration of the profit track. I'm afraid some positions will be redundant and certain people—yes even some senior executives—will have to seek a new level they will have to be managed out. People with the wrong attitude will not make the cut they will be downsized. I don't like to say it I do not but here is the honest truth in terms. In the argot. The blunt truth is that it won't be a soft transition. In the end it has to be acknowledged—well. Sometimes there just aren't any good remedies for that moment in the corporate life cycle and sometimes you can't give someone— with the best will in the world you cannot give someone the ending they would like.

I don't know how else to put this and it is totally your choice that this is where we are—your choice from start to finish do please remember that as we embrace the forward aspect of our dealings—I'm just saying in the end there's no way around it:

Heads will roll, Mr. Eiger.

Heads will roll.

Sharkey is still staring at me and I'm obviously not going to take him home with me. I mean what would I do with another mouth to feed?

So I get some Saran Wrap and I tape the cut end to the floor and I tape the roll to his hands.

Sharkey says: "What the fuck are you doing?"

"Well Sharkey I am leaving now and I do not want to blow up your balls."

"Oh that's great Jack I really—"

"But at the same time I do not entirely trust you to be measured about this situation when the adrenal glands start working their mojo and so on. All kinds of weird biochemical shit is about to break loose in your body Sharkey and your decision making is going to suck so I am first of all going to urge you to do NOTHING for twenty-four hours and then I am going to explain to you what's happening here okay?"

"Okay."

"So first of all I am putting the phone I am using as a detonator—which is still live okay so please don't—okay—in the other room. All you have to do is wait until someone comes in and get them to switch it off. Then you are all good. And I am going to call your cleaning service in about an hour and then you'll be fine and as I say maybe just take a personal day. But in the meantime Sharkey I cannot emphasize this enough do NOT stand up. If you stand up the static charge on the Saran Wrap will almost certainly induce a current in the detonator cables and your balls will explode."

". . ."

"True fact."

". . ."

". . ."

"Saran Wrap will do that?"

"It is science Sharkey I am dating a scientist."

I walk to the train station and honestly I halfway expect to hear the sound of Sharkey's balls exploding but I do not so I assume he has abruptly become wise. I call his cleaning service and book them in for five-ish, which is the first time they can make it today. I get back on the train.

Man, Europe is just totally civilized this is the only way to travel.

Doc says: "It does not matter. We do the job."

"But Doc we have no client—"

"Of course we have a client."

"Who tried to kill us. It was a setup."

"It does not matter if the client never wanted the job done. We rob the bank. We bring our employer exactly what he asked for. If he then refuses to pay us that is a problem for him but we—we are the Seven Demons. The robbing of the bank follows inexorably from our hiring as day follows night and one breath follows the next as death follows life. That is all that exists in the world for any of us because we are the Seven Demons. That is what we do and what we are and it is what Volodya died for and that means something to me. Is that clear?"

"But—"

"Is. That. Clear."

"Yes Doc."

"I will rob the bank. I am entirely capable of doing that as you well know. You will go and be as loud as possible so that everyone is paying attention to you and while that is happening—"

"Wait I'm the distraction?"

"You are the right hand everyone watches. I am the left one, which empties the pocket."

"I do not want to be the diversion."

"I know but Price when all this is done there you will be. Everyone will be used to you and you . . . you are the razor blade taped between the fingers."

". . . Yes."

"You will make a miracle for Volodya. For all of us. For me. You will fully express our disappointment."

"I can do that I guess."

"You can. The liquid nitrogen wedding was one of the most awful things I have ever heard of and that is what I want from you right now. Only more so. Like that but with actual malice Price. I want it to hurt."

"Are you . . . okay?"

"No I am not. Do you understand me? I am not okay."

"Yes."

"Make a horrible plan Price because if you don't I will."

"Okay."

"And I do not have your restraint."

"I'm sorry I think you said you do not have my restraint?"

"Please think about this carefully and realize as I say it that I appreciate the magnitude of the assertion and I am factoring into it the fullest understanding of who and what you are: No. I do not."

Doc buys a giant electronic whiteboard and writes HOMER at the top. It is the HOMER board. There is a column for stuff that we need and another for stuff we have dealt with and another for stuff that we haven't.

I write FUCKING HORRIBLE REVENGE on the agenda section of the board. Doc says yes quite so. Then she makes a new page on the board for robbing the bank and everyone writes a list of things they would need if they were going to rob the bank their own way.

Saul:

Full architectural and system diagrams

Pressure diving equipment/biomedical suits times seven

Two commandos

Three bulldozers

Demolitions and entry options tbc

Mi-26 "flying crane" helicopter or best option

Saul says: "Jack I feel like I should say this is not a good way to do this. Like do this head-on and you are in a land war for like seven hundred miles of escape route."

"That would be super cool though."

"It would be a cool movie Jack it would not be a cool plan."

"I am very disappointed in you Saul with your common sense and your shitty practical approach."

"You're welcome Jack."

"Doc Saul is fitting in too well can we kill him?"

"No Price we cannot Charlie and I have spoken of it and we find him aesthetically appropriate also he shares the babysitting."

"What baby—oh. Oh haha okay we will ignore the unkind implication that I am an infant. And proceed show me your stuff."

"Aw boss I am moved but I think Doc would object—"

"Charlie—"

"Hey you are all embarrassed by the sexy talk that is sweet—"

"Doc help me—"

"She's right Price it is kinda sweet—"

"Thank you Doc I think it is sweet that you think it is sweet—"

"Come ON man that is literally what I said but you guys are bumping uglies so—"

"Hush Charlie your crime parents are talking—"

"Ew no I do not want to have come out of Doc's crime vagina—"

" . . . "

" . . . "

" . . . "

". . . If anyone ever mentions even the notion of my pos-

sessing such an organ again that person will immediately die
is that clear?"

"..."

"..."

"..."

"... Yup crystal."

"Yup."

"Yup."

"Oh yeah."

"Lucille."

"Then I will proceed."

Doc:

Three large pigs (live)
Neo-scopolamine (Belgian Heverlee variant) 200 doses
Aerosol dispersal unit
Tranquilizer guns
Gun guns
One Festung security employee (high rank) to be
    secured before visit
Others to be acquired on-site
And one helicopter

Charlie:

Supercomputer time
Detailed base code for Die Festung
Caffeinated beverages
Alcohol
Cocaine
Water bed
Norwegian men's biathlon team

Supercomputer time
Trunk broadband access
Fast car
Awesome dress
Casino chips
Walther PPK with silencer
Custom genetically tailored MDMA variant
Eye patch
Snakes
Supercomputer time
Lightsaber
X-wing
Droids
Metallic swimwear
Supercomputer time
Hot tub
35 mm film projector
35 mm print of *Koyaanisqatsi*
Moty's auto hyper lubricant (Thailand)
Romy Tarangul
Supercomputer time—

"Charlie I sense your attention is straying—"
"No boss my plan is just real baroque is all—"
"Okay carry on—"
"Naw I guess that'll do it."
". . . Ewwkay."

Rex:

Eight times Massive Ordnance Penetrator (MOP)
Eight times Massive Ordnance Air Blast Bomb
    (MOAB)

Eight C-130 Hercules aircraft for delivery
Marshmallows

"Rex I am not certain that the contents of the vault will survive your plan there. Also the marshmallows will burn. A lot."

"Oh I was not going to cook them sir I like them as God intended."

"Okay but how do we complete the mission Rex?"

"I figure we just get this stuff then tell them we have it and what we're gonna do with it and they can either open the fucking doors or we'll do it and then go with Saul's exit plan."

". . ."

". . ."

"That is the most grown-up thing anyone has said Rex and that is alarming."

"Yes sir."

"Seriously Rex I got to respect this approach it is real Demony."

"Thank you sir."

"I am not sure that it meets our present needs Rex but I think next time we will start with you."

"Thank you sir."

". . . Carry on Rex."

"Yes sir."

Lucille:
LUCILLE!

". . ."

". . ."

". . ."

"Yeah who knows actually that might do it."

"..."

"..."

"What about you Price?"

"Naw Doc I am still collating our many options."

"Well get it done. In the meantime I have a thing."

"Yum yum—"

"Silence!"

She does not look jokey so I silence.

We sit in the long room and Doc says to everyone: "Do not be like Jack."

That seems harsh to me but Doc is speechifying and I do not want to be rude.

Doc says: "We already have Jack we do not need everyone to be Jack. But we are the Demons now and not anything else. That is the only thing that matters in this moment. Where we are? Who we were? These things are not relevant anymore. This job needs to be everything and I'm telling you how you get there. You do not choose to be like Jack. You choose to be like you as if you were hopped-up on appalling Jackness like fucked-up on a toxic testosterone psychotropic methamphetamine Jack serum."

Rex puts up his hand. "Um I do not know how to do that."

Doc nods.

"Open your eyes and look at the ceiling fan I will administer it now."

"What—"

"I cultured this out of Jack's blood this morning. That means it also contains Volodya. Look upward Rex you will feel a slight pressure as the needle goes in."

"Uh-oh gosh well uuhhhhhttttt oh gosh I feel sick."

"Rex it is only a needle. There. Now. Who's next?"

"There. And there. And here—"

Doc. Injects. Her own. Eyeball.

That's my girlfriend right there.

". . . You are populated with Jack's microflora. With Volodya's. You are a little bit them and so am I."

Charlie wants to know if that will actually do anything.

"I have no idea. Perhaps. There is an element of magical thinking. But you will feel different and you are different. The degree of difference is unknown. You are all, biotically speaking, Jack. Except you, Price. There is obviously no point giving you a serum of yourself so I have made this one for you."

"What is that?"

"It's us."

". . . It's a big one ain't it?"

"Don't be a baby."

"I am just saying Doc everyone else got a little tiny poke and that is like something you would use to make a cow pregnant and we all know how I feel about cows."

"Jack?"

"Doc?"

"Jack."

"Doc?"

"This injection contains all of us who are alive. I cannot give you Volodya because he is dead. But you do not need me to do that because he is already in you because he gave you his blood when he knew he was dying. He knew he was dying and he chose that and I do not think you thanked him."

" . . . "

" . . . "

" . . . "

" . . . "

"I am not crying."

"I know."

"Into my fucking eyeball Doc I am ready!"

"In fact this injection goes in your gluteus muscle."

"What right here in front of the anarchists?"

". . ."

". . ."

". . ."

"Of fucking course it does, typical log-cabin motherfucker, all right you guys fuck off to work while I drop trou for the dead Russian asshole. Jeez Doc you just had to didn't you. I mean where's my fucking dignity in all OW OW OW."

So what do I do now?

I have like a mood or a modus: I'm Jack. I'm the Price you pay.

That's it.

(Wow. Little head rush there. Demon juice got some kick I guess.)

I mean Lucille doesn't really have skills either he just hugs people and they die of his giant knifepuppy affection but somehow that does not bother him. Well I say somehow . . . it's because I burned out his brain using drugs and electric shocks and turned him into a giant knifepuppy because I wanted to.

That's my modus in action right there I guess and now here is Doc and she says I am the guy to make the appalling shit happen.

That's my modus too I guess.

I mean it's not what I want. I am just a guy trying to get along.

I sit by and my leg hurts and I wonder what I am going to do.

Stabbed in the fucking leg by a fucking kid.

Stabbed with a fucking oyster knife like a fucking joke criminal.

Stabbed by a child.

What am I?

I'm a guy without a log-cabin motherfucker to my name is what and I don't know who to talk to about it. Like who to make representations but also like who to talk to.

I'm the first of the Seven Demons. I have all of them in my blood right now. I think you could cook an egg on my balls. Volodya would do it he would stake me out and cook an actual fucking egg and he would claim it wasn't weird just some old Ukrainian survival thing.

When man is losing that much heat, is no alternative in cold night.

(Head rush.)

Fucking post-Soviet log-cabin motherfucker I think he just made that shit up. Fucking universal donor bullshit.

I leave the coffee and I go and stand behind the awful bar and stare into the stupid mirror between the Japanese whisky and the French vodka.

"My name is Jack Price and I am the Price you pay."

But I'm just not feeling it. Who the fuck is that in the mirror? Got some crime face going on but who the fuck?

"My name is Jack Price."

"Hi, I'm Jack, and I'm—"

I mean the thing is it was funny one time but once you pay a price it is paid and that's it. Otherwise it's a subscription.

I am not a fucking subscription.

Looking at that face. I dunno man who the fuck owns that face? Some guy. One time was a coffee guy. Then he was a smartass coke guy. Then he killed a bunch of folks. Some stuff happened in between whatever. Then his friend died his employee and he was evidently not ready for that to happen.

How is it he was okay with his lawyer that he was actually a little bit in love with how is it he was okay that she got shot in the side of the head and he was fine with that but this is not okay? Who thinks that way?

Who?

"My name is—"

I'm not feeling it.

Yeah well Jack would you like to phone a friend?

Sure why not I got lots.

Lots of friends.

Only want to talk to one of them.

"Hallo yes this is a post-Soviet log-cabin motherfucker and I am a little bit dead forever right now please leave a message beep."

"O you're deceased? Well gosh that's embarrassing I forgot—man is my face red—"

Face arms legs fuck I was fucking covered in blood so—

(Head rush. I think I may be high. Demon juice high.)

Okay come on come on my name is—

"MY NAME IS"

"My name is FUCK IT"

What am I ever supposed to do with this?

You know what Jack why don't you call someone who isn't dead?

Outgoing VoIP call:

"Hi It's Barton hi I am VERY RICH in a water bed right now who's this?"

"Hey Barton it's Jack Price."

"Jack Price?"

"Jack Price, Barton."

"Jack who?"

"The guy with the plane. The bad guy, Barton. I have had a not good day do not make me come over there and murderize you for being you."

"O Banjo Telemark? The artist sir?"

". . . Yes. Yes I am an artist Barton."

"Okay sir."

". . ."

"Sir?"

". . . I am thinking Barton. I will require your input shortly."

"O. O okay just uh—that's a little tricky right now sir there is stuff going on—yowow mama Calliope—I'm just a little distracted sir—"

". . ."

". . ."

"Fog of crime."

"O my saints and kittens—yes sir fog of crime sir—"

". . . did you say saints and kittens?"

". . . um yes sir I was greatly moved—oh my—now I am a little self-conscious sir—damn it I will beat you like a four-egg omelet—not you sir I am talking to Calliope—"

"Barton I would send you more money but you cannot possibly spend what you have."

"Oh thank you sir I guess."

"Is there anything revolting you need that I can arrange or pay for you seem like a nice person there are certain aspects you might balk at."

"No sir I'm real contented right now sir you see—oh—oh YEEEebob be a little kind there—I'm fine sir—just a little matter of—"

"Barton I do not think I need to know what you are doing and I fear you are about to tell me so I am going to go. Call me if anything comes up."

"Oh very good sir okay O yoooyooHOBA—"

"Bye now Barton."

Call disconnected.

See there's two ways of doing something so that no one knows it's happening. There is the one where you walk on tiptoe in the dark and if the lights come on you have a problem like—

Well I guess you get stabbed in the leg with an oyster knife.

But then there is the other way of doing something that no one knows is happening. Fog of crime. That is when you fill a room with light and noise and women in sequins and men in top hats and ten thousand elephants and while all that is happening and everyone is staring at the show—

You stab someone with an oyster knife.

Sometimes it's about the modus and that is good. Sometimes it is all about process. But other times you fucking mainline your Ukrainian and the blood of your criminal associates and you just fucking do it. That is also some kind of truth.

Sometimes it is about the vision and my vision right now . . . (Wham.)

That was more than a head rush. I think I just exploded out of my own face and—

I can see worlds of crime. They are all around me and I am them. I am space and time I am coffee I am cocaine I am universes. I am gods and I am—

I am Demons.

"My name is—"

Yes.

"My name is—"

Say it.

"My name is Banjo Telemark."

Let me show you my art.

Ringedy ring.

I am busy being full of worlds of crime so I let it go to voice mail.

Ringedy ring.

Voice mail.

Ringedy ring RING RING RING okay fine FINE what—

O it is Sharkey.

It probably is not the ideal moment to take this call because I do not feel diplomatic and Sharkey, well you know: Sharkey has cause to be a little annoyed. In fairness—well if I had it to do over—

Naw I guess it would go exactly the same.

VoIP encrypted: accept y/n

"Hi it's Jack I'm a little busy right now but go ahead."

"Jack it's Sharkey."

"Hi Sharkey I am glad to hear you well. I am right now doing a thing so I cannot undertake any new work if that is why you are calling also I am stoned out of my gourd on Demon juice—"

"You're a dead man you fuck."

"Okay well that is disappointing I was hoping we could move past this Sharkey and go back to being friends?"

"Friends you shit you wanna be FRIENDS now?"

"I can't say it's like my dearest wish man but yeah that's where I was heading I mean we gotta work together and it's basically my default like, you know, a stranger is a friend you haven't—"

"You put DYNAMITE ON MY BALLS—"

"In fact it was not technically dynamite. That's like that stuff in cartoons. This was way more, you know, professional and grown-up. And I gather from the fact we are talking that the service have, you know, I guess unlimbered your scrotum. So—"

"Dynamite. On. My. Balls."

"Okay I get where you're coming from but you know Sharkey I was real upset and I needed your attention and you got this attitude like you've seen it all and done it. I figured that actually had not happened to you before. And see here we are and it is fine and we can work together. I was upset with you over you know your client betraying me and killing my friend but I have moved past it and you still have your moving parts so—"

"You're gonna put dynamite on my balls you fuck? You're a dead man I am going to kill you with my own hands. KILL YOU and I will juggle with your fucking balls and I will have dogs and the dogs will—"

"Sharkey I have to say your timing is not great we are right now holding a sort of a wake for a colleague and I feel like your mood is a little disruptive maybe even disrespectful."

"FUCK YOU—"

"Okay man I'm kind of done with this little chat let's talk again when you're more even tempered—"

But la la la Sharkey is angry. The dogs will either eat me or fuck me or both I really have no idea I am not listening. I mean honestly how are you gonna do both at once? Hello: SPINE?

"Sharkey it is Jack have you killed me yet or am I still screaming?"

"You're fucking dead right now Jack. I am connected you know who I am connected to? To fucking Ottavio Leopold Calvanese you fuck you remember him—"

"That is a real elegant fellow there Sharkey."

"Yeah you tell him that see what it gets you."

"Sharkey."

"Yeah you walking dead man piss-pot motherfuck?"

"Sharkey are we not going to do business together anymore?"

"FUCK YOU JACK I am coming for you I am gonna come for you Jack you're dead D E A D is what you are you COME TO MY HOUSE—"

"It's really more of a duplex but anyway you're saying I should count you as an active like enemy like even if I had some massively financially rewarding thing coming I should not come to you and cut you in that would not make it better. We're just enemies now over this whole thing? Because man I thought we were bigger than that."

"Dead Jack. Dead."

(Mute call.)

"CHAAARLLLIIIIIEEE?"

No answer so I go back in the room with the board, which I will not call the board room.

"Charlie Sharkey is calling and he is pissed."

"Oh dearie dear."

"Also he is—I got to say this man I feel like he's mostly coming from a negative sort of place and—did I say I was basically high on you guys like your mitochondrial sexy hormones—"

"Price that is not a real thing JESUS you're burning up what the—"

"I am filled with worlds of crime Doc."

"Yes I imagine you are—"

"I see paradigms. Socially."

"Price—"

"But that is not the point I cannot keep Sharkey on hold forever he is going to become unreasonable well no actually he is already—well never mind that I mean but professionally speaking for a moment Sharkey is aware of my continued being aliveness and I do not think he is our friend. Like he is now officially a loose end. Charlie I wanted to ask you is he—"

"Yes boss."

"Seriously?"

"Yes he is."

"The stupid on this guy Charlie it burns."

"I know boss we should have factored that in to our decision making."

"Yep no question that was an operational flaw will you mark it down?"

"Yep already done. You wanna explain to him?"

"Yes please—Sharkey? SHARKEY. Sharkey."

"Yeah the fuck dead man?"

"Could you schschfffp ffkkkffsch I cannot hear you?"

"IS THIS BETTER YOU FUCK?"

"Yes it is thank you."

"YOU ARE GOING TO BEG ME JACK."

"I am genuinely saddened by this turn of events man but I got to ask although I already know the answer: Is it possible that you are so appallingly dumb you are calling me on the actual phone I left at your place as a detonator?"

"Wha—"

SNAP.

Because once the phone has exploded the rest of the pretty enormously loud bang noise does not get transmitted. It is safe to assume that although Sharkey's balls are completely preserved from this sad sequence of events his brains do pass through his other ear at something approaching the speed of sound.

I mean it's not like we didn't all know this was coming, but I tell you I am seriously concerned that the legacy crime world is woefully slow on uptake of the digitally mediated workplace environment.

FOUR

"DOC WE WILL NEED A DEAD GUY AS SOON AS POSSIBLE."

"Put it on the board—"

"There is not time for the board—"

"There is always time for the board that is how we know things have been done they go on the board and then they are crossed off the board and—"

"IT IS ON THE BOARD NOW, TEACHER PROCESS LADY WHO IS NO FUN—"

"Excellent I will take care of it—wait a particular dead guy or—"

"No no this is just housekeeping we will need a dead guy to be me I have just exploded Mr. Sharkey and also I feel the stirrings of a plan in my crime testes."

"No."

"No?"

"I say no to crime testes Price I am drawing a line. In fact I am actually drawing a line. Here—"

Doc writes a little column in black along one side of the HOMER board with NO at the top and writes CRIME VAGINA and CRIME TESTES and then CRIME with square brackets and a variable N to mean any sexual or reproductive body part metaphorically invoked to indicate an instinctive reaction.

"Yeah Doc that's fair okay okay but I feel a plan."

"Good. Now re: exploding Sharkey—Calvanese will be unhappy—"

"I know yes there will be consequences but we will make nice later. But you see where—"

"I do, Jack."

"We dump the dead guy and we let him be found as if we did not mean him to be found. Jack Price bled out and died. I am now BANJO TELEMARK—"

"O God—"

"No Doc it is genius do you not see the fog of crime the vistas of possibility the Kircheisen Art Fair the strategies and tactics of disguise the sheer brutal invitation to chaos Doc it is all there I AM BANJO AND HE IS ME AND WE ARE—"

"I will get you a dead guy."

"Cool."

"I wish to register my dismay."

"Noted. Can you—can you make it look right?"

"Of course I can."

Of course she can.

I am dating a woman who can.

Who can do anything.

Who will do anything.

Anything at all.

So that is all great but we are of course living in someone else's house and at a certain point she was always going to come home.

"WHAT THE SHIT ARE YOU DOING HERE BITCH?"

Charlie says: "Oh fffudge."

I am a little surprised by fffudge but okay.

"BITCH I WILL RIP OFF YOUR BITCH HEAD AND STICK IT IN YOUR SKINNY ASS! AND THEN I WILL

FEED YOU TO MY FUCKING GOATS IN FUCKING
PIECES AND THEN I WILL SELL THE GOATS TO FUCK-
ING OLIGARCHS FOR TUSCAN-STYLE SHIN MEAT
AND THEY WILL EAT YOU AND YOU WILL GO INTO
THE SOIL SHAT OUT BY THE EXPLOITERS AND THE
SLAVE OWNERS YOU FUCKING WHORE OF THE
PATRIARCHY—"

The woman is tiny and skinny like that statue by Canova
that is totally indecent they should not show it to the youth.
She has black hair tied in a topknot and sprayed solid so that
it looks like a Venetian chandelier resting on its back. I do not
think she is pleased to see us but to be honest no one is these
days and it is starting to drag on my bonhomie but even so—

"Um well hi I am Banjo may I know your—"

CLICKCLUNK

The gun is—honestly how does everyone have these things?
They are like these cool bespoke firearm situations even Lucille
had a gold-plated gigantagun one time before I threw it away
and I—I just I guess I don't really like the idea of having a
signature gun it feels needy. Like I am the king of openhanded
chaos I do not want that shit. But at the same time undeniably
you cannot get openhanded chaos out and wave it at people
to make them shut up and in my life right now everyone but
everyone seems to do this.

The artisanal firearm right now being used as punctuation
is called a Donnerbüchse, which is to say a thunder gun, and it
is basically a weaponized recycler. It is a cone with bang bang
at the back and an open mouth at the front and you put any
old crap you happen to have in and then pull the trigger and all
your chicken bones or nails fly out and rip pieces off whoever
is in your way. Many people who are shot with one of these
things who do not sustain fatal initial damage are killed by the

very many fucked-up infections they contract in unexpected body parts because that is what happens when you get shot with a chicken carcass and a bag of nails. Another way of thinking about a Donnerbüchse is that it is a handheld unidirectional pipe bomb.

"Fuck you Flavia," Charlie says which is not helpful.

"Charlie I will ask you to refrain from offering conflict resolution at this time and maybe just make nice."

Charlie says: "Sorry I meant to say hi Flavia."

The lady with the thunder gun is called Flavia.

"Fuck you Charlie what the fuck are you doing here?"

"I am here with Banjo he is making art."

"Fuck Banjo and his art. The banjo is an instrument of oppression, a blackface parody."

"In fact that is not accurate it was popularized in the U.S. largely by a blackface act but it owes its origin to a wholly non-European heritage and it is authentically—"

"Shut up you talkative asshole or I will blow your fat face out of the fucking roof of my house."

"Yes ma'am wait fat?"

"Sure you don't like me calling you fat face. That's your fat-face problem whatever. Now Charlie take your friend and fuck off out of the Black House—"

"I think I'll talk to—"

"You will not fucking talk to him Charlie or I will fuck you in the mouth with this and then I will pull the—"

A voice that can only be described as big says: "CHARLIE?!"

Flavia says: "Schafscheiße."

Charlie says: "Eat me Flavia."

A guy comes through the door of the Black House lounge area who is bigger than the voice. He's even bigger than the Donnerbüchse.

Charlie flies across the room and lands on his chest like a limpet. Not like a sex limpet, like a little kid, like a BFF, and then they start howling like wolves and shouting.

"ARROOO!"

"ARRROOOOOO!"

"BARROOOOO!"

"ARROOOOO!!!"

"BARRRUUUUUUNOOOO!"

"CHARLEEEEEE!"

"BRUNO!"

"CHARLIE!"

"BRUNO!"

"CHARLIE!"

"BIG GUY! What are you DOING right now I heard you were all up in the Fascists' face, man?"

"We are ECO-WARRIORS Charlie! We have found the religion of the living earth! We are the Class Army for Nature we are plugging polluters in the river like factories and chemical plants it is FANFUCKINGTASTIC. They vent shit and we catch them at it! But do we engage in snitching? NO OF COURSE NOT THE POLICE ARE THE DOGS OF THE CAPITALIST APPARAT! No! We plug the outflow with Z-Vat and we send their shit right up into their ass like a fucking fountain. The FOUNTAIN OF PLANETARY JUSTICE I am making shirts! SCREW YOU BOHEMIAN GROVE!"

"NO GODS NO MASTERS!"

"TINY SMALL!"

"BIG GUY!"

"TINY SMALL!"

"BRUNO!"

"CHARLIE!"

"LUCILLE!"

(Everyone looks at Lucille who just seems really pleased to be included.)

Charlie says: "Wait what is Z-Vat?"

Flavia says: "O for shit's sake—"

Because Bruno is all over that question and he and Charlie—

—with an actual cannon pointed at them—

—they geek the fuck out.

I tell you love is strange but when you see it you know it is there and if Flavia cannot see that she is gonna be one unhappy lady.

"Z-Vat. Zuckerwattebombe!"

"Like . . . cotton candy bomb?"

"Like from a fairground! But not for eating! For oil well problems after Deepwater Horizon. Rapid expanding foam-fiber cement. It makes a plug. A Swiss product very effective also clean. So then the shit backs up in their pipe and into their factory and they have a crisis and the authorities come and find out what they are doing and they go to jail. Obviously our action also is illegal but they do not know it is us."

"They don't?"

"Of course they imagine it is us but we do not give them proof huh? And they have much to do somehow they do not find time to investigate difficult question of who takes a direct action. There is absolutely a file. It is a priority file because we are repeat offenders. But at the same time it is not time critical. There are files that are time critical even if they are a lower priority. So it is completely natural and respectable that they cannot confirm their suspicion."

"Bruno man—oh man—this is Banjo he's good people he's like a rock star of art man you're gonna love this."

"How come I don't know you are coming to Bern?"

"I just figured you know we didn't—I mean I kind of left—Flavia was—"

"You want to bust my balls?"

"Bruno—"

"CHARLIE YOU BUST MY BALLS?"

"Bruno we all know where your balls have been I got no intention of touching those hirsute fucking danglers get the fuck out of here."

"There was a time Charlie when—"

"Yes there was Bruno yes indeed there was—"

"HAH! CHARLIE!"

"BRUNO!"

"CHARLIE!"

And that right there this time is for sure a sex limpet. There are sex limpet tongues and after a while someone starts reciting that Japanese poem about parting the wet grass.

"Charlie you stay the night? I—"

The Donnerbüchse goes off into the wall. I'm not sure what it's loaded with but it smells like hell.

Everyone looks at everyone else for a while because it just smells so terrible.

"Get the fuck out Charlie," Flavia says. "Leave my brother alone you are bad news for him."

And actually once someone has pulled the actual trigger on a Donnerbüchse full of whatever the fuck that was you don't want to sleep in their house anyway.

Charlie has to promise Bruno she will come see him to discuss the Fountain of Planetary Justice, which I assume they will do naked and which I will of course not allow for operational security reasons also because Flavia is a fucking nutjob with an eco cannon. I mean we don't have to move out we could just kill her. Then we could kill Bruno although I'm sure Charlie would not like that and we could kill all the others but then what? When people came looking for them we'd have a whole thing and we can't just murderize the whole of Bern that is not what we came for and people would talk in the wider community they would say it was uncouth.

Not that there isn't a kind of gothic chic in a house full of dead anarchists but they're incidental. There's just no need for that and who knows when you might need a chemical plant enema'd or something and then you'll be like O shit I know someone who wait no goddamn it I had Lucille hug them to death and burned their house down damn did I not update my contacts app that is SO DANG ANNOYING.

I get this all the time actually I had a birthday reminder two weeks ago for my friend Leo that I shot.

So fine we plug into the Demon money moneys and buy a house, which is not supposed to be possible at speed, but giant jet money in shell shapes speaks a special language and accommodations are made and by the time that is done, and we move ourselves out of the Black House, Doc has found a guy who looks like me.

I ask her where she found him and she says she just scraped Tinder and fed all of it into a bunch of software and bing. I ask her what his name was and she says she does not know.

He looks a lot like me. Little bit sadder and tired maybe but I guess that will happen when you show up to your date at her rental apartment and she anesthetizes your leg under the table and cuts your femoral artery open.

Guy died without ever knowing it was happening. Didn't even finish his funny story but Doc says she knows the punch line and it isn't that funny.

She tells it and Charlie says it's pretty fucking funny but not so you'd fuck someone it's not that funny but under other circumstances not so awful that you'd kill a guy for telling it and let him bleed out into an IKEA carpet. Saul—Saul is here now and has got a kind of an eager-beaver thing going on—Saul thinks it is not funny but he acknowledges as how you could think it was funny it's not like he thinks its evil.

Saul carries the dead guy because: eager.

It's halfway dark when Saul carries him to a freight yard and we set him up. The yard is big and the shadows are long. The trains are just paler shadows because there's no passengers. The lights are the old kind, orange gold, or maybe they're modern and the company just makes them that color because it's the color those lights ought to be.

They'll find the dead guy at the next station when he drops into the mail chute. He wasn't married I guess that's something but that doesn't mean no one's gonna be sad but they'll never know what happened because he just vanished off the face of the earth. He up and decided to go backpacking in India and he got a job and now he's settling down and he's moved to somewhere and no one knows.

Make up whatever shit you like Charlie took care of it.

Somewhere in the yard a guy blows an actual whistle and the train starts to move. Cold metal wheels on cold metal rails.

I watch Jack Price go out of the freight yard into the world and then we go home and cross him off the HOMER board.

Detail is important is what I'm saying. Detail is everything, which is why Banjo Telemark is seen to drive himself across the Swiss border on a Maltese passport and the vehicle he is driving is ancient and has some scratches and a bunch of tour stickers all over the rear. It is that avocado color beloved of the makers of porcelain bathroom furniture in the latter part of the twentieth century and it probably gets worse petrol mileage than an actual oil fire but it is also undeniably an original 1966 Citroën DS21. The Basel border guards get the misty look of men seeing childhood drive by slowly with some kind of a countercultural asshole at the wheel and they do not know whether to give me a hard time or salute but in the end I am so damn friendly they cannot help but smile and wave me through.

Plus also behind me there is a minibus driven by a sharp-faced woman in a business suit and she is a medical person of obvious impatience and it pleases them to make her wait a little while they show the DS some love.

Charlie went to actual Malta for this passport. She did deep Charlie things there. It is a good passport. It is a whole life. You could fall into it for hours.

Through Basel and down to Delémont where Banjo stops off to take in a canvas by the noted Gérard Bregnard. With a little help from Charlie, Banjo's invitation to the Kircheisen Art Fair has finally caught up with him and by happy coincidence he is even in Europe. Of course he would be delighted to come. He is thrilled by Kircheisen, by its conceptual weight. He considers it to have extraordinary artistic gravity. He is dying just DYING to meet Hans Eiger and understand his unique Kunstgeist be very careful how you say that.

I am Banjo Telemark. I am an Ambiguitionist that is to say a maker and vendor of bespoke bewilderment. My atelier is the world and in my atelier nothing is solid and every truth you think you know is also a lie.

I am Banjo Telemark.

Let me show you my art.

MURDER ON THE RAILWAY is the best Swiss tabloid headline ever. There is an outrage against the Federal peace and also too there is misuse of infrastructure and offending both of those things together is like stealing the crown jewels, which please note the Swiss do not have because that would be some feudal bullshit and they do not approve.

Although one time they stole the ducal hat of Burgundy.

Yeah ducal hat yes. Yes the Swiss and yes stole I know I know it is off-brand it is not my fault history is filled with this shit.

MURDER ON THE RAILWAY tentatively identifies the dead guy as Jacob Morgenstern Price an international hoodlum and professional murder artiste formerly a dealer in really excellent bespoke artisanal cocaine—

"Thank you Charlie—"

"One day boss we will raise the stallion up once more—"

"That sounds dirty—"

"It was dirty boss it was a dirty dirty bad pony and you could ride it all night without getting a sore crime—"

"Charlie—"

"Crime buttock—"

"I am blind now, blind in my brain parts. Silence while I read our clippings—excellent bespoke artisanal cocaine but more recently the kingpin of transcontinental death squad the Seven Demons who reputedly keeps a man in a cage on his executive jet—shit did anyone feed Sean?"

"Yes boss we have a service."

"How do we—no do not tell me. Good fine good. Oh wait oh shit—"

Because there in the opposing column is Agent Hannah explaining how she came to lose track of the felon and she has two very purple eyes and gosh she is very pissed. She has also opened a case file on the Seven Demons and she is all over that shit. Well she is welcome to be all over that shit because our money is ghost money and when Charlie got hold of the financial software she straightaway created a boojumajizzle called a fractal self-replicating iterative shell net, which is basically a little tiny robot brain which runs around the world creating empty companies tangentially linked to one another and to unavoidably real objects like the jet but also to random crimes and natural disasters. The boojumajizzle then runs incremental amounts of money around and around the system so that it looks like a real thing and entire law enforcement agencies could waste decades untangling it because it is like a headphone cord the moment you leave it alone for ten seconds it turns into a hair ball again.

All the same it would not be good for Jack to walk into Agent Hannah at any time in the future especially given as how she seems to be not entirely persuaded of my deadness.

"Smart lady."

Doc says: "Huh."

"What huh?"

"That is her?"

"The agent yes that is her."

"Attractive."

"No?"

"Yes. Diametrically contrasting with me in physical structure and psychosocial sexual cues."

"Had not noticed that at all gosh is she really?"

"Price, for there is no need to be coy about it, she is eminently bedable. I have said to you before I do not require you to have no sexual contact with other women it is simply that there is a high percentage chance I will murder them if you do. It would appear you engaged in some close combat at least."

"Yes but that was in the line of escaping. Come on Doc—"

"It's not as if I won't murder this one anyway."

"Why are you so keen on this idea it is freaking me out?"

"Vicarious desire perhaps or maybe an instinct that it might be advantageous to the group. Sadly now that you have made her look like an Aryan coati I suspect your chances are greatly diminished."

"Aw come on that will totally fade in a few days—"

"Nonetheless a stumbling block on the road to coitus."

"Yes well I'm sure that's a sad thing for all of us."

"I'm somewhat relieved actually I had wondered why you did not simply kill her when you had the chance. You are perfectly capable."

"Because—"

"Yes?"

". . ."

". . ."

". . . Huh."

"Exactly."

"Enough of your sexual adventurism, science barbarian! My art is calling!"

"I am sure that it is."

FIVE

"HALLO MR. TELEMARK HALLO HALLO I am Inge Désirée MY GOD what a pleasure I had NO IDEA you had accepted! HOW splendid I believe this is your first conventional fair, huh? We are quite honored actually to have you here. No, you must not be modest, that is entirely inappropriate! When the fair is over you may be self-effacing, huh, but not now, no. Not at all. You must make genius quite loudly. Let us be the platform for what you want to say!"

In fact Frau Désirée spent the last two days trying really hard to uninvite Banjo Telemark whom she has never heard of but somehow the press release went out and he has an invitation which is unquestionably signed by her and somehow Banjo is here and that would be a terrible fuckup except it turns out he is this important secret brand artist whose work is all about the fluidity of understanding and context in a blah blah blah I do not know Charlie made me say it.

We are in the big office on the outskirts of Bern, a warehouse by the river converted into a business space for Eiger's in-town business. The reception is here because Kircheisen does not open its doors until the actual festival and we are still in the art foreplay.

I do not really know the art world but Charlie does. Charlie before she murdered a woman and opted in to the Demons was a kind of a rising star of making pictures with a pencil, although in fact it is a stylus, and as well as being an internationally wanted criminal Charlie also still writes and draws an independent comic book called *Giant Egg,* which is all the time winning awards. In *Giant Egg* all the usual superhero and supervillain crap happens except that at the given point in the action at which generally a guy in black and a woman with hip dysplasia would kapow all the bad guys instead a huge mid-brown egg the size of a compact car smashes through the ceiling and does nothing at all. No one knows what Giant Egg's power set is because as soon as this happens the dynamic of the situation changes and the bad guys just stare at the egg and reconsider their life choices. Giant Egg's silent and motionless inexplicability stretches out over them. I have asked Charlie about *Giant Egg* and what it means and Charlie says it is a reflection of our interiority.

Charlie's interiority has recently secured a merchandising deal and now you can buy shirts and mugs and your own plushie Giant Egg full of crushing uncertainty to hug while you sleep.

Charlie speaks art and now so do I. It is not hard to speak art mostly it is body language and occasionally you have to say something is fraught or unachieved or if you are feeling really nasty you can say it is ludic. No one knows what ludic means so they will either panic and agree or use another word such as composed and then you can discuss whether composed is really the right word until they go away.

Do not say postmodern because although no one knows what that means either almost everyone thinks they do.

Frau Désirée is thin like a garden rake and ageless. A lot of Swiss people are ageless. They hit fifty and that's all the aging they're prepared to take and if age wants to do more than that it can fucking come in person and it better come loaded for bear.

Banjo Telemark meanwhile is a piratey arthouse mother-

fucker with three actual gold teeth and he carries a cane with
a skull on it. Doc has put gloop into—like IN TO—my face
to make my forehead more prominent and my lips fatter. She
swears this stuff will dissolve in a couple of months and I will
be the same but you know: Doc is Doc and plus also she has
always wanted to rework my face into aspect ratios conform-
ing to her personal triggers for sexy evilness so I may just never
be the same and that is fine I was not so attached to the old me
that I want to make a thing about it.

Frau Désirée is right now talking art and I say something
about fashions in self-actualization, which is apparently a sort
of low jibe one can throw in and she laughs and tells me I am
yoshing. I do not know what I have said and nor does she and
I guess that is probably what art conversations are like. She
palms Banjo off on a geezer called Herr Doktor Doktor Paul.
In high Swiss formal you give everyone all their titles in a line
because missing one out is rude. Herr Doktor Doktor is old
like fucking horse-drawn carriages. He must be a hundred.

Consider that for a second and understand what he has
seen. He is old enough to have seen the actual Second World
War as an adult. It happened all around him. Then he saw the
moon landings and Vietnam and the end of the Cold War and
now whatever the shit this new thing we're doing is that is so
utterly dick.

"I have dementia," Herr Doktor Doktor Paul says. "Do you
have dementia?"

"We're going straight to that? We are not going to talk
about how was my flight?"

"Did it crash?"

"No sir."

"Then who has time to talk about it?"

"Hah."

"I am ninety-eight years old frankly I barely have time to sneeze. I was at a funeral last month and the priest asked me if I really wanted to go home or just sit and wait for mine."

"That is some hard-core priesting."

"Catholic humor, it is edgy."

"I'm an atheist."

"Yes well, you try atheism when you can feel God pulling your penis."

"I—wait what?"

"It is how God calls you home to judgment. He pulls you out of your body by the penis."

"I was not aware of that."

Herr Doktor Doktor shrugs: "It is not common biblical teaching."

I like this guy. I ask how it is having dementia.

"It is fucking shit. Even if you're rich and they cannot kick you out for saying the word penis. You know why it is shit?"

"I'm guessing because dementia?"

"HAH! Yes. You are quite right that is why. But also because fucking young people finally get to tell you everything they want you to think is true and you have no way to be sure one way or the other. From moment to moment any fucking thing could be happening. The entire universe is malleable. When I was young do you know what we were afraid of in this country?"

"That the Germans would invade?"

"Sure maybe them. I was going to say the Soviets in fact but them too. Then later it was all about the Turks. The Turks were coming to miscegenate us. But it turns out the Soviets didn't give a shit and the Turks are very good at being Swiss. So now there are Swiss people with Turkish beginnings who worry about all the Croatians coming in. I suppose that is progress of a kind."

"I guess."

"It is crap and you know it. But you know what my grand-kids do now? They take turns making shit up. Once a month they fuck with me. They take turns. Opa Opa the Russians have come! Opa it is Sharia Day you must dress and comb your beard! Yes Opa this is how it has been since ninety-one do you not remember? Switzerland is an Islamic Soviet now. Little vermin! I went to the opera in a fucking kurta."

"How was that?"

"Drafty around my balls but I'm guessing real Muslims do not go commando to the fucking opera. Lying little shits. They are beautiful. I love them. What do you do again? I forget."

"I am the leader of a global criminal syndicate wanted in pretty much every country on earth. I kill people occasionally but mostly I'm just trying to get by because you know every-one has to have a thing that they do. Next week I'm going to rob a bank for three hundred million euros but mostly because I just really want to."

"Oh you're a fucking artist?"

"Yes sir I am."

"Call me Paul."

"Paul."

"Banjo."

"Paul."

"Who's Paul?"

". . . You almost had me."

"HAH. Good. You met Eiger yet?"

". . . No I have not. But I know his work."

"You should meet him Banjo he is a loathsome Arschloch."

"Oh good I guess all the best people are here."

"Yes Bern is not large and there's a lot of entertainment but only one party like this. Eiger . . . did I say we don't get along? I think to be honest he hates art but he is the owner of the venue so we all pretend. Even his family and they mostly don't like him either. You understand hypocrisy of course."

"I'm a fucking artist Paul."

"HAH. Come on, then."

I follow Paul and I go and meet Hans Eiger.

Eiger is not talking. He is in a group of people who are talking and you could think that he was joining in but he is not. He nods and laughs at all the right moments. There are noises coming from his face that sound like words but they are the noises his brain makes while it's waiting to start again. Engine idle you can see it. Hans Eiger hates this crap.

"HALLO HANS this is Banjo he is an artist."

"Hallo Banjo that is an interesting name I am Hans Eiger."

"I am so delighted to be here Herr Eiger I have heard so much about your mountain."

We shake hands. Eiger is still not present. He doesn't even bother to squeeze my fingers to pulp or eyeball me. I am an artist. An ant. He smells of some sort of rich masculine scent like iron and leather and goat blood but there is something off about it like—

"Yaaaawuh what have you heard of Die Festung?"

"O it is my absolute—it is my nemesis Herr Eiger you know I am an Ambiguitionist I specialize in situational ambiguity in the induction of doubt and your facility—I hear it is all about certainty."

"Yes! That is quite true in fact it is—"

He looks at my face again and there it is: his brain waking up. Eiger, like a snake half waking inside his own skull and peering out of a socket.

"Have we met before Herr Telemark?"

"Were you at Burning Man last year I was part of the group wearing only stolen footwear reconfigured as clothing—"

"I was not—"

"Then it is more likely you have seen my photograph recently I have permitted myself to become famous although I have reservations about the commercialized Nietzscheanism implicit in celebrity but anyway as soon as I received this invitation I had to come immediately. I wanted to see the installation and of course to put a piece into the show."

The snake has gone back inside. Art talk will do that.

"And what is your piece?"

"O I have not made it yet Herr Eiger but I think already there must be scrap metal iconic Swiss items. Infrastructure, agriculture, homogeneity must all be expressed and questioned."

"Your work is to undermine?"

"O by no means to examine Herr Eiger. In many cases that amounts to the same thing owing to the hollowness of modern systems you appreciate—so many of them—they are simply Ponzi schemes they rest on nothing. But something with solidity is revealed as absolute by my interrogations the Rock of Gibraltar piece for example—"

(I can hear Charlie breathing heavily she is going to have to make one up and add it to my cover by tomorrow morning I am a bastard—)

"What was demonstrated there was the solidity of the stone beneath the tottering British Imperium of course the fantasy of a gunboat trader nation but as with Gibraltar so with Kircheisen the real is made more so—OH Herr Eiger I have—I would LOVE to make something that was specific to the location would you permit that?"

"I could not allow the use of our corporate branding of course—"

"NO no no I do not mean to imply your sponsorship no that would be inappropriate of course but something—I understand your facility is defined by impenetrability perhaps something to invoke that I see I see I SEE A TRAIN OBLITERATED AGAINST THE MOUNTAIN I SEE—Oh I am sorry that was loud sorry madame I trust that will come out—art you know it is percussive—"

"This does not seem—"

"Allow me to persuade you. Show me your beautiful facility I must touch it I must see it I must lick the salt from the stone I must sir—"

"You must what—"

"Yes yes I will speak to Inge. It is decided sir. I am so THRILLED to have met you. Paul, you are a genius you were quite right quite right I am SEIZED that is what I am—"

I go to embrace him and again that weird mix of manly man and something weird and like rose water chocolates as he fends me off like NO I HUG NO HIPPIES and I—feel—

I feel someone behind me and there is silence of scrutiny and I turn and I see—

Nothing.

There is an empty space where there should be a face and a torso.

Weird.

Then I look down into eyes like the sky.

Evil Hansel is wearing a little tiny suit today. It is double-breasted and blue, and unlike Eiger there's no flower in his lapel. Instead there's a little tiny pin of a Swiss flag. I actually cringe a little inside like I can feel that knife in my leg. Blood slurry in a winter gutter, slowly tipping down into the drains and sewers underneath. He smells like pool cleaner and limonene or his mother washes him in blueberry air freshener. Perhaps she does.

"Hi little dude who are you?"

"Hallo," says Evil Hansel. "My name is Marcel."

"Really?"

"Yes."

"I'm pleased to meet you Marcel I'm Banjo."

(Sky eyes don't blink.)

"Do you know my grandfather?"

"No I— O wait you are Hans Eiger's grandson?"

"Yes of course."

"No I don't know him we were just talking I want to do things to his mountain like—I want to make art there."

"Oh. You are an artist."

"Yes."

"Oh. Well I hope you have a rewarding time here at our festival and that your work is productive for you."

"Do you like art?"

"I prefer to work with Lego and so on. I also like movies."

"Good for you."

"Yes it is. Thank you. It was a pleasure to meet you."

And that's it. Of course that's it. Evil Hansel does not care what the fuck a stranger does with tires and old cowbells on his opa's mountain. And I am a stranger. Jack Price is dead and my face is full of Doc juice and he does not know me at all. He does not look back.

_____

Charlie makes me do much art shit. I drink apple juice and pretend it is champagne. I drink a lot of it and establish a reputation for an iron stomach. I flirt with old ladies and young ones. I talk art finance with suits and art concepts with anyone in jeans. All bullshit all the time.

And everyone knows it. Evil Hansel, even Evil Hansel knows it. Over by the buffet table there is a little heap of clothes and a shock of psycho *Sound of Music* hair, and a couple of Lego figures have fallen out of his hand onto the floor. One of the waiters is nudging them back toward him. Yeah. Sleep well kid. Crazy little fucker.

So yeah. Art bullshit.

After a certain point you just gotta pee.

"I gotta pee."

"Thank you boss you don't need to keep me informed on micturative matters."

"I do not know what that is."

"It's peeing."

"I know that."

"Boss—"

"Yeah—"

"Go pee please."

"Yes."

Some things you just don't see coming. Things like that I take out my penis and point it at the urinal and—

WHAM.

Because there is.

A gun sight.

On the urinal.

A fucking sniper sight.

Printed.

On where you pee.

This is a hilarious joke for executives. It is good for your pelvic floor to control aim and flow and also it is a feedback trick to reduce splash and therefore janitorial costs. Seriously. This is a thing. Porcelain semiotic design is a thing now.

But I have just been shot at and my friend is dead so I see—

The interior of the mail van—

"Price I got to go now. Okay I go but you just—"

"Don't leave me here you Soviet prick I am stabbed—"

"I got to go now—"

"You live an untidy life—"

Agent Hannah bears down on me I am thinking about sex—

Bunnyboner—

"Wash me—"

"I am Banjo Telemark I am Banjo Telemark I am—"

I'm fine I'm just a little shook up is all it's—

Then WHAM again but this is a different not just impact but weight. That's not a hallucination that is something around my neck and it is heavy and I fall—

"You are him," Evil Hansel says. "You are the man."

There is just no way a kid Evil Hansel's size can tackle a guy like me I mean NO WAY so he hasn't. He has tied a curtain rope around the nasty enormous ornamental vase on the wash table and thrown a noose over my head and kicked the vase on the floor. Now I am lying on the ground and looking up at him and he says:

"You are him."

"What the fuck kid what—"

"You are him. I see you."

"Of course you do you're fucking nine."

"Yes. I am."

And he is nine. I mean that's the point isn't it kids do not see the world the way we do. They see clearly because they don't have that thing telling them impossible things are impossible. He just saw me and now—

I'm lying on a men's room floor tied to a stoneware vase with a chipped base and he's got the fucking oyster knife again JESUS FUCK this is embarrassing I will get cut AGAIN—

I could die here. I mean it's not likely I can still probably—

Get dead of infant.

Dead of oyster knife.

Dead of being too fucking stupid to stay alive.

"YOU YOUNG MAN ARE IN SO MUCH TROUBLE RIGHT NOW COME OUT OF THERE."

O God bless you Charlie you are o GOD BLESS YOU—

Her hand comes in through the door—

"EXCUSE ME SIR I DO NOT MEAN TO INTRUDE—"

Rex comes in like a wall and bundles Hansel out and then I'm standing and it's all done it's done but fuck

Fuck

How careless can one guy get—

I am doing this like I used to and it is not working and I—

Fuck this needs to shift to paradigm shift or I will get all of us dead.

Outside Charlie says, "I WILL BE SPEAKING TO YOUR MOTHER ABOUT THIS. WHERE IS SHE—OH IT IS YOU IS IT MADAME—YOUR SON—YOUR SON IS A SEX PERVERT MADAME HE TOUCHED MY—HE—YES HE TOUCHED MY BOOB—NO HE ABSOLUTELY REACHED

RIGHT UP AND IN WHEN I WAS LEANING DOWN TO SAY NICE THINGS ABOUT HIS LITTLE SUIT—LIKE A FUCKING OCTOPUS MADAME—"

She keeps saying boob over and over again.

"BOOB yadda yadda yadda BOOB! And furthermore blah blah BOOB blah ALSO I THINK HE TOOK A PICTURE WHERE IS HIS PHONE—"

Evil Hansel is a psychopath. He is terrifying and short and totally dangerous as shit. That with the vase was fucking golden. He's a godhead genius fucking horror show.

He is also nine.

If there is a hell for nine-year-old boys, it involves being accused of being a sex pervert by a lady with whom some part of you would really like to be a sex pervert but you do not entirely know what that is.

(BOOB! and la la la)

So that's great that's just perfect Charlie is a fucking rock star. I am not dead and then I go outside and I see Evil Hansel looking at me like the end of the world and that is perfect too.

I see his mother making her apologies and she is not alone she has a friend with her a member of her I do not know what let us say cookery club?

And the friend is perfect too but not in a good way. No no not at all.

"I am so sorry about this," Evil Hansel's mom says, "I will speak to him about it but I am quite sure it was a misunderstanding. Or perhaps it was not and he will require therapy and so on. In that case as his parent I am at fault. But please lower your voice it is not appropriate to shout he is a child."

That is quite a speech and I have to be a little respectful of Hans Eiger's daughter here she is quite a lady and I wonder how much she knows about her old man but I do not wonder very hard because I am looking elsewhere.

The cooking club buddy of Evil Hansel's momma is a fine figure of a woman and someone has done a really excellent makeup job for her but if you know what to look for you can absolutely see she has bruises around her nose and eyes where some shit-heel criminal hit her with her own handcuffs. She looks away from what is no doubt a maternal nightmare to gather strength and her eyes skitter across the room and—

And—

And across my face—

And they stick—

Just for a second they stick and even though she doesn't get right now who I am. My altered face will stick in her mind and worry at her and sooner or later she will know.

It's definitely time to leave this party.

We could not entirely stay at the Black House forever because it is full of anarchists and they have no sense of boundaries anyway even if Flavia had not shot the wall with a stinky hand cannon. Also with the best of goodwill it has to be said that not every anarchist is a committed son or daughter of Kropotkin some are just your average screwhead with a fondness for piercings and cheap drugs and if confronted with the opportunity to earn large sums of money by trading information with the evil global corporatists they would take the money and laugh all the way to Coachella that is just people.

And soon we will need to start doing the kinds of things that leak and whisper and get back to places you do not want them to be.

So I have bought a pig farm and that is where we are going

now after the party. Like a big version of Martin's shack up the mountain it is totally authentic wood-frame construction Rex is professionally intrigued. Dark wood with lines on it. Smells of years. Shaped like a T with room for all of us albeit little rooms like cells. Firepit and a stove for cooking and really good water pressure coming down the mountain from the Kircheisen peak and we can look up and see Die Festung and know we are going to fuck it up.

All mod cons because this is Switzerland you can go off-grid here if you want to but you never have to they will bring the grid to you so we have Internet and three-phase power.

And pigs.

Doc and I have the bedroom on the end of the T and we sleep and listen to the sound of the river and the rain on the roof and in the morning early we wake to livestock and the natural world and I could stop here. I could just stop and be this person forever. I have a bajillion squidzillion euros and a new identity and a new face and why the fuck not who would look for Jack Price here now that he is dead?

Volodya would, I guess. But even he—I mean sooner or later you leave business undone.

He'd get it.

I wonder if Doc would—

Oink snuffle. OINK.

Sidebar I bought a pig farm. You will recall that Doc requires pigs for her evil plan and it is not easy to buy pigs individually just for shits and giggles especially in Europe where they care about the welfare of animals—

OINK snuffle oink OINK—

They say Hey Jack why do you want this pig? And you say that you want to use it to rob a mountain fortress and if you grant (what is obvious) that you do not know but it does not seem impossible that the pig will get exploded or liquidized (because: Doc) then they say you cannot have the pig in fact you cannot have any pig ever.

But if you say you want to buy a pig farm that is different because then it is obvious that the reason you want to buy a pig farm is that you want to farm pigs.

Oink snuffle oink.

Oink oink.

ZNNNEEEEzzzznaaaarrrrRRRR—

Oh yeah I also—

Oink snuffle oiZZZZORCH—

SQUEEEEEEEEE—

I also bought a—

ZORCH SQUEE ZORCH squee ZORCH gggggtttgg—

I have—

ZORCH splat.

. . .

. . .

. . .

I have also bought a hyperviolent Kircheisen door through a shell company in another shell company in another shell company and lalala. So now we have both pigs and robot death door.

Oink snuffle—

It turns out these things should not be stored in the same room.

SQUEEEEOINK SPLAT—

"Price!"

"Sorry Doc."

"Stop killing my fucking pigs!"

"It was not me it was the—"

"Stop THE DOOR killing my fucking pigs—"

"You have A BAJILLION of them Doc plus also too they actually make more if you just leave them—"

"Not as quickly as you are nuking them—"

"I am not nuking them the door is not my responsibility I AM BANJO TELEMARK I do not sully myself with mere robbery for hire—"

"You are now also my pigman. Stop nuking the fucking pigs—"

"I really want a nuke like an actual nuke by the way—"

"NO we have discussed this. Also IF we had a nuke, which we will for many good and sufficient reasons NOT, do you think for one second you would be allowed to have the codes does that strike you as a good plan?"

"No now that you say it kinda not I guess I am not the guy you would—no basically you are the guy for—"

"I AM and I do not want one and do NOT change the subject my PIGS—"

"Bajillion pigs—"

"I have—I had—twenty-four Price now I have nine I need at least three at this rate I will have to buy more and people will fucking notice if we are getting through twenty-four pigs every three days that is—"

"It is the door Doc it is super-duper sensitive—"

ZORCH SPLAT—

"PRICE!"

"Charlie shut the door down for now just let the pigs eat."

"All eight of them."

"Sorry Doc."

The X8 does not like Doc's pigs at all.

Bad door.

———

Breakfast bacon. Not our bacon. Do you know nothing there is a whole curing technique this is bacon from—also too electrocuted pig is not always all that tasty there are hormones—

Bacon and fresh juice and horrible UHT milk in coffee and—

VoIP Incoming call.

For Doc.

Because I am dead.

Accept y/n?

y

Speaker on.

Doc says:

"Go ahead I am listening."

"Doctor. It is Ottavio Leopold Calvanese."

"A pleasure to speak to you."

(Doc is looking at me because this is totally my fault.)

"Indeed so Doctor and yet you have presented me with something of a problem."

"I have?"

"It does appear that you have murdered Mr. Sharkey."

"I understood him to have exploded."

"He did."

"In fact our express preference was for a resumption of normal business practice after a lapse in his professional judgment. What happened is a matter for regret. I have no idea what exact chain of events might have precipitated such an outcome."

"It is an interesting happenstance that he was somewhat at odds with you."

"Correlation is not causation of course."

"But you do possess a demolitions expert."

"Doesn't everyone?"

(Doc mutes the phone.)

"This is your fault."

"Don't give a fucking inch Doc."

"I thought conciliatory."

"No Doc not conciliatory fucking full force forward. If you blink he will fuck us."

"I do not think so."

"I do it is old-school alpha-male stuff I swear I swear I—wait okay—okay what would Volodya do if he was Calvanese?"

"..."

"..."

"Fine."

(Unmute.)

"... Doctor ... I was under the impression that this was to be a quiet venture."

"So were we, Mr. Calvanese."

"Let me be clear I will not tolerate further outrages."

"I see."

"You will restrain yourselves until you can decently depart the country."

"I'm afraid we have business here."

"You do not."

"We do."

"Regrettably Doctor I must insist."

"Must you."

"I must."

"Since we are speaking in terms Mr. Calvanese I must ask you an indelicate question."

"Please if it will clarify matters for you—"

"Were you involved in this?"

"I beg your pardon?"

"I believe I was clear but in case I was not: my companions

and I have recently lost a good friend to what we now know was a setup. We were brought here with an eye to our elimination. We take this very much amiss Mr. Calvanese and of course we do not imagine you would involve yourself in something so . . . low . . . but since we are now speaking without restraint—"

"O but we are not—"

"That is not an answer—"

"Well then no I was not involved but it occurs to me as the smooth flow of business is perturbed that I understand the urge—"

"It is not the urge that is the problem it is the indulgence."

"Do not make this more difficult than it must be for either of us, dear lady."

". . . Ah?"

Well now it turns out I didn't need to say anything at all. You do not do Dear Lady at the Doc and keep all of your body parts. Now I am waving at her to calm it down and she is not interested. I am a little concerned. If it was anyone else like Charlie maybe I would ask Doc to maybe tranquilize her but Doc is the person I would ask so—

Maybe we should just knock her on the back of the head before this goes any further.

Calvanese is still talking he has literally no idea the shit that is about to fall on him—

O my.

Fall on him.

Huh.

That is—wow. That would be a thing. Inappropriate of course in the circumstances but . . . wow.

I stare into the sky outside the window and see universes of crime.

O my.

While I'm distracted, Calvanese says:

"I regret to remind you Doctor that we are on my home ground. Resistance would be met with overwhelming force. You are remarkable people. You are not gods."

"No."

"I am glad we understand one another."

"Do we."

"We do."

"I am considering my response Mr. Calvanese."

"Excellent."

"I do not wish there to be misunderstandings between us."

"That is perfect Signora—Dottore—I am so glad."

". . ."

". . ."

"Do you eat beef Mr. Calvanese?"

". . . What has that—"

"I promise you will shortly see."

"Then yes. I do."

"And as a man of commerce and culture you are no doubt also aware of the formidable power of European beef agriculture on the formation of global affairs?"

"I am."

"Then let me in turn be quite clear: if you ever attempt to instruct me again Mr. Calvanese or if the expression Dear Lady so much as occurs to you in my connection you will wake the following morning to the news that Italian, French, and Spanish cattle are falling victim to an appalling infection: a hacking cough which grows so powerful that the bones of the chest are snapped by the muscles and by the end of forty-eight hours the heart gives out. The animal dies and the meat is polluted with bile and stress. The global freight system will abruptly be subject to scrupulous checks. Individual travelers will be banned from entering or leaving certain countries without a quarantine period to prevent the spread. In fact it will be much too late. By the end of the week every continent and country will be affected as it emerges that the condition is airborne and almost impossible to detect during an early, notable infectious stage. Life will become vastly more expensive and annoying for everyone until a cure is found, and of course all and any contraband operations in any field will become almost impossible. The global economy will be plunged into a recession. International commodities crime will be drastically affected both by the increased difficulty of operations and by the decline in disposable income among most demographics. My kind of crime of course will be facilitated. That is to say that both radical medical research and bespoke political, economic and personal violence will be in great demand. In addition there will be a measurable decrease in carbon emissions as beef farming effectively ceases to be a viable undertaking, which I regard as a long-term benefit to the human species as a whole. Pro bono if you like. But like many large banks and some nations your organization will be unable to withstand the stress and will dissolve into warring factions and effectively cease to exist. Before it does so however your brothers will receive information from me to the effect that all this is your fault and I imagine they will kill you quite thoroughly but also knowing the stylings of your microsociety also any family you may have. So by all means Mr. Calvanese do take a few hours to consider your position. And please understand that the scenario I have described to you is only one of my options and you will notice it is remarkably devoid of human casualties.

You are not my enemy Mr. Calvanese and therefore I use a light touch. Do you see?"

". . ."

"I will take your quiet for the sensible contemplation of new and important information. Do please call again."

CLICK.

Yeah.

That'll do it.

I say: "Nice bluff there with the cows Doc."

Doc says: "I never bluff."

Everyone gazes at Doc for a long, long time.

And Doc gazes back.

Rex goes to talk to a guy. Doc offers to drug the guy but Rex says there is no need. The guy will just talk because that is what happens. The guy was the foreman on the Kircheisen build but that is totally a coincidence. They will meet in a snack bar and they will be two guys in construction talking about construction. Rex will tell the guy about the time his brother's firm accidentally shished an imported corgi with a scaffolding tube. He will talk about the times when the plans just weren't doable because plans are always not really doable in the actual universe and fixing that is part of the contractor's job. Then the guy will tell Rex about Kircheisen. He won't mention the name and Rex won't have heard of the place but still.

Somewhere—Rex says—somewhere something went off spec because it always does. No build ever survives contact with the site. So somewhere they ran into stone they couldn't break without fucking up the stability of the mountain or they found a watercourse and they worked around it. They found a huge fissure. They found a void. That shit is what happens and what it means is that somewhere there's a place where the Kircheisen Festung isn't as strong as it should be.

Saul goes with Rex because Rex does not speak German but in the end it turns out that Rex and the guy both totally speak construction and beer and sexy-time dancers.

Yeah there are sexy-time dancers in Bern if you know where to look.

Nighttime in the pig farm is dark like nothing in the city. This is werewolf country like deep night so deep that the moonlight throws a shadow on the valley wall and we will be inside it until 3:00 a.m. You have not seen dark unless you have seen dark in the shadow of a mountain. Away across the valley there is a twinkling collection of lights, which is a whole village, and it is dwarfed by the empty blackness of the forest and the rock walls. I listen to it and try to hear the world. Behind me in the farmhouse I can hear Saul clumping around with weights on his arms and legs. He says is practicing for the JIM equipment. Everyone else is asleep.

Except me.

I look up at the place we are going to rob.

Somewhere up there Hans Eiger has a little apartment and when I think of it I think of Frank Lloyd Wright and a sunken firepit in the middle of the room and a yellow '60s majolica vase as high as a man with bulrushes in it. There's a classic leather recliner and a deep shag circle rug and a picture window which looks down into the valley—

And right on the balcony by the wind chimes there's a sniper's nest with a vintage anemometer and I can see him lifting his rifle and—

I dream about the Demons and the whole thing of being their boss is a giant monster that loves me and it picks me up and puts me in a hole so I will grow and the rain comes down and water comes up over my head and I still cannot get up because this huge Demon hand is holding me under and I start to drown and I wake up choking because there is Swiss goose-feather-pillow funk in my throat.

Doc turns very precisely on the bed and puts out one hand until it touches my shoulder and that is all.

But it is enough.

Always remember that Evil Hansel and Agent Hannah are a sideshow.

It's all about Volodya.

Do the job.

And submit the bill to the client.

. . .

. . .

The Client.

"CHARLIE! WAKE UP!"

"I am awake why are you shouting—"

"WAKE FROM HOGGISH SLUMBER MINION AND GREET THE DAY—"

"O shit you are perky. It is the middle of the night—"

"This is not PERKY. That is surrender talk. I am JACK and I am filled with joy to all mankind I bring horrors—"

"I do not think that—"

"SILENCE I require your measly intelligence because I cannot do this thing."

"What thing can you not do that is so fucking—"

"Find Mr. Client."

"What?"

"Find Mr. Client Charlie do it now."

"Mr. Client was Eiger you said."

"I said Eiger was the client. He was not MISTER CLIENT obviously because I met him and when we looked at the nice pictures of Mr. Eiger I would have said: O SHIT THAT IS OUR CLIENT. Do you see how I did not say that and please do not say maybe he was wearing a cunning disguise that is not a thing that can really happen."

"You wear disguises all the time you wore one this evening—"

"My disguises are TERRIBLE they only work because people are not paying attention. Did you notice an ACTUAL CHILD saw through my disguise today and tried to kill me? That is how well disguises work in the real world Charlie. I am a master of not being a fucking idiot. I would have noticed that Eiger was Mr. Client so who was Mr. Client? WHO?"

"I do not know."

"You are a digital wizard find out."

"Find out?"

"Find out."

"Just like that?"

"What I said."

"Like go into the marina restaurant computer system, which is likely not even online and then find an image on their shitty horrible CCTV, which they do not clean and somehow feed that into a giant sky computer and get a name from it and say Oh Boss lookee I have magicked you this?"

"Yes like that."

"It does not work like that at all anyway anyway most likely Eiger just hired some guy."

"Just hired some guy?"

"Just hired some guy."

"That is stupid."

"THAT IS EXACTLY WHAT YOU WOULD DO BOSS—"

I would do that. I would call an agency and pay a guy to be Mr. Client. Like: Hi Sharona I am Bobby DeLindt from Highdown Casting in Santa Monica hi hi hi it's good to talk to you hi. Yeah okay so we are doing a thing here. Stay with me Sharona. I know it's outré but we're doing a VERY bespoke reality game for a high-level client it is not our USUAL thing at all but you know money talks and we need a guy and he has to look legitimately top-drawer is what I'm saying because he is like the face for the game—

And so on.

And that would work fine.

It would be okay.

You'd maybe have to kill the guy right after.

You would not want him backtraced in a situation where you were assassinating the fuck out of a person with friends.

But still.

But that guy that I met—he was not that person. There was nothing in that guy that was for hire. There was nothing in him that said he was part of a plan. Any plan he was into would be part of him not the other way around. He was a boss. Not necessarily The Boss like no one is ever entirely The Boss.

But that guy . . . he was not anyone's sock puppet and if you tried to make him that well that would be on you.

I tell Charlie to find Mr. Client and I go back to bed.

In fact I do not go back to bed because as I walk down the corridor toward the bedroom I hear a strange sound from outside. It is sort of conversational and gentle but it is also very very lonely and sad.

It is Rex talking to the pigs.

"Hi Rex."

"O hi Colonel hi."

"Just Jack is fine Rex."

"Sometimes it feels wrong to me sir."

"Sure man if that's what you want."

"Yes sir."

"You having a little quiet time I guess?"

"Yes sir."

"Okay then."

"Yes sir."

"You know Rex sometimes I come out here—well I guess you don't need to know that."

"No go on sir."

"I don't want to interrupt you man we all got our thing."

"No sir I would appreciate it."

"Well okay sure but you are not to laugh even though it is kinda funny. I mean it's not funny but it is kinda. Yeah anyway anyway . . . Sometimes I come out here and I you know I sit down or I lean on this rail and I talk. Not to myself that is cray cray so I talk to the pigs."

"You do?"

"Yes Rex I do. I feel like they really understand more than we know I mean Doc—now Doc tells me that pigs are real smart and they form emotional attachments and so on—but you know Doc is more of a dog person. She has Tycho and they have a special bond and I do not really do those. I mean I do them with people you know this. I feel for you guys you are my guys but I do not understand how anyone would vest that level of affection in a dog. It is a dog. But these pigs . . . I come out here Rex and I see something in their eyes. Not like a human something but a pig something that is still very real and meaningful."

"Huh."

"Does that seem strange to you Rex?"

"Kinda I guess."

"O it does?"

"Yes sir. Weird as shit but that is life I guess. Other people's lives are weird. I mean your relationship for example with the Doctor that is weird to me also. Like she is this terrifying evil doctor, and you are you, and you scare one another and you drive her crazy and then you do weird sex things and that makes you happy. In my life that would not be a sound basis for a relationship but I tell myself: other people's lives. So that I get but talking to pigs is a little beyond me."

"Huh I really—you do not talk to the pigs at all?"

"No sir I just come out here and I watch old war movies on my telephone."

". . . Uh."

"I am very much a fan of *Cross of Iron* sir directed by Sam Peckinpah."

"I did not see that coming."

"He was a man who understood the truth of armed conflict in a way which cannot be equaled by generations thereafter. Few of the modern school for example were in Vietnam or Iraq they are tourists."

"I guess that is true."

"But after then when it's real quiet out here and dark and I—well I talk to Billy sometimes."

"Uh-uh."

"I figure I have some stuff to make up for on his account sir. Atonement I guess."

Billy is Rex's brother who was shot by Fred the Head. Fred was trying to make a point to me and indeed at the time Fred and Doc were still working together. What happened to Billy is one hundred percent on Fred but Rex and I avoid discussing it in general lest we encounter areas of personal friction and compromise our smooth working relationship. This kind of polite reserve is the heart and soul of shared criminal enterprises in an environment in which people have a professional history which will not always be aligned. It is just best practice.

In this present situation however with Rex talking about atonement it behooves me—and I do not, do NOT like to be behooved in this way—but it behooves me to probe the mood a little because in general anyway you do NOT want your criminal colleagues to be talking about atonement and also well because Rex did know we were coming here and could theoretically have alerted Hans Eiger to our arrival. I would not like to think that Rex was responsible for Volodya's death but maybe he might could have intended me or Doc to die instead and of course when you are dealing with an old white guy— Hans Eiger—he will very often assume that the old white guy in a given group is the guy in charge and shoot him first even when perfectly clearly the boss is the younger and more attractive person in the middle.

No, not Doc, me. I am talking about me.

I do not think Rex sold us out.

But I have responsibilities. I am behooved and here we are.

Rex asks me if I think it is odd that he talks to his dead brother in the middle of a pigsty in the middle of the night with only a hyperviolent robot door for company. I say that I do not.

"No Rex that is—we have never really talked about Billy."

"That's fine sir."

"I—I'm not real good at processing emotions and shit like that Rex."

"No sir it is not masculine sir."

"Uh-huh. No. Definitely it is the masculinity which prevents me from doing that you are right. But I guess . . . I liked Billy. He was my friend. I'm not going to say he was always easy to be around what with the depilation and the coke and so—"

"He was a tremendous asshole and would always hit on my girls when we were kids together but I loved him and I miss him now he is gone and sometimes on the one hand I just need to make sure he is okay with it that I—that I am here with you sir."

"Because I was part of what happened."

"O not that I just figure he would say REX YOU ASS-HOLE YOU ARE RICH AS SHIT NOW GO TO VEGAS IN A LIMO."

"That is true he would totally say that. He would think we were all assholes for not doing that all the time. Do you—do you want to go to Vegas in a limo? Or we could totally go to Monte Carlo it's close and it's pretty much the same."

"It is?"

"Stuffier I guess. But still basically everyone is for sale and no one wakes up looking as pretty as they go to sleep."

"I was never much of a one for gambling and—that actually was I guess one place where Billy and I would argue—like there are limits and you know fun is one thing, but at a certain point just a hug—I mean I like breasts as much as anyone sir but there's a limit to the number you can actually do anything with."

"I guess there is, Rex."

"I figure that number is probably six."

". . . Huh."

"But sometimes also I think of the Cause sir. Billy was a soldier of the Cause even though he did not know it."

(In fact obviously there is no Cause as such and Billy was

therefore completely right that he died for nothing except my cocaine business, but in Rex's understanding of the world it is all about the Cause.)

"Billy was burned-out on war sir. He could not hear about it. He was a hero but he was also, you know. He was Billy and he was not ready to the fight anymore. So I figure he gave you up sir to whatever extent he could."

"That is okay Rex. That is why we have information compartmentalization."

"Yes sir but all the same the enemy nearly got you and so I feel like I got this debt."

"Not to me Rex."

"No sir to the Cause."

We sit and look into the shadows. Every so often a little light comes on to indicate that the door has noticed something and would like to kill it. It is a green light to indicate that it knows that is not allowed, but it flickers a little, which I figure is the door saying that it fucking will one day. One day it will figure out how to switch itself on and then it will kill us all.

"So you see sir I talk to Billy and maybe I say all the things I didn't say when he was alive because he was too damn loud. And I tell him I'll pay his dues."

"And what does he say?"

"He's dead sir so you know he does not say anything at all. I guess that is death."

We stand there and after a little while he cries. I do not say anything. Nor does he. Then he politely goes inside and leaves me in case I want to discuss anything with the pigs.

SIX

BANJO TELEMARK DOES A FEW INTERVIEWS with art papers. Mostly he has time on his hands. Banjo lets it be known he will walk the streets of Bern and travel the train network. He will touch the truth of the country he is visiting. Ambiguitionism—Banjo says—requires knowledge of an underlying truth that critically speaking does not exist but which in the everyday is all the real that there is. You can only know a nation by its roads and rails Banjo says. By eating in its roadside cafés and listening to the voices of post mistresses and bus drivers.

Banjo talks a lot of shit but that much is true.

While Banjo goes on his little spiritual journey between the cheese maturation huts—that is an actual thing—between the cheese maturation huts and the light industry all along the valley floors, I watch Hans Eiger.

I watch Hans Eiger for three days. It is very boring.

I watch him and think I should have shot him by now.

Pop.

Zing.

Splat.

But then what?

Then he's just the guy who killed a Demon and got shot in the head. And that is fine.

But it's pedestrian and he will still have won and that is not allowed.

Hans Eiger must be inundated. He must be drowned on his mountaintop in a sea of Demons.

People have to wince when they say his name.

They have to say: "Hans Eiger O SHIT that Hans Eiger O SHIT that guy is—WOW HAS ANYONE EVER BEEN MORE DEAD?"

They have to feel his death as a tenderness in their crime vaginas and crime testes and whatever else these people have.

Like what you feel when you see a guy hit himself in the eye with a hammer and you hear something go crack and just for a moment you feel that crack in your face and your nethers get that feeling of ice water like an electric shock of sympathy.

If someone has a name that is just a little bit similar—like to say like I don't know like Franz Peyser—that should be enough. Franz Peyser should be out of a job in organized crime in Europe in the whole fucking world and no one should ever know exactly why but they just know in their fucking souls you can't be near that guy or your eye will explode.

Like that.

So I don't shoot him not that I would personally shoot him I'd find someone who knows how to use a long gun and

Pop.

Zing.

Splat.

But I do not do that instead I watch and I remember that I am very bad at waiting.

Hans Eiger goes to one menswear shop actually a tailor and he buys bespoke menswear. He takes meetings in hotel conference spaces. He has calls in the business suite. He knows people and people know him. He is a face.

Whatever man he is a dandy of some sort no doubt.

Evil Hansel's mother lives in a duplex on the river she is legit and she is married to a guy from Gibraltar and she sees her father but it's not like they're close.

Eiger drives a German automobile with a customized engine. When he is at Die Festung he stores it in a secure garage by the cable car. In town he parks it at the Commodore Hotel.

He eats at a particular table at a particular restaurant where they know him. They know how he takes his coffee.

He has an apartment in Doha on the sixty-first floor of a steel-and-glass tower called Karlsbad House.

He does his high-street banking at a Swiss private bank that is designed to look like a small family firm and has branches in 101 countries. Every week of his life is defined by a schedule that is insofar as he can make it exactly like the last one.

I know how to do this.

I know.

"Hi I am Banjo Telemark hi I—yes the artist THAT'S RIGHT gosh I am so flattered that you—oh in the *Neue Zürcher Zeitung* right yes that photo OMIGOSH that photo is so embarrassing—what is it you say here HERR GOTT NO'MAL—aha hahaha ahah—yes anyway my GOSH what they did to my chin in that photo no really I am shy oh then just one selfie just one but just for your personal site—hi yes this is my manager Dr. Brunhild Hexenjammer—listen I—well thank you I would like to order suits for all of my team yes also the women but in the men's style—yes—yes—well I appreciate both the—no the timing is important it must be immediately but I appreciate—yes here is a check by way of persuasion— yes that really is a lot of money it was paid to me by the sultan of—yes he very much is a collector. Yes so I would like them all to have something a little special I leave that to you and them there are five of us in total but as I say—"

And that is Eiger's suit delayed until after the fair.

It doesn't matter at all he has plenty. It doesn't matter at all. It's not substantive.

But it is the world come calling.

"Good morning sir."

"Good morning Mr. Telemark."

"Good morning."

"Yes you have said."

"Indeed so well to business then. I wish to open an account."

"Very good here are the forms. You will also require certain—oh I see that you have prepared well—"

"Yes I like to be expeditious in financial matters—"

"That is excellent but we will also require one—"

"Yes here and also I think recently there has been added a—"

"Yes indeed thank you that is most efficient I do respect such—"

And so on.

Because when Charlie fakes your existence you do not just get a little book with a picture in it. There are people in Valletta who will swear they went to school with me. There is a construction company on Gozo where I did my first job during the summer vacation there is a girl there who broke my heart and has always regretted it.

You can go and ask them. They'll tell you all about me. No ambiguity at all.

"Thank you so much I have one question can you provide digital account access?"

"Oh yes of course that is just modern. You also will need this it is called an American name quite unusual they say: a dongle."

"Excellent."

I cannot go to the school because the lady has seen Banjo and Banjo is hard to forget. Charlie cannot go ditto. Doc does not want to go but I put it on my section of the HOMER board so she goes.

Horrible fucking revenge.

"Welcome to the Dorfschule Kircheisen how splendid you are coming here to live that is excellent."

"O yes we are very excited our employer is proposing to invest in the region. We are so to speak the advance guard."

"Ah an invasion!"

"Oh yes quite so an invasion from St. Gallen!"

"The worst kind my God!"

"Yes you shall be quite overrun!"

"Ahaha!"

"Ahahahah!"

"Ahahah!"

"Ah."

". . ."

". . ."

"Perhaps you might wish to see the school?"

"Oh yes indeed it looks quite perfect on the website—"

"And how many children—"

"Four—"

"Four my God such riches congratulations—"

"O yes we are quite entirely fecund."

". . ."

". . ."

"Gosh well yes. Anyway here we are this is the classroom and—oh how pleasing here this is Erna she is teaching here as an interim measure she is quite elevated we are always delighted to have teachers so qualified—"

She is Hans Eiger's daughter is what. Agent Hannah's friend.

Evil Hansel's mother.

Erna is a researcher. She has just divorced a ne'er-do-well husband and is considering her options. In the meantime, of course, she is teaching, because she does not like to be idle.

She is delighted to meet us. She is the more astonished to learn that Doc is a research scientist by training and that she is looking on behalf of a colleague for someone with—well how remarkable—with exactly the kind of experience Erna has herself.

For a post in Sydney.

Six months with the possibility of tenure thereafter. It is all very short notice but it's a dream job. Erna must consider carefully of course. Take all the time she needs.

So long as it's less than a week.

Lindemann Auto is the Swiss version of one of those places where they take street cars and turn them into race cars. They will put skis under your running boards so you can drive your SLK across a lake. They will turn your Bentley into a boat they will—they will secret agent your shit right up. But they will also just maintain your nice car for a lot of money. Hans Eiger brings his car here because it is the best engine place in Europe and only Magnus Lindemann himself is permitted to work on it.

Turns out Magnus has a son and the son is called Otto and Otto is a solo cellist.

And by end of day Otto has just been booked to play a single concert in Beijing but there is a requirement that his father personally introduce him on the stage.

Magnus doesn't have to be asked twice because family.

Gosh this would just be an awful time for Hans Eiger's car to break down.

"Hello Mr. Telemark welcome to the Commodore how can we assist you?"

"Well to be honest—to be honest I have been sleeping in the Black House and at an agricultural building I have recently acquired and it feels—how can I put this—it feels obvious."

"I see."

"It is obvious because I am a countercultural person. I am an Ambiguitionist I specialize in tearing down the world's certainty."

"Yes quite so."

"I am concerned that I have—to be candid—that I have allowed people to become comfortable with who I am to think that they know me by my dress and style by my very disrespectability. And so . . . I am going to change my mode."

"And you wish—"

"I wish to stay here at the Commodore for the next two weeks. I will require accommodations for five persons two of whom will share a suite."

"That is quite in order—"

"I also have some vehicles we will need to park here and—how are your relationships with local restaurants?"

"They are excellent—all this is quite—perhaps you could provide me with—"

"Ah of course let us say a cash payment in advance and of course here is a credit card for your security—"

"Oh I note that it is—"

"Yes indeed there is in fact no limit on that one."

"Welcome to the Commodore, Herr Doktor Telemark, and may I say I have always admired your unique and penetrating formulation of the artistic experience please inform the staff of any requirement you may have."

"Herr Telemark?"

"Yes what can I—oh."

"Herr Banjo Telemark of Valletta, presently resident at the Black House and the Bauernhof Müller?"

"Well gosh you gentlemen are strikingly official."

From behind me Agent Hannah says: "That is because they work for me Mr. Telemark."

"How excellent madame but I do not believe we have—oh wait you are friends with the mother of the sex-pervert child?"

Agent Hannah twitches just a little.

"The boy is blameless, Herr Telemark, as you must be aware."

"Madame I know nothing of the matter I was not witness to it but I do eagerly await its fullest explanation to the satisfaction of all parties concerned now if you will excuse me—"

"I would really like to talk to you, Banjo Telemark."

"Well that would be lovely I am sure but I am working right now."

"This is how artists work?"

"Yes my practice is of its nature quite ludic."

"Does the name Jack Price mean anything to you Herr Telemark?"

"Why yes of course he is a renowned international criminal terrorist famous for cunnilingus."

"I—what?"

"What what?"

"You said he was famous for what?"

"Cunnilingus. Apparently it is a thing with him. I read where it is all he does when he is not engaged in acts of terroristic mayhem. He is obsessed with the act with the close engagement of lips and sex organs with the whisper the moan the gasp the slow gathering rhythm and the exhortations and the grip of hand in hair and shoulders on wide thighs. It is his

calling, his service, his hunger for the sudden unexpected wonder at the edge and then the thrashing and engorgement and
the gathering thunder of the heart and the fractured awareness
of inexorably approaching climax and finally with the absolute rigidity of ecstasy and the single poised moment in which
all things are beautiful. In that way as with his horrible acts of
senseless violence for money he is an artist."

". . . Oh."

"Yes."

"Where ahem where did you read this precisely?"

"I frequent the Internet madame it is known."

"It is?"

"In certain circles insofar as one can believe anything."

"Is there ah is there any more information? Of a useful
nature?"

"I despise utility I am an artist."

"Of course."

"However I believe it is possible that his lover the Professor
is—"

"The Doctor—"

"Is that not a character in a bourgeois British television
program?"

"That—no—well—I quite like—"

"The Doctor then as you say she is apparently possessed
of deviant attitudes and strange lusts also involving drugs and
electricity. Certain of my colleagues speculate that they take
lovers together I believe the term is delta. But it would almost
certainly be fatal to be the amusement of two such people."

"No doubt—"

"Fatal but I venture delicious thus caught between fear and
anticipation in an arena where shared pleasure is life. The des-

peration. The permitted and desired violations of norms. The slow galvanic spark. The—"

"No thank you I—no I am sure I can read that later not that I will require that detailed a—"

"One never knows what may be critical in a work of art, madame. Thus you may profit by knowing of the vile yet astonishingly accomplished sexuality of these monsters, just as I have made it a practice to meet denizens of the demimonde where I can find them and it may not surprise you to know that such folk gossip like old people at a café table. Thus the cunnilingus of Jack Price is a topic of endless fascination of course but—I mean for example did you know that the head of the FIS's illegal assassination section is presently having an affair quite unsanctioned and unprofessional with the Dutch ambassador to Madrid?"

"No! I know Madame de Jong from her time in Bern that is quite remarkable—you're not serious—"

"I assure you it is the talk of the underworld this season and has been since the pornography festival at Cannes when they were caught on a certain yacht—"

"O I believe I heard something about that but I had thought it was just a rumor—"

"I KNOW it's so completely—"

Agent Hannah draws closer and her hand lands on my shoulder like old friends like confidential chat like that. I take a breath and I can smell her. The vinyl holster the automatic the herbal deodorant and sweat the whisper of lipstick grease. I know what she would taste like if I put her in my mouth. I know because these tiny particles I am smelling are also on my tongue we are within one another now already as we have been since the fight.

I hear her breathe in and I know she is tasting me too.

I do not randomly lick the agent of the Swiss Federal Investigative Task Force known as the Einsatzgruppe JONAS because that is not how professionals do.

One of the other agents makes a little noise like are we interrupting his fucking important thoughts and Agent Hannah scowls at me like this whole thing is my fault.

"Herr Telemark that is not germane. What of substance do you know of Jack Price?"

"Nothing of substance, I suppose. He was reported dead a few days ago I saw it in the paper."

"I believe you are lying to me."

"Then you too are living in my art. To be honest it can be lonely."

"Jack Price is not dead."

"Found art. Ambiguity is wonderful."

"I know that he is not dead because I saw him alive. I almost captured him but he escaped me. Now I am to believe he subsequently bled out."

"But you don't?"

Agent Hannah says: "Be seeing you—Herr Telemark."

"And may I know your name?"

Agent Hannah looks into my eyes and then away and she says:

"Yes. I think you may. And if it should turn out that you see Jack Price—if he is alive—do be so kind as to tell him to get out of my country or I will put him beyond the opportunity to practice his skills. All of them."

Agent Hannah turns and walks away into the Bern evening and the flunkies go with her.

Well shit.

The next morning is golden in Bern and the natural world sings in the trees and although the anarchists have done their thing the cycle of life continues because in the pits on the far side of the river the bears are fornicating as bears do. They are not real discreet about it.

GNARR! GNARRK HRONK! WHUF WHUF WHUF HRONK!

Go at it bear fuckers. Raise the roof.

The world turns and no doubt that is nice but I am working. I am working with my modern butchered consumer electronics and my anarcho-socialist ice kobold security to do crimes.

There are places on the interwebs where good children do not go. One of these places is called G-Bread. Do not ask me why it is called G-Bread. It is because of the witch's cottage in the fairy tale. These people are deep into their dark-fantasy-lifestyle choices much of their technological security revolves around magic circles and naked chanting. Mr. Friday and Mr. Dory look at this place the way a consultant ENT guy looks at you putting a paper clip in your ear to scrape the wax out.

No but seriously do not put that shit in your ear it is not okay.

So in consequences of some poor admin decisions and a lack of basic competence, G-Bread is where you commission bored Chinese kids to run DNS attacks on your neighbor's email and then because the whole place leaks like a slug's asshole you go to jail. No sensible criminal person would ever go to G-Bread but I guess not every terrorist is a fucking ghost mastermind like in the movies so maybe they do.

Never do crimes on G-Bread.

But just like a nude masterpiece hidden under a crappy picture of a vase, so there is something under G-Bread. If you enter the wrong password three times and you remove the numbers from the end of the resultant URL you get sent to another place and if you enter the right password there you're in Halcyon, and Halcyon is the place where your ENT guy goes to get laid with ophthalmologists.

Dirty dirty dirty ophthalmologists.

Not literally but that could also be arranged on Halcyon.

On Halcyon I have posted an offer: If you commit any serious crime anywhere in the world and publicly identify yourself as Jack Price you can claim an extra ten thousand dollars.

If someone is arrested in the commission of such a crime and you free them with violence you can claim one hundred thousand dollars.

If you are a member of the law enforcement community and you free them you can claim seven million four hundred and eighty-one thousand nine hundred and forty-one dollars from a total remuneration pot of one hundred million dollars.

If you can supply evidence of someone gaming the system you get a full ten million dollars on presentation of their polished skull on a stick.

I did not want to be too forward about this so I have used Sharkey's login information and his bank account that seems only fair because I did try really hard not to explode his balls and it's not like he had any descendants other than those formerly resident as potential in said balls. At least not that I know of but actually he probably did and I make a note to put someone on that.

Then I get up and jump in the river instead of showering and I discover that the river is glacial meltwater and my penis is very unhappy with me.

Lucille swims for half an hour he is secretly made of walrus. When he emerges his walrus man parts are like sweet potato. Doc looks at him through infrared goggles and says his groin is actually two degrees warmer than the rest of his body. This is autonomous urogenital thermogenesis and very interesting scientifically speaking. Doc says I should really look. I tell Doc she is a genius and a woman of tomorrow and I do not look at Lucille's appalling nethers through high-tech surveillance gear that is not my jam. I go and make art.

But on second thought I do make Doc take pictures because art is where you find it and the more mysterious and horrible the better and if there is anywhere in the universe more mysterious and horrible than Lucille's sweet potato walrus lovesack I do not know where it could be and I do not want to.

"Boss it is impossible."

"Nothing is impossible."

"Actually boss—"

"Yes all right lots of things are impossible what impossible thing is this?"

"The thing."

"What thing."

"The thing that you said."

"What—"

"The guy in the marina. Boss he is not there. There's pictures of the back of his head and like that. But he does not want to be seen."

"Is there a picture of his ear? I read where they can do ID now with just ears—"

"Boss. I am the nerd in this conversation. There is no good picture of his ear also the availability of ear comparison data is not great."

"So we have just his back?"

"Yeah shoulders head and butt—"

"How are there pictures of his butt?"

"Like in his suit from behind? The bellhops in the marina hotel wear body cams—"

"Oh so not like his actual butt—"

"No not his actual butt that would be weird—"

"If we had his actual butt could we identify it?"

"If we had his actual butt we would have the rest of him or else I guess it would not be so much an issue anymore boss."

"But if we just as a matter of curiosity if—"

"No."

"Seriously?"

"Boss—"

"Yeah okay. It's just he worries about his body mass index so—oh."

"What oh?"

"Soup."

"Soup?"

"I am going to kill him with soup Charlie."

"Um okay?"

"Not with soup maybe but definitely because of soup."

"Yes?"

"Soup and emeralds Charlie. These are the key things here. I must go now."

"Where?"

"Bogotá."

Some things you got to do in person. There's no phoning it in there's just showing up. Often they're little things like this but you still got to go and it can only be you.

Can't take the Demon plane they will be watching that. Gonna be some guy named Urs in the bag-handling line who has a friend who has a friend who works for Eiger. A woman called Charlotte who works passport control. Someone.

Happily I have close relationships in the international pilot community I can draw on so I will just go now and fly fly fly—

"Price."

"Hi Doc I am just going to Bogotá—"

"Yes no doubt whatever but you also have a thing for me."

"I do it is—"

"No Price not that thing."

"Always that thing."

"Eh-eh Price no now is not the time."

"You brought up my thing and my thing is partial to you so—"

"Well yes I too am partial to that thing."

"O ARE you o good let us repair to a bedroom and—"

". . . This will not get you out of doing that other thing I was talking about."

"There are no other things there is only—"

"Price."

"No indeed quite understood."

"Excellent bring the klister I have an idea—"

". . ."

"Do not say anything about finding the klister."

"No ma'am."

Klister is a kind of ski wax for when you want to go real slowly and no of course that is not what we do with it you are an idiot. But if you put klister on your skin you can lean on a wall and not slip down it even when normally you would slip down it and with the right understanding of sexual physics and good core strength Doc is correct that you can have basically hot spider lady sex.

She puts my back against the wall walks up it holding my

hands. She stalks me as if she is going to eat me. It is the most fucked-up appalling thing I have ever seen.

She puts one foot on my chest and flips through the loop of our arms and slides down. I can smell the wax and the sweat on her spine. She puts both her palms flat on the wall and I cradle her as if I'm a chair. She rolls her head back to bite my neck and I feel the agony of the stress position and then the first touch of—

Amnesia.

It's quite a long blackout and when I remember myself again she's still kissing me and I realize that this time she didn't take any and she knows exactly what she did and I hear her chuckle in her chest and she—

Amnesia.

"Doc—"

"Yes yes—"

"Doc I really got to go—"

"I said yes I KNOW—"

"You are not helping you are—"

"Fine but you also have to do that thing."

"Tell me."

"The Kircheisen system runs on some ancient bullshit code it is security by obsolescence."

"Charlie cannot break it?"

"She can but not until she understands it and it will take too long. She needs a manual. Or better I think it is customized so the fastest thing is if we just ask the coder."

"Well we can totally do that why—"

"We do not know who that is it is part of the obfuscation—"

"I am not—"

"Price! I put it on the board."

"Yes?"

"That is how it works I did the school you do this. Fix it."

"I am not a computer person!"

"Speak to Friday."

"But—"

"Board."

"But—"

"I am right now buying a dozen military-grade plasma cutters for rescue work we will not be doing under an oil rig. Speak to Friday. In person he will like that you are flying anyway doing your whatever."

"It is not nearly in the same direction Doc—"

"It is on the board Price. Look there is Jack written underneath it is a Jack thing."

"I—"

"The board says so Price it must be true."

". . . Yes ma'am."

"Good."

"Can we do the amnesia thing and this time you—"

"No. But I will tell you what I will do."

"O yes?"

"I will show you what I remember."

"O will you?"

"Yes. First you see there was—hhhhhsssst. Yes. There was that."

"And now this?"

"Well—w—welllll no no last time we first did—"

"Hnnnn yes I see—"

"Not yet but now—"

"O o o"

"In-o o indeed o hoo o O"

"O"

Amnesia.

"Hey Mozart!"

"Fuck off Jack it is Rossini."

"Is that like a religious holiday in Assholia?"

"And when you get to Fuckoffistan just keep right on fucking until you come out the other side."

"You want to earn some money real fast?"

"I won't have sex with you Jack."

"Eight million seven hundred and five thousand five hundred euros untraceable."

". . ."

". . . Mozart are you there?"

". . ."

". . ."

". . . Ten million."

"Fine."

"Fifteen."

"What?"

"Fifteen million you said yes to ten real fast."

"Twelve."

"Done. Get in here and take off your clothes."

"I do not want to have sex with you."

"You're a fickle bitch Jack I hope you're still going to pay me."

"I want you to fly me to Bogotá."

"For twelve million dollars?"

"Yes."

"Do we have to bomb it or something?"

"Would you do that for twelve million euros?"

"Sure why not."

"Huh."

"Now why the fuck do you look like I shat on your puppy?"

"I feel like you massively overestimate how awful it would be to have sex with me."

"Yeah I'm sure you do get in the plane I'm supposed to drop orphans on emergency medical equipment in seventy-nine hours."

"I think you have that the wrong way round."

"Yeah I'm sure you do get in the fucking plane."

Because this is the world now this is the thing: everywhere is just a few hours away. Mozart's plane is not super-duper fast but it is fast enough. It has nasty military seating the way they make seating by averages and that way it never actually fits anyone in particular it is always averagely uncomfortable for everyone. She has bolted some sort of stereo system onto the back of the flight deck and there is an actual hammock and an espresso machine where the forward galley would be on a commercial flight and otherwise the whole thing is just a heavily armored cigar of metal without windows. It's like a submarine for air. The instruments are all like science fiction advanced and no doubt Charlie would be super excited but I do not really care about that stuff and all I can see is the little cubbyhole with the hammock and the books and even there are pictures on the ceiling and this is about the loneliest little mobile house I have ever seen.

"This is the loneliest mobile house I have ever seen."

"I'm an introvert I do not like people very much."

"I hear that and I respect it do you want me to go sit in the back?"

". . . No."

". . ."

". . ."

". . . So how did you get to be like this rebel pilot lady?"

". . ."

". . ."

". . . Bad timing I guess."

"What bad timing?"

"Are you always like this?"

"Like how?"

"Like chatty."

"Well we have hours right?"

"We do I was thinking we would spend it in tranquil contemplation of the majesty of the earth from altitude."

". . ."

". . ."

". . . So now that we've done that—"

"O God I'll tell you when we pass over Iceland."

"Are we going to pass over Iceland?"

"Absolutely not."

"So you will never tell me."

"Nope."

"And we're not passing over Iceland at all that was like pilot humor?"

"Sure whatever."

"O because I have friends there."

". . ."

". . . Whom I will not wave at as we do not pass over Iceland."

". . ."

"..."
"..."
"... So how—"
"O my God—"

The thing is that lying is hard and truth is easy and there is this idea in the world that the best lie is the one that is close to the truth and that is beautiful bullshit and I will tell you why. That kind of lie is the most usable lie. It is easy to remember because most of it actually happened just like that and for most people in most situations that is all you need. But in any professional situation where a lie must be sustained in the long term where it must conceal a truth from a person determined and capable in the field of finding that truth then the lie must touch the real world exclusively at those places where the interface can be controlled. Deep lies are all about control and you cannot control a hybrid lie because any time you need to give further detail you risk giving detail which can be used to penetrate the lie.

"O hi Richie I saw you out with a blonde last night—"

"O hi Jack yeah my cousin Anna was in town from Potsdam—"

"O that is lovely have you been out there to visit?"

"Yes I have it was great Anna is like a tour-guide-type person and we stayed in this really terrific hotel—"

See what just happened there is that Richie fucked-up. Anna really is a tour guide from Potsdam and he is sticking as close to the truth as he can but oops his cousin is from Potsdam so why was she staying in a hotel with him there?

So if you are telling a lie that matters you do not want to be retrofitting it to the truth on the fly, which is what you will have to do if it touches the truth all along its length and now this feels dirty anyway ANYWAY you cannot do that you are not that smart and you think you are but you're not. You will get busted because you will say something like:

"I recently had excellent ajiaco in its native setting."

Did you now? Well that is interesting because ajiaco is a delicacy much favored in Bogotá like if you were to look at any tourist guide it would say try the soup and do you know what else is in Bogotá? No not cocaine that is a fucking stereotype. What is in Bogotá is the Emerald Trade Center, and if we think back we find ourselves saying: What was it that Mr. Client wanted us to steal but emeralds?

Now it is possible that that is all so much bullshit but I am willing to bet you that when Mr. Client said the word emerald his entire fucking soul was wearing the same dopey grin as poor dumb Richie staring up in his mind's eye at whatever he and Anna-not-his-cousin did in the Alimony Auberge.

I will bet you enough money to pay Mozart for sex that Mr. Client was here in the last month talking to people in or near the big sandy building with the green glass frontage.

Bogotá is a kind of a triangle running along one side of a bunch of high bits and there are rivers and a road that runs north–south through town and it's a city like any city you would know it's got ten million people and skyscrapers rising out of neoclassical cement construction like World's Fair stuff like LA. There's some old old Bogotá too like colonial and the thing you need to get right now is this is a fucking. Capital. Of the world. It's Paris it's Madrid it's Hong Kong it's not some fucking stage set for your personal narrative and it is complex as shit. I have been here before when I was in coffee because have you met coffee of course I fucking came here. And the thing that you do not do when you are approaching a capital city with its own way of doing things is blow into town like a giant hornet and land on everyone's food and scare the shit out of the tourists because even a hornet eventually outstays its welcome and gets blatted under someone's boot heel. That is why I am not here with Saul who has some employment history in the region or Rex and his explodophilia or even worse with Lucille who just likes to slice things up very small with his love. It is also why Doc and her I Will Kill All The Cows are presently chillaxing in the spa pool at a hotel in Zürich sourcing whatever thief shit she requires and Motor Oil Charlie is working on Eiger's dongle—

Yes yes she is and she is not happy with my dongle humor—

—so that leaves me to hitch a ride with Mozart and be real calm and conciliatory and not get neck-deep in shit in a place where they do understand appropriate responses to freelancing plus also too not everyone here was a huge fan of the management structure around—i.e., me being the only shareholder in—the Pale Peruvian Stallion and that is not stereotyping that is commerce.

So softly we go.

"Hi I'm Jack Mahboubian hi."

"Hi Mr. Mahboubian welcome to the Zebedee how may we assist you—"

The Zebedee is a luxury hotel and also a festival of Daliesque architectural batshit whose website features a digital composite image of that woman from the *American Gothic* picture holding a board meeting with men in episcopal purple one of whom has the head of a snail. For some reason I cannot place at all it is very clear they are all about to have sex and they will then all die of her appalling children hatching from their heads. The presence of this image is never explained and probably never should be but I just totally wanted to stay there. I even created Jack Mahboubian as a bespoke Zebedee-friendly cover identity because Persian New Zealand casino entrepreneurs are exactly the kind of person you can imagine staying at the Zebedee. Mozart is also staying at the Zebedee and in fact she is even more appropriate to the place than Jack Mahboubian, and several of the weird naked rock-climbing videos and collage art pieces viewable in the bar area look like she could be in them.

"Hi hi the room is lovely I am a particular fan of the box jellyfish tank are they defanged in some way?"

"No Mr. Mahboubian they are authentic but the tank is sealed and made from surplus space shuttle glass so it is perfectly safe."

"O that is excellent are they also for sale?"

"A local artisan Mr. Mahboubian I will get you his details—"

"O thank you thank you and a more trivial and banal request I am visiting the Emerald Trade Center today by I wish very much to eat ajiaco can you recommend a few places that might be convenient to the location?"

"O of course—"

Short list.

"Hi Jack Mahboubian hi I hear you have the best—no the BEST ajiaco in town I read where it is mmmMMM! Can I get a little—I am having a party for my investors could I—thank you so much—"

Except that half the time I am doing all that in Spanish because yes I speak Spanish of course I fucking do it is the one of the world's languages plus also did I say COFFEE yes I did.

And yes of course they can help me out and little by little
it goes:

"Well of course my friend was in here like a couple months
back very sophisticated guy excellent taste looks like—maybe
you remember—O well never mind—"

—never mind never—

—never mind—

—never—

"O you do?"

"Yes I think I do was a French guy maybe?"

"Yes of course he was now he told me—he told me you
were super-duper expensive—"

"No of course we are not! Did he really—"

"Yes he said—well to be honest, looking at these prices I
wonder if maybe you overcharged him by like an extra zero
I'm gonna laugh at him for not noticing he is a rich man—no
don't worry about it seriously the guy is so damn rich—O you
have well I guess of course you have records yes I would be
delighted to give him a message to call you say he paid by
card? Why yes OF COURSE there he is François Leclerc you
are so right and look he just has no fucking idea what he is
talking about—or—you know what I bet he was joshing me
like trying to keep you guys to himself! Because this ajiaco is
SO GOOD could I try the Bandeja Paisa if I come in tomorrow
I would like a table for eight yes I would be delighted to pay
in advance—"

François Leclerc.

Mr. Client.

Hi there I'm Jack.

SEVEN

AND THAT IS THAT AND THAT IS WHEN you leave the party. No one in Bogotá has any idea that the first of the Seven Demons is in town or that the former maker of the Pale Peruvian Stallion is here or any of that and that is how we like it so we leave everything in our hotel room and we just fly out again.

Except that we do not because Mozart is in a bar fight so first I go in and I fake arrest her and drag her out and put her in a hire car like she was a prisoner and she spits like a fucking cat and then we drive off to the general approval of a bunch of guys feeling nauseous and ballsmacked and two dancers who are evidently twins and to be honest I completely understand how that kind of shit can happen but now it is very much time to leave because under no circumstances do we wish to attract attention or get held up at the airport.

Giant fucking jet privileges do not apply to Mozart's flying turd in the same way as they do to Fred's porno plane.

I do not try to bribe anyone it is a mismatch to offer at this time do not ask me why it is an instinct.

They look at our passports and they look at us and one of them says something about how we're fucking and we've stolen the jet and they all laugh and Mozart says something in gutter Bogotano which implies I have been chemically castrated and they all freeze and then start laughing and we are through and it's just my imagination that behind us somewhere someone is putting two and two together because we're on the runway and gone and then it's just flying time.

"Thanks Mozart."

"Go to hell Jack."

"O you're still an asshole?"

"Fuck you Jack."

"Soooo I almost forgot I need to go to Iceland on the way home can we detour for like three million one hundred and—"

"Yes five will be fine—"

"So tell me the whole life story thing while we—"

"No—"

"Come on I feel like we bonded—"

"We did not bond you're an asshole—"

"So're you—"

"I am a motherfucking LADY—"

. . .

. . .

. . .

"Mozart?"

"It's fucking Rossini—"

"Iceland is definitely up from here—"

"Which of us knows navigation?"

"I am right now looking at Google Maps though—"

"Fuck you Jack that's bullshit let me see that—yeah no you're right hang on—"

"I am?"

"Of course you're fucking not don't be absurd."

Mr. Friday is the not-boss of Poltergeist. He likes fishing and Scandinavian art-house cinema and he has exquisite taste in hair liniment. When he speaks he sounds like Santa Claus if Santa was increasingly concerned about the role of the Global South in the production of cheap plastic Christmas toys. He abhors violence and has strong views on social responsibility and he is totally calm even when his BFF is putting an iron spike in someone's brain. Be like Mr. Friday. Do not be like the person with the double-vented head parts.

Doc says that I get along with Mr. Friday on some kind of deep psychological level she does not think is rational. Doc says that some aspect of my self-expression speaks to Mr. Friday's suppressed desires and he responds to my wishes in ways he would normally refuse to contemplate.

I do not think this is true but Doc has charts so it must be that is science.

Mr. Friday stands in front of a smoking hole in the ground, which is evidently his house. I say:

"This was absolutely nothing to do with me Friday hand on heart."

Mr. Friday looks round.

"O Hallo Mr. Price! I had heard that you were now deceased."

"I have also heard that but I do not think it is true."

"Oh ho ho oho yes oh oho."

(Do not laugh like Mr. Friday. That laugh is just fucking creepy like going to an empty house in a storm and the woman who owns it is entirely hairless and dresses in black net and she says to come in and that's when you notice she's had that thing done where they bifurcate your tongue and you can never quite see her feet and when you wake up you find a man-size-shed snake skin on the second bed. Which is completely unfair on Mr. Friday who I think is a genuinely moral person in an imperfect world.)

"Do not worry Mr. Price I know this was not you it is an aspect of our geology here. From time to time there is a move-ment in the earth and the strata of rock change. Yesterday there was water in my basement that was the wrong kind of water. So I moved my furniture out into the street and went to stay with friends and last night my house exploded."

"It did."

"O yes. Superheated steam from the bowels of the planet. It is invigorating. We will build a new house at the end of the road and put my furniture in it. That is Iceland. It is how we do. Oh hoho hohohoh. What can I do for you?"

"I am seeking your wisdom Mr. Friday."

"I am happy to offer professional help of course."

"Aw that is very sweet. I miss you guys also."

"It is a form of words Mr. Price you are not absolutely at the top of our list of preferred customers on account that you are a fissure in the strata of society and also a bad egg."

"I—wait—a bad egg?"

"Indeed."

"A bad egg."

"Yes Mr. Price."

"O well excuse me the Duchess of Croquet called and I believe she would like her idiom back."

". . . Now inexplicably I feel remorse. Oh very well. Come and we will walk to my new house."

We walk to Friday's new house. It is also a hole in the ground but it is not smoking and there are people doing things that look like things that will make a house happen quite soon.

"What do you need Mr. Price?"

"I need to find a programmer. In Switzerland."

(Obviously you do not list the precise name and address of the programmer of your fortress for exactly this reason but there is a limited number of firms operating in Switzerland who handle this kind of work and programmers are not in general humble monkish types they are programmers and that means they are a kind of artist whose art winkies are so engorged that they require canvases costing millions of euros. Every programmer is waiting for a Great Pyramid.)

Mr. Friday says that he will not help me hurt anyone.

I say that I am not going to hurt the programmer all I want is to have a perfectly nice conversation.

"Why do you want this information Mr. Price?"

"Aw Mr. Friday I wish you would not ask me that or if I would tell you that would have to be you know just between friends."

"We are not friends Mr. Price."

"We're not but all the same man we got history is what. Like deep history."

"Horrible history."

"Yeah but Mr. Friday in this world you know sometimes that is the most reassuring kind."

". . . that is both true and appalling."

"Yeah well I'm an artist now."

"You are?"

"Yes I am known as Banjo Telemark—"

"O really I have seen your work in—wait that means it has never in fact existed—"

"That is the genius of my ambiguity Mr. Friday—"

"Mr. Price?"

"Yes?"

"You are proposing to crack Die Festung."

"No I mean that would be entirely no of course not also too Jack Price is deceased I am an artist why do you ask?"

"You are."

"If I was going to do that, is it something you would be upset about?"

"In fact we do not like them. We believe in freedom, they in perpetuation. We are in fact a revolutionary movement albeit an incremental one they are deeply conservative to the point of stasis. It is an incompatibility. Mr. Eiger and his ilk—"

"Ilk."

"Yes his ilk. Cornflower men. He and his sort—they appear to be Swiss but they are not like true Swiss who are compassionate in surprising moments and directions. They are the other thing. The closed door and the sneer. The cancer that hides in the body of the Gemeinde there is a similar issue elsewhere even here. When people are afraid they espouse severity. The Cornflower Men make them afraid and then offer them answers."

"That was real stirring but I am not entirely—"

"They are a little bit Fascists."

"How little?"

"Quite a lot actually."

"I'm going to do me things to these guys."

". . ."

". . ."

". . . It seems I am constantly in the position of helping you because you are pointed at monsters more horrible than yourself. And yet each time I do this you become more . . . you."

"Seriously man I have a job I just want to get it done and they are being unreasonable is all like they—Friday they killed Volodya the sniper I mean that guy . . ."

"He was appalling. He made ham from the dead."

"Man don't start with that he absolutely did not it was just ham we had this whole running joke about that it used to make him laugh."

"You cannot actually believe that."

"O shit Friday did he really make ham out of—Jesus never mind I just—all I want is to get this job done okay and these guys are putting themselves in my way when I—you know I totally tried to do it the respectable way but there are issues of—"

"You propose to annihilate them."

"Will you help?"

"Do you promise me that the programmer in question will not be harmed?"

"Yes."

". . . I believe we should define harm."

"Friday—Friday man I'm not—okay I have been off my game that thing with the lady whose car we stole is well she is not alive and obviously there was the unfortunate business with Mr. Sharkey's exploding face but—but when—let's say when I am in control of the environment I do not wish to make people die that is not my thing."

"You derive no pleasure in random killing for its own sake. That is true."

"Well so here we are I am asking you as a service to I guess local humankind to help me here so that no one has to get so much as a nosebleed—well I say no one but obviously I'm excluding from that certain un-Swiss fucking Fascists who will probably fall from a great height onto a pointy object or something—"

"Do you also understand the reasonable bounds I require in exchange for this information?"

"No serious physical discomfort or damage no death little or no loss of earnings no serious long-term emotional or psychological trauma."

"That . . . is correct."

"Within the obvious limits like if I don't know if this person has a shotgun under his bed in some ultra-Swiss thing that I do not know about—"

"Yes of course self-defense is respectable even in a criminal context if not legally understood—"

"Okay."

". . . Okay yes."

"You people are awesome I am just so grateful."

"Do not thank me please it makes me feel soiled."

"You're an asshole and you've given up everything about who you are to do this one dirty thing and I can't believe you're helping me. Aw that came out cold man I did not mean that to sound cold."

". . ."

"Honestly Friday I really do like you guys and if you like I'll give you a hug to get you through this weird little moral crisis you're in but I get the sense that would not help. Right? Am I right? Yeah so maybe hug Mr. Dory and get back to me when you can okay?"

". . ."

". . ."

"When I talk to you Jack Price I believe I have woken from a coma to find I am living in a locally made experimental film."

"Ain't that the world these days my friend."

"Thanks Rossini that was horrible here is money bye."

"Did you just call me Rossini?"

"I am an asshat lady but I know the difference between the *Marriage of Figaro* and *The Barber of Seville* and you did right by me so yeah I did."

". . . You need me again, you call, that's fine. But call me Mozart okay?"

". . . Sure Mozart I will."

"Now I'm going to go park my plane in front of your plane again and maybe draw a giant penis on it in ultraviolet paint."

"O screw you."

I go before she says in your dreams or some such because Mozart is a nice person and very useful and I cannot have Doc murdering her for loose talk.

Doc still has the same number of pigs. The door has been well behaved. Lucille has been watching it to make sure.

Every hour of every day.

Door vs. Lucille. Lucille vs. door.

Rex says that neither of them has blinked.

Back to Eiger. Back to the job.

"Hi Charlie how's it going?"

"It's going boss that I will say."

"Are you in yet?"

"God LORD boss butt-plug joke much?"

"What?"

"Oh my God never mind yes I am in."

Charlie vs. the dongle for Eiger's checking account: first to three falls.

One.

Two.

Three.

This is how truly modern bank robberies happen and it is the best way. You just steal a few cents from every account in the ledger and put it all into a new account, which transfers every month to another external account, which immediately forwards it to one of those banking jurisdictions which do not keep great records and then you spend it. Kids' stuff.

Or you don't steal anything because that was never what you were there for in the first place.

There's one more thing that Hans Eiger does every day. He goes to a tobacco shop. It is not one of the grand ones it is quite small and even a little bit scruffy but even so when you go in there it smells of respectability. It smells of old men keeping secrets and it smells of government. There is a mezuzah on the door frame and a morbidly obese dachshund on a cushion by the till. Hans Eiger does not ever buy anything in the shop but every day he goes in and he inhales one cigar and then nods to this little guy and the little guy nods back.

So this time when Hans Eiger goes out I go in. I figure the little guy for maybe Armenian but when I wish him barev dzez he snorts and says his mama is Beta Israel so we talk coffee. Ethiopian coffee is serious coffee. Weak-ass North American barista brew is like a ballet shoe and Ethiopian coffee is like something handmade in leather for the president of a Russian bank.

We do not talk about Hans Eiger at all and still less do we talk about cigars even although these are some fine fucking cigars and they should be respected by the mouths of beautiful women because that is the best thing that can happen to a cigar. We talk coffee like two old men remembering great sex they once had with girls they wish they'd hung around for and fallen for and I wish Doktor Paul was here because he would love this.

We talk for like two hours and then the little guy says it is time now for me to go and I say thank you yes it is and I buy a cigar, I tell him give me his favorite and I guess that he does. I do not know what it is and he does not tell me. Doc will smoke it sometime Doc loves a good cigar and it is a good cigar.

Doc is beautiful when she smokes a cigar. It is a thing do not judge me.

I do not fuck with Eiger and the cigar shop because he does not buy anything here and that makes me pay attention but also because I like the little guy and his shop and there is no need to break beautiful things just to upset bad people who like them.

I fuck with everything else though because I am petty that way.

First it turns out there has been a fire at Karlsbad House in Doha. This is a thing that happens very occasionally there in the new buildings. They are building very fast and they bring in labor from overseas and it is not always the case that those workers are well treated some of them die on the job and in this case indeed someone evidently died and was lost in the super-structure and his corpse caused a short circuit between two phases and la la. Only one floor was affected and the building suppression systems were excellent and performed above spec.

But now it seems Hans Eiger's apartment will not be available for his use in the near future. Insurance will cover it of course there will be no—

But well. There you are that is inconvenient.

I do not know who the dead guy was. Rex does not tell me when he gets back. He looks a little haunted. A little more like a Demon than he did. Saul asks me if he is okay.

"Yeah he's fine."

"He doesn't look fine Jack."

"What are you his mother?"

"Just getting the lie of the land Jack."

"Rex was just some guy. Lost his brother to criminals. Wanted to do right by his country."

"Look where that gets you."

"Right?"

"There's an issue around group cohesion when a given component of the group is allowed to feel disconnected and—"

"What are you like the most heavily armed shrink north and west of the Atlas mountains here?"

"I am a commando it is the skill set—"

"I really do not feature Marine Force Recon talking group dynamics in the Humvee—"

"That is because you are an effete criminal snob with no working knowledge of the complexity of—"

"And you're a hairless ape with a cannon fixation—"

"I have seen you looking at my guns you want guns as big as—"

"Compensating for—"

(Zzzzzipp.)

"Good Lord Saul what am I supposed to do with that?"

"I am married I am just making a—"

"Why am I seeing all of the team junk this week—"

"WOW Saul that is your actual—"

"Charlie why are you here—"

"Should I also—"

"LUCILLE?"

ZZZZii-

"O GOOD GOD NO—"

"No seriously boss should I show everyone my crime vagina now is that a thing we are—"

"Price why is there dick everywhere NO CHARLIE that will not be necessary also those words I HAVE SAID—"

"Doc can we go away somewhere please to an island and never meet any of these people again?"

"After that I will be seeing all of them every time I close my eyes what is WRONG with—"

"Hi what'd I miss?"

". . ."

". . ."

". . ."

"Hi Rex."

"Hi Rex."

"Hi Rex."

"Nuffim Rex hi Rex."

"Uh. Okay. Well gosh Saul has a very impressive penis."

". . ."

". . ."

(ZZZiiip.)

"That is very kind of you Rex and in no way connected with what I am going to say now which is that we are going to go and get wurst as men do there is a Schnellimbiß that I know. There we shall sit and take the air and drink beer."

"O okay Saul that is nice I guess."

Saul takes Rex to get wurst he says it is good for broken hearts. Doc gives me the face that says I am basically landfill with biohazards please get my shit together.

I tell her I have a name and I see her smile.

I put on my Banjo and give an interview to a Spanish newspaper about Ambiguitionism. I claim not to know anything about it. I claim to be a wanted terrorist and murderer. I say that I am here to rob Eiger's bank.

The interviewer thinks this is excellent content but it wants some visuals so I take him into the pig barn and show him the X8 and he photographs it exploding a pigskin in the shape of a pig full of what he assumes is not actually a pig.

It is a pig.

Doc is not happy about this because now she has only seven pigs but you can buy pigs on the Internet and anyway it's not like we need more than one pig. I am an evolutionary pressure is all, we will end up with the smartest pig for our job and that is the pig that we want.

I watch Hans Eiger go to his garage but his car will not start. There was a strange noise in the engine in his drive home yesterday. Now the key turns and nothing happens.

I watch him call Magnus Lindemann and find out that Magnus is not at home.

Hans Eiger takes a taxi to pick up his suit, which is not ready. He is very sensible about it. It is the sort of thing happens and he understands commerce.

He is standing in the street when someone from the Karlsbad calls to let him know about the fire. Hans Eiger is not happy now and he is almost terse. Then he takes a deep breath and I can see him master himself. He finishes the call and sighs and decides to go for coffee.

He sits and drinks a coffee. It is not his practice to drink coffee at this hour but he does it anyway and he has a little schnapps in it to make it fertig.

He calls his daughter to tell her about his day. Erna tells him she is thinking of moving to Australia.

Hans Eiger does not respond well to Erna and she hangs up on him.

He goes to lunch.

In East Germany it was called Zersetzung: biodegradation. Those assholes would destroy your whole life in little tiny ways before you realized you were under attack. Some people never realized at all. They just died in the gutter thinking the universe was a horror.

That would actually be fun. I could take years over this. Make it a project.

But it wouldn't rob the bank and you have to have certain standards.

"Boss I have him."

"Eiger?"

"No not him: Mr. Client. Your man Leclerc."

". . . Tell me all Charlie."

I am doing the thing where you steeple your hands with your fingertips on your forehead like they are containing your intellect and your rage. I am just trying it out because it's a villain thing. I quite like it although I have this urge to futz around with the corners of my eyes because they feel like they have grit in them and I could just poke it out and get rid of it and then go back to my steepling. That is not like sticking a fucking paper clip in your ear it is perfectly safe although if you do it after a commercial flight you will catch something because Doc tells me the primary route of infection on aircraft is surface to hand to eye. Anyway the steepling maybe doesn't work for me but I am trying it.

It's going to freak the shit out of Charlie so there's that.

"Tell me all, Charlie. Tell me all."

"Ooooh show-and-tell!"

Sometimes the villain thing is harder than you'd think.

Here is Hans Eiger as a strapping young soldier and here is his brother in arms François something or other we do not know because this was in the fucking stone age before the Internet. The guy is Belgian and he went and joined the Legion with an eye to sidestepping some past mistakes and when he was discharged he took a French passport in the name of François Leclerc, which is somewhat like being a French John Smith. While he was in the Legion, though, Frankie made friends with (picture) a bunch of nice guys including (picture) Hans Eiger and they were you know soldiers together and then after they were soldiers of fortune maybe a little bit and it is unkindly suggested (picture) they were running heroin from Iran through Kosovo and up into Europe with the assistance of assorted fuckwads (picture picture short clip) and these fuckwads were of a Nazi persuasion (arrest photos) that is to say new Fascists with an ethnic beef (riot burning cars men shouting at tiny brown kids on a bus) and old Nazi blood looking to capitalize on the fanboys (*New York Times* profile seriously motherfuckers you're WHAT now) in order to rise again, and the criminal element among these guys just love to deal heroin from Mesopotamia into their own countries because they are so motherfucking patriotic. They do this with maximal violence because it is not about money with them although they like money it is about power and specifically the power to fuckwad as much as possible like this toxic masculinity we hear so much about these days that is entirely their jam.

"Boss I am right there with you but their failure to model a more positive manhood to the youth is not our primary concern here—"

"I know Charlie but completeness and detail are important in a holistic criminal environment—"

"I haz much details here it are: they are dicks. With tattoos."

Charlie is full of true facts.

(Slideshow. Some of the dicks with tattoos have tattoos on their dicks and this cannot possibly be pleasing to the old guys like: what is Fascism coming to, millennial Nazis have no standards they probably eat avocados like the Socialists and then where are we and la la la.)

All the same here is Frankie Leclerc being a fuckwad at a demo in Greece and here is Frankie palling it up with those NATO guys who went to jail for drugs and here is Frankie with the Brothers of the White—I don't know I'm saying maybe Roosters?—the art is awful—anyway they are a motorcycle gang. And here is Frankie with the Count von Badfuckyourself and the Count is known to be the new man in respectable far-right politics in Mitteleuropa and here he is with Bishop Hatlikepeniskirchen who totally reaches out to the poors and understands why they do not like the Africa coming to these green shores of the northern Med that is just good economic sense and entirely compatible with the Christianism and pretty soon I would like to vomit in a bucket please.

And here is Frankie with a bunch of metal suitcases flying out of Bogotá on a Moldovan emergency medical courier passport and here is our dear friend Hans Eiger hugging him at Basel airport and welcoming the great man to Switzerland and Hans Eiger is a good Swiss and this is after all a medical emergency so it would be rude to overcook the security discussion that would just be inappropriate.

One billion in emeralds from a conflict zone moved through Colombia into the Kircheisen Festung.

Mr. Client lied to me.

He also told me the truth.

Moohoohaha.

Here is my truth: Frankie Leclerc is a very bad drug dealer.
That is to say that he is a bad man which I do not care about but
also very bad at dealing drugs. You can tell because there are so
many arrest records and outstanding warrants and such for his
people. You can tell because in this dog-eat-dog world of Inter-
nets and dark websites and that Frankie is using conventional
analog methods and guess what his overheads must suck bigly.
Bribes and lawyers and hits and such yes. Frankie is not clearing
anything like the kind of money in those cases so Frankie . . .
Frankie has backers and backers are a thing they are an issue
they are like investors shareholders they expect results and a guy
like Frankie . . . he does not like someone jogging his arm. So
now we begin to see what Hans Eiger and Frankie might have
in common now they are all growed up and serious men. Hans
needs to advertise and Frankie needs to get out from under and
what might they achieve together?

But Hans Eiger cannot be hanging around with men like
Frankie Leclerc surely because Frankie is a bad guy there is
paper there is a trail and somewhere there is a file and a dozen
of those alarmingly competent Eurocops like—

Oh.

Ohhhh yeah.

So now that I know all about his friend I get my Banjo on
again and I go and have lunch with Hans Eiger.

There is only one place in the city where Hans Eiger will eat
lunch it is called the Hirschen. He eats there every day at the

same table. He never books. He just comes at exactly the same time and he eats the same thing.

I do not sit at Hans Eiger's table.

I sit at the table opposite.

I order the salmon.

Hans Eiger absolutely hates salmon. He cannot stand the smell of it.

The steam blows from my table over his because that is why I chose this table.

I can see him hating it but it would be remarkably inappropriate in almost every way for him to object so he can't.

I eat my salmon. It is excellent. I make little noises.

Omnomnom.

Hans Eiger sits under the stuffed badger and the crossed wooden skis and he eats schnitzel. It is reputedly the second best schnitzel in the world but only because the Kronenhalle in Zürich always and forever holds the top slot and you cannot go to the Kronenhalle every day from Bern and still get anything done with your morning.

Hans Eiger eats his schnitzel and smells my salmon and I look at him and I say:

"O hai! It is me Banjo! You are Hans Eiger I claim my five dollars!"

"Excuse me?"

"It is a joke a very old one hi! We met at the art thing with Herr Doktor Doktor Paul how are you?"

"To be honest Herr—"

"Banjo Telemark—"

"Yes of course Herr Telemark I am having a difficult day and I wish to repose—is that how it is said?—to repose myself and consider and so forth—"

"O I totally understand I am right now making art—hey listen—hey actually can we talk I want to rob your bank—"

"What?"

"Obviously not for real! I would not tell you that. That would be insane."

"Obviously."

"I want to rob your bank—like conceptually—like I want to bring in bulldozers and so on—real actual physical bulldozers that you would never ever allow like American monster machines that Chinese thing they use that lays like a half-mile bridge in a day that kind of—and have fireworks for demolitions and music like 'The Imperial March'—and maybe performance artists in swimsuits eating fire and someone dressed as a bear because you know Bern—"

"I do not think it is appropriate to the reputation of my bank—"

"BULLDOZERS how cool would that be and also maybe actors in commando outfits and we could have pink paintball and—"

"Inappropriate—"

"BULLDOZERS—"

"NO—"

People are noticing our little chat now and Hans Eiger does not want that because Banjo Telemark is not someone he wants to be seen talking to. Banjo is harshing his Swissness buzz.

"I get that but I think you're wrong like how cool is a bank that is so fucking confident that it allows an artwork about—like we would have a giant inflatable Dillinger—"

"Please speak in a more measured—anyway no—"

"You could kill it! Shoot it with a cannon! You have just seen off a robbery it is like the gossip of the whole town—"

". . . What gossip?"

"I am Banjo Telemark Herr Eiger I am connected up the wazoo I know you just shot some motherfucker with a cannon from your battlements and that is exactly what I am talking about—"

"No Herr Telemark—"

"No?"

"No absolutely not where would you hear such a—"

"I hear all things Herr Eiger I am special that way—"

"That is slanderous in the extreme you would do well not to repeat it to a third party it is a disgrace actually—"

"But it would not be un-Swiss sir not at all—"

"To discharge a firearm in a public place—"

"Completely safely you are a crack shot—"

"Against an unsuspecting adversary—"

"A wanted murderer—"

"You sound quite enthusiastic Herr Telemark perhaps you should do this—"

"O do you think so they do say art is violence and mine possesses a unique—"

Something is bugging me and I cannot think what it is like a familiar something like a flavor in the air like a coffee I have drunk like perfume and I am almost there I almost get it before the thing happens but I don't and—

And that is when a voice says:

"JACK?!"

Hans Eiger's face goes cold and flat as his mountain.

Back in the day when all I wanted was to put my foot on the face of the whole wide world of coffee—before I was called the Cardinal but after I cut tight around the Sandberg Benin Cartel and dry-gulched those fuckers so that we got rich and they got the other thing and people were starting to pay attention—back then, I was stabled with a guy called Ronald Platt because every straight razor needs a strop.

There is a whole subclass of execs in the world who are there so that they can get fucked when the house burns down and you know what they say: if you do not know who that person is in your company then that person is you. But I never had time to fuck Ronnie up for my transgressions because of the Hamburg Flamingo Incident.

There was this bar like a rooftop bar in Hamburg. This was in the '90s so no one thought it was weird that it was themed tastefully on *The Perfumed Garden,* which is a fifteenth-century book on fucking written by a guy named Muhammad ibn Muhammad al-Nafzawi. These days it is tolerably unlikely that a bar in a European nation would theme itself on an Arabic sex manual because you know there's just a whiff of something a little culturally insensitive there plus also the world's relationship with the, you know, Mysteries of Exotic Islam have shifted since Mike and the Mechanics had a hit with "Seeing Is Believing." But back then even a decade later it was absolutely supercool to have German university students dressed as genies and houris and cheeky mujahideen and what all the fuck else prancing around bringing hookah pipes and affogato to the finance community. Do not ask me how the fuck that was okay I am not a hospitality person I do not even like people.

It being Hamburg there had to be a twist and the twist was that there were flamingos wandering around and if a flamingo stood on your table the house bought you champagne and the houris made a huge fuss about the whole thing.

Well enough but your flamingos for some reason don't like to stand on tables especially they do not stand on tables covered in ashtrays and bottles of Cristal. It turns out that flamingos despite being associated with excess because they are pink they are real homebody types they do not appreciate bad smells or strong liquor and in fact these flamingos were depressed. They were becoming agitated and I think we can safely say even if Ronnie Platt hadn't've come along they'd still have shut the place pretty soon. There is nothing sadder than drinking champagne with four dozen silent flamingos standing around in the grip of an existential crisis.

But Ronnie man Ronnie. Ronnie was a generous asshole and he could feel the sorrow and he figured to fix it. Ronnie figured that the flamingos were sad because they were captive and the night after I told the head of Lindo-Michaelsen to kiss my ring if he thought I was buying his crappy fauxlombian—I could smell the deceit on the fucking paperwork and I left him holding that warehouse full of shit and Jeni Sutton called me the Cardinal—the night after we were in the Garden. Ronnie was not real rational on account of having actually washed himself in vodka on the advice of some Swedish naturopath. He looked at one particular flamingo and it looked at him and some kind of thing passed between them like brotherhood and Ronnie shouted:

"FREEDOM!"

And he picked it up and he ran.

Ran like the wind.

To the edge of the building and launched this flamingo into the air so it would you know like have an advantage. The whole thing was just beautiful and there was actual background music which was a Pashtun cover of "Take My Breath Away."

But of course it was all not great because the flamingos were clipped to keep them on the roof. Ronnie stood there with this deep connection burning in his face and he and the bird made eye contact and there was certainty and complicity between them and the bird spread its wings and Ronnie shouted FREE-DOM! again.

And the bird fell seventeen floors and landed on a school bus.

No one died but you know the whole thing was not popular in general.

And obviously when I say no one I do not include the flamingo, which definitely for real died, along with Ronnie's career.

So this is the face on the kindhearted total lack of intellect who grabs me in a hug and shouts my name right there at the top of his voice and of course he does not say Banjo.

He says Jack.

Eiger is listening now.

"HI JACK OMIGOD JACK PRICE? MAN IT'S MEEEE RONNIE FLAMINGO MAN HOW AREEEE YOUUUU?"

When Ronnie talks is the moment when everyone else pauses for breath so his whole thing his whole too-loud thing goes out like an air-raid warning? Nope. Because that is how it is when your world turns to one hundred percent asshole and you have stood there too.

Now you can see in my face I want to kill him. That is actually the danger with being a Demon is that every problem starts to look like the kind of problem where that is the best answer. Leaking faucet? Kill the plumber. Traffic on I-9? Kill the other drivers. Like that guy's car? Easy he won't need it. Network cancels your favorite show? Well sure how many of them gotta go before the rest get the fucking message that the world needs more Dichen Lachman not less?

Quite a few actually, as it happens, which surprised me, but never mind that right now.

"OMIGOD JACK SOO COOOOOLLLLL WOW MAN NICE THREADS HEY IT'S ME FLAMINGO RIGHT RONNIE FLAMINGO JAAAAACK EHEY RIGHT HAMBURG AM I RIGHT?"

Kill this asshole it would be

oh

so

easy.

But probably not ludic.

I am Banjo Telemark. Banjo Telemark the artist who lives for confusion and bewilderment and this right here is found fucking art it is Banjo gold disc. It is immortality.

I say:

"OOOOOOMIGOD FRIDA KAHLO I AM YOUR BIGGEST FAN!"

And I kiss Ronnie Flamingo on the mouth.

With tongues because hell it's Frida fucking Kahlo.

The staff at the Hirschen are totally relaxed about sexual orientation but they do not like shouting or artists or public tongues that is not their jam.

They sit me down and they kind of hoosh Ronnie away like hoosh hoosh back to his own table.

Eiger says: "Jack?"

I say: "Man I have no idea what that was about. That guy thinks he knows me."

Eiger says: "And he is wrong."

"Of course he is."

"I think it would be best if you left now Herr Price."

"Price, what Price? I am Telemark. Man I have just no idea who this Price guy—wait is that the guy you totally shot in the face?"

"Your speculations are unwelcome Mr.—"

"Banjo—"

"As you say."

I say: "So man I feel like I have upset your equilibrium man but Hans—baby—I really want to rob your bank call me it will be great."

And I go back and I eat my lunch and then I pay and I leave.

I pay for Hans Eiger's lunch too which is a nice gesture and also too it means he won't find out for another few hours that someone has broken into his day-to-day bank account and stolen thirty-one thousand francs and his bank are saying it is all his fault for setting his password to P4SSW0Rd.

If that was actually his password that would entirely be his fault that is a shitty password.

His password was some crawling alphanumeric horror no sane human being could remember but once Charlie has your bank's dongle and an idea how the whole thing works that is not really much help.

Hans Eiger will check out Ronnie Flamingo and he will find out that there really was such a guy and that he knew Jack Price. But then he will also find out that Jack Price was not then known as Jack Price and then he will find out that Ronnie Flamingo died in Gozo in '06 before Jack ever went by Jack.

I do not know what the fuck a dazzling urbanite like Ronnie Flamingo was doing in Gozo I am guessing it is not a good story.

Gozo is the island next door to Malta which is where Banjo Telemark is from.

The guy who just got Frida Kahlo'd is an actor I flew in who now includes on his résumé the information that he worked four years ago on a live project by the famous Ambiguitionist artist Banjo Govinder Telemark.

Eiger will find all of this out.

And it will drive him batshit.

It is totally ambiguous. Banjo Telemark is an actual prankster. A known international bullshit merchant who specializes in fucking with you in the name of art and that is precisely the kind of art Hans Eiger particularly hates. Art should be painted on canvas and have ballet dancers or squares of red and yellow and blue that is just what is right.

All this means I am obviously not Jack Price even if Hans Eiger and Evil Hansel did not kill Jack Price last week, which demonstrably they did. I am some hairy asshole bullshitting my way into the art scene to make money and get laid and right now I am bullshitting Hans Eiger because he hosts the festival. It is obvious.

And yet he knows in his bones he knows it in every fucking crag of his craggy fucking mountain face that I am Jack Price and now he has to kill me again. He just knows it because of course he does he's not a fucking idiot.

Now that he has thought it he cannot ignore it and at the same time he knows he fucking knows that my whole jam the whole entire thing that Banjo Telemark does—Banjo's entire bullshit—is the creation of ambiguity and if there is one thing Hans Eiger fucking hates it is ambiguity and now Mr. The Art Of Ambiguous is fucking with him and he cannot he absolutely cannot fucking overreact right now because if—oh God if—if this is a demented fucking art-house prank and he goes for it and he somehow gets Candid Camera'd firing a long gun at a chortling anarchist reject with gold teeth—then o God—o God all that reputational zing and boom he has just murdered his way to will burn up like mist on a summer day and—and—and—

Soon he will also find out that all around the world men and women called Jack Price are committing crimes because there is money to be made in doing so and he will know that this is something the Demons have done because Jack Price is dead and they want to hide that fact.

Or I did it to make him think that.

Does that mean Banjo IS Jack Price or that Banjo is part of some conspiracy BY Jack Price or that Banjo has tapped into the Pricegeist or or or—

But the thing about Banjo is Banjo is this obvious tremendous try-hard asshole. Banjo is in Hans Eiger's face. In the macro Hans Eiger needs to be strategic and wise and he can do that but in the micro—

In the micro he has to beat Banjo Telemark.

He has to beat Banjo so that the river of the world can resume its course.

And the only way he can possibly do that is by playing Banjo back at his own game. Roll with the joke. Be funny. Funny is not his natural home but he can be funny of course he can be funny fucking otters do it on the Internet all the time. Cats climb on Roombas how fucking hard can it be for a man like him?

He can roll with the joke.

This will make perfect sense to him it will seem like a message from God. Because right now the whole world is fucking with Hans Eiger and there is nothing he wants to do more than fuck it right back. It is like a dare. It is everything he is.

Security. Strength. Certainty.

He is going to make two mistakes right now. The first one is actually not a mistake it is a sensible thing to do but this is my oeuvre. He is going to phone a friend.

That is fine and dandy. It will hurt him in the end because I am a fucking artiste but that is not his fault that is me. But the second . . . oh Mr. Eiger oh in his soul he knows it is wrong and yet he cannot but do it anyway.

He is going to let me put bulldozers on his mountain.

Not today.

Probably not tomorrow.

But soon and for the rest of his life.

EIGHT

THIS IS THE CALM BEFORE THE YOU KNOW WHAT. We are waiting for Mr. Friday to come through. While we do this we are in a resting state of readiness. I am the stillness I am the lake water the river the sea I am—

I am very bored.

In fact although I fucking hate this part I approve of it enormously because robbing a bank is what? It is PROCESS Uncle Jack yes that is right. It is not fucking black suits and guns and spooky masks it is process and it is HOMER and process and that is how we do not die. Doc is arranging aerosol-dispersal anesthetic for elephant conservation in India, which coincidentally is also useful for wide-area pacification of security forces on mountains. Doc wants to narrow the focus of delivery and I say JUST ELEPHANT TRANQ THE WHOLE FUCKING CANTON—

But Doc says she has it so she has it. She does. I trust her. I tell her so.

She has already solved the issue of how to get loot off the mountain at the end of the job she is going to have me distract everyone with exciting drones which of course Banjo Telemark will have as part of his ART and which everyone of a law enforcement persuasion will assume have been hijacked or co-opted for this purpose, while in fact the real work will be done using the cable car. Then we will just load the loot into a big container truck marked as roofing supplies and drive it away.

I say the cable car is a boring way to leave a fortress you can only get to by cable car and Doc says yes, it is, that is the point.

I leave Doc to be very grown-up and I feed her pigs and do not let the doors kill any of them and I go to buy junk for my special fucking-with-Eiger-horrible-revenge show.

"Hi my name is Banjo Telemark I wish to buy your junk."

"No we are—we recycle we do not—this is where junk comes to—"

"Madame I wish to buy many tons of junk I will pay enough to recycle many more things it is for art. When the art has been viewed I will return the junk to you as junk if no one buys it you will get free junk plus money. This is a good thing."

"Yaaaawuh and what do you get?"

"I get art madame I do not need money. Rich people are forever giving me money for art but part of that process is scarcity. This art can be ephemeral so that my other art is expensive."

"That is good business."

"I am an artist that does not mean I must be an innocent adrift in the world madame."

". . . What junk do you need?"

"Auto parts and airplane panels also any ethnic Swiss schlock you may have."

"Ethnic—"

"Many of your fine hotels and eating establishments and so on here feature cowbells and such also many cows but I am assuming there is ultimately wastage and recycling of same."

"Yes that is true."

"I wish to buy cowbells and aluminum car parts for use as art. Ideally in this quantity which I have written on this paper."

"This is a large quantity but . . . yes I suppose it is possible."

"Excellent here is money. Please deliver half of it to this address here and half to the Kircheisen Festung for the art fair marked to my attention."

"O you are with Herr Eiger?"

"He will be thrilled I promise you."

He will not but sometimes art is really just for the artist I guess.

Charlie is not bored Charlie is fine. While I was in Iceland Charlie went to see Bruno and she is very excited about eco-terrorism and she would like that we take a few weeks after this job to do some pro bono environmental work. Bruno evidently understands Charlie very well because he took her on a job under the water and they plugged Z-Vat in an illegal outflow together and had sex in the water—not the outflow water some clean clear water upstream—and then had sex on a barge in front of some sort of boat-safe smokeless stove. I do not entirely get how you have sex in a dry suit but if anyone can do it that person is Charlie. Charlie figures we could kill the Japanese whaling industry in a month and move on to illegal logging in the Amazon next year and in this she has Doc's cautious agreement because it is undeniable that if the earth catches fire and falls over then being rich will be considerably less fun than it is now and Doc feels this is a very real scientific possibility owing to feedback and shit that I do not understand but I trust Doc. If Doc says this is bad it is bad and Doc does so that is fine.

All the same it is not good for Charlie to get too euphoric so I make her come with me to rent bulldozers.

"Hello I wish to rent bulldozers. Also other heavy plant. Have you anything in purple I do not like the yellow."

"We have a very little red and some green that is all."

"If I was to arrange payment would you permit me to respray? I would of course reverse the process after my show—"

"Show?"

"Ah yes I am an artist—I work at scale which is why—"

"Oh, you are that Banjo Telemark yes of course how FABulous and what are you making—"

"Art of course ahahaha you see—"

Charlie hangs out with Frau Anton to discuss bulldozer regulatory blah blah blah and I am at a loose end so I go back to Eiger's cigar shop and I buy another cigar. The little guy asks if I liked the first cigar and I tell him I haven't smoked it yet. He asks me why I want another one and I say that I like the process of coming in here and buying cigars I don't really like to smoke. But the smell of the place and the vibe and so on that just makes me feel comfortable and happy like there's a good world somewhere under this one that I can find if I stand still.

Which is actually sort of true but I don't know that when I start saying it only when I finish and then I am embarrassed and I still don't know why Eiger comes in here because he also does not buy any cigars.

Maybe he also just likes to come in here and be with the little guy.

Maybe we have that much in common.

I do not ask the little guy about Eiger and we don't talk about coffee this time we just—

We don't talk about anything at all for an hour. We just stand there and do things in the quiet of the shop.

And then I leave and he does not say goodbye.

I see Volodya across the street just going into a shop. It is a hat shop. I run across the road and nearly get hit by a car. There is a lot of honking and shouting in Swiss. Swiss is a great language to be pissed off in.

I get to the hat shop and go inside but of course it is not Volodya it is a fat man from Sion.

I nearly kill him for having the nerve to be a fat man from Sion and not my friend.

I cry a bit instead. I sit down to cry on a bench and I see something so I duck my head. There's a noise like ZVOVVvv above my head and something lodges halfway through a metal sign pointing the way to the Bärengraben: a metal marble the size of a human eye.

I look across the road and I see Evil Hansel with a heavyweight fisherman's catapult. With the right projectile these things are lethal up to forty feet but they look sort of scampish. Scampish such that a small boy might carry one without getting arrested and such.

Evil Hansel looks at me and shrugs. He doesn't even reload. His face barely registers anything at all.

We stand there and look at one another across the road for a while. Then a bus comes and he's gone.

I slightly like this kid.

I mean he stabbed me while his grandfather shot my friend. It's not like we could ever be friends.

But Volodya was right man this country has interesting people in it. People and stuff I guess.

I go back to the pig farm and I wait for Doc to notice I am there. Rex has disarmed the door and now it looks kinda sad. It is a murder door with no murder left in it.

"Hi door."

LOOM

"Hi door my name is Jack how are you today?"

LOOM

"I hear you man but there has to be something that you want like something that you can't get just with the opening and the closing."

LOOM

LOOM

LOOM

"Yep I guess in the end that is really just your whole thing isn't it?"

LOOM

"That and the killing—"

"So if I just—"

"If you were activated and I reached out and—"

ZzzzzZZZ-CLICK

"Wow. Yep."

CLICKACLICKACLICK

"I feel ya big guy."

LOOM CLICKACLICKCLICK

"Yeah let it all out that's right—"

"Price?"

"Hi Doc."

"Price are you talking to the door?"

"No?"

"Mr. Friday called it's time to go."

"Go where?"

"A place called FischFisch."

FischFisch is hard to find because if it was easy to find there would be a risk of un-Swissness. Once you know there is a place like FischFisch you almost have to have an opinion about it and having an opinion on something that is not your business is not Swiss. The avoidance of that situation by obfuscation and deliberate blindness is absolutely a form of high polite Swissness all by itself.

"Hi I am Banjo Telemark and this is totally my jam."

"I am sorry sir you cannot come in it is a private club."

"Big guy I can totally come in I am a renowned artist."

"You cannot come in."

(Guy has a neck like a structural steel and giant ridiculous arms. He is just so obviously a tough guy and now I have déjà vu.)

"This is weirdly familiar you have a really huge neck is it possible that you are a fan of French film noir and a student lawyer?"

"No."

"No?"

"No."

"Well that is the thing about déjà vu I guess it is not a reliable guide to tangible reality."

"Reality cannot be said to be tangible sir the truth of the universe is not observable and in any case takes place at a level below the Newtonian human understanding and in many ways also above it our scale is habitable but not relevant to

the extrinsic cosmos. Even if it could the tactile is mediated by
fallible sensory apparatus."

"... In like ten seconds I am going to walk up your face like
a cat on a curtain and bite off one of your ears."

"That is quite unnecessary Herr Telemark I am yoshing you
the management is delighted you have come."

"What is it with the yoshing in this country wait Doc did
you—"

"Get in the club Banjo."

So here under the Hotel Kieselstrand's original art nouveau
ballroom there is a modern-built art deco bar called the Jahrhundert and it is only when you go through Jahrhundert to
the private dining area and down in the executive lift that you
come to FischFisch, and FischFisch has a heavy velvet door
and when you get beyond that door and take a seat it becomes
rapidly apparent that FischFisch is a sushi bar wherein you can
throw sushi to attractive somewhat naked people somewhat
dressed as seals or indeed dress yourself in a manner of wet
foot-binding plastic flipperslipper and bark for your futomaki
from the preternaturally attractive hospitality team who are
themselves wearing a cutaway interpretation of Yupik hunt-
ing gear that has as much to do with the original activity as
the chaps of a woman riding an electric bronco at Joe Lariat's
Rodeo Grill in Miami, Florida, where I have not been and nor
should you the pie is awful.

FischFisch offers numerous other sushi-based activities that
have names in Swiss German I thankfully do not understand,
because this is the most bespoke and salubrious fetish establishment on the planet. There is literally not one surface here
from which you could not eat your dinner, and indeed people

mostly are although technically I am not sure a person can be a surface.

All of which is very educational and Rex in particular appears to be learning a great deal and much of it stuff he would acquire in no other way. I do not know if this place is culturally appropriative or just so fucking weird as to belong to some other category of shit for which previously I had no name.

We are here because Elena Riccardi comes here with her husband twice every month and she is coming tonight and aside from being a really good amateur golfer and obviously some sort of fish fetishist she is also according to Mr. Friday the true and only software designer for Die Festung at Kircheisen.

Doc says:

"Charlie you have experience in this culture—"

"I what now?"

"You are polyamorous Charlie you put it on the website—"

"Boss lady! That is not this! This is like a whole scene. It has scene-y-ness and rules and stuff that I cannot possibly know. Sure I mean sure I advocate and accept the boning and adoration of more than one person within a consensual and acknowledged frame of emotional and sexual rules toward a fulfilled but unbounded sense of self but this is just WEIRD—"

"In fact this is only unusual you do not know weird until you have had sex with Price—"

"Doc this is not something we need to—"

"Really boss lady what—"

"Well for example he recently asked me to give him a sub-dermal tracheal stent—"

"DOC THAT WAS PROFESSIONAL yes I asked about it in bed but that is not—"

"It was undeniably weird though and I was postcoitally nude at the time—"

"Van der Graaf lady calls my conversation weird—"

"Hush you will arouse me—"

"Van der Graaf van der Graaf van der—"

"ENOUGH Price enough be professional Charlie—"

"Yes quite right Doc. Charlie be professional we are on a clock here the lady in the fish suit is waiting—"

"What I'M the one wasting—no never mind—FISH SUIT BOSS Jesus how can I put this in Jacktalk let me see yeah okay yeah I am an expert in coffee right and these people they are buying and selling pork belly and I do not know one fucking thing about what turns on their pork belly horn okay? What the fuck ever is going on over there with that sashimi—this is not my universe okay?"

"Fine we'll just busk it how hard can it be?"

Doc does not even bother to reply.

"ROCKS AND WAVES AND DISHY FISHY—"

Walk across the floor. Smile. Swerve and turn. We are moving through the crowd we are browsing taking it in we are—

"I do not want to know what is happening with that mackerel sir—"

"COLD SALT WATER HOT SEA LIONS—RAAAWR! O BABY RAWWWR—"

I do not know this band they are kinda Elle and the Pocket Belles but dirtier and more oceanographic I will guess they are bespoke.

"RAWRRR PENGUIN PENGUIN PLEASE BE GENTLE—"

"Hi— O I'm sorry I did not meant to intrude—"

"WHEN YOU'RE REALLY FISHY SPENT YOU'LL—"

"That is fine just fine don't worry about it—"

"May I say that you look lovely in that fish suit—"

"Thank you this is my husband Oscar—"

"MIGHTY HUNTER SALT SPLASH SPLISHY—"

"So enchanting well I shall be on my way o wait look here is my friend Rita Langstrumpf she is as you see quite elegant—"

"Banjo I will fuck you up. Hello I did not catch your name madame I am—"

"Ow gosh you have sharp nails Madame Langstrumpf—"

"QUITE SOME LOVELY FISHING TALE—"

"I am so sorry they are part of my jouissance I did not mean to scratch—"

"O MY! BABY WHAT A WHALE—"

"Yes I quite see o goodness it is hot in here I feel quite—"

"Darling are you quite all right you look faint—"

SLOOSHTHUD

"We will need medical attention I must call the manager—"

"BABY BABY FISHY DISHY—"

"That will not be necessary Herr Oscar here you sit Madame Langstrumpf is indeed a doctor in her working day please be discreet on that score obviously FischFisch is not entirely reputable in the wider community—"

"O of course o o in fact I also feel a little . . ."

THONK

"Charlie you could not catch his head?"

"I thought there was a pillow this divan has one of those stupid boards—"

FISHERMAN SO STRONG AND BOLD—

"Is he alive?"

"Of course it's a board not a spike he's not even gonna have a bruise—"

"Very well then let us help Elena out of here."

We are helpful. We are solicitous.

We are good citizens. That is a very Swiss thing to do. And that is how you do a kidnapping in a fish fucker club.

WANT YOU IN MY CARGO HOLD—

Which is fine.

Until we are leaving and we are away from the music—at last AT LAST my God one more line and I was going to—and someone squashes into my arm with what feels like the upper surface of a mostly naked breast and says all breathy:

"O Mr. Telemark I am so glad to meet you your art—it moves me—it touches me deeply Mr. Telemark truly it does—"

"O well thank you so much madame I do—"

I am paying attention to the breast area and I do not notice the hands and TINK the cuff closes tight like tight. I look round and—

Agent Hannah is wearing a clever disguise something in a Nunatsiavut fall style cut real short like to the—you know groinal region—so that you can tell those are not regular cop undies they are something impractically tiny and appropriate to the venue but I am not looking because VERY professional. She's grinning her sexy Aryan dolphin grin. Agent Hannah is totally the winner in this moment but at the same time she is not thinking properly because she's smug about this and because she is used to working in a pantsuit, which is where things get—

—a little weird—

—because as she closes the cuff on my other hand behind my back, she leans into me and lifts with her core, and my hands—my fingers—are pressed or—or driven really let's

say driven—against the bare skin of her thighs and her—
somewhat minimal and as it transpires incrementally mobile
undies—and—um—how to say this without saying pussy—
her personal intimate undercarriage—which is receptive to this
situation in a way which I think comes as a surprise to both
of us.

Which means that as she cuffs me there is a definite I guess
you would say nontrivial interpersonal connection of the sex
kind—

There is no getting away from this Agent Hannah touches
me inappropriately with her clitoris.

I do not move so much as an eighth of an inch.

And then I fucking swear to you I feel her weight drop—
her body drop—and lock rigid, and for one second her mouth
opens and she exhales in an O and she shakes in place like if
I'd wired her up to the alternating current.

I don't know where she is right now but I'm definitely having a harpoon issue.

Doc looks back over her shoulder what's the delay Jack let's
go there is kidnapping to do here—

And she—

Sees—

Everything—

Everything at all.

Her eyes are terrible dark and deep and I have promises to
keep and deaths to die before I sleep.

Doc smiles so wide I think she will swallow the world and
she looks at Agent Hannah and I see murder happening right
there in a thousand different ways inside her head and Agent
Hannah sees it too and then Doc swirls away out of the door
leaving me handcuffed and holding the arresting officer by the
soft parts of her highly trained federal investigating cligeva

and Agent Hannah does not remotely try to change that as she leans in against me and says right into my ear so that I can feel the traces of her teeth on my skin:

"Do you know what you got wrong, Jack Price?"

I do know and she isn't really asking. She says it differently this time because pronouns:

"You forgot to kill the taxi driver. But Jack? He didn't forget you."

Oh fuck it I completely—fuck. She's good. She's really really good.

Serious harpoon issue.

Agent Hannah steps back and my fingers are removed from their little Aryan dolphin Valhalla and they are behind my back so thank God I cannot put them in my mouth that would be totally inappropriate.

I tell myself Agent Hannah is having some similar dialogue with herself vis-à-vis her own thighs and now that is in my head and—but she is all business now she slips into a pair of gray sweatpants and a blue cop jacket as we get in the car and I am hooked to the chassis in the back. Half-inch steel hoop like for military-grade croquet.

I am so totally going to Swiss jail.

I actually to be honest I do not think that will be all bad.

I mean it is Swiss jail I am sure there is great dental and all kinds of due process and Doc will get me out in two shakes of seal's—

We do not talk about that now.

Swiss jail will almost certainly feature minimalist neutral design palettes and basic comforts and hygiene I figure also acceptably nutritious food and punctilious attention to prisoner well-being and reform. Because this is not fucking Louisiana this is the canton of Bern.

I'm guessing maybe a selection of educational and morally improving TV channels like maybe I can find out that whole deal with the ducal hat.

And you got to remember I am Banjo Telemark quite demonstrably and Jack Price is dead and the money dear LORD the money and the lawyers which will fall in a great appalling crash upon this situation . . . I got maybe three or four hours of this shit to deal with.

So I stare out of the window at the river and the mountains and I close my eyes and think about swimming in the cloudy blue-green water in the moonlight and how cold and sharp that would be and saunas with burning yellow lights and cutting a hole in the snow and Doc rising up naked out of the river as Agent Hannah passes by on her way in—wait not passes by, passes through as if they are both made of molasses—they ripple through one another and stop and then—

Then I open my eyes and see the truck.

I said that Eiger would phone a friend and he has. Of course he has. And who has he called? He has called François Leclerc of course that was always the plan. He has said—brash and loud to the bad people we do not like and in their language because he needs them to believe he is their man here their guy on the ground their absolute solid rock in the Canton of Bern—he has said: I have a hippie infestation boys there is a long-hair jerking my chain will you come deal with it for me?

And they will that is totally their jam. If there is a hippie problem they are just all over that. They love a hippie problem. Beating up on hippies is like a fucking traditional activity although in certain parts of the world you have to be real fucking careful about it because there are hippies and hippies and some hippies turn out to be log-cabin motherfuckers after all and—but an art hippie is just a hippie and they love that sweet bloodhoney.

So they are here to help man just to help out a buddy. You can tell it is them because they are so very fucking precisely ethnic. If any one of them had so much as a midbrown hair he has dyed it that straw-piss color you see in colorized photos from the '30s. These guys are nostalgia walking and they are here to do me wrong.

Well okay not walking per se that is not what they are doing. I sort of reckoned they would come in their black suits with their perky flower badges or in that paramilitary crap they wear to make themselves feel like real soldiers and not basically drug remoras. I figured they would in the first instance try to scare the shit out of Banjo Telemark or at least send the screwheads in first with bats to beat him down because as we have mentioned Hans Eiger does not want to accidentally-on-purpose murder an artist howevermuch of a dick that artist might be. Because advertising. But of course that constraint now that I think about it does not entirely apply to his deniable friends here and these guys are not walking and they do not have bats that I can see.

They are riding.

In a big fucking terrifying truck of death.

Which I admit I did not absolutely plan for.

This is not Humvee country they do not have those here. Humvees are all about an American kind of war porn that is sort of WWE and militia cool and rap and rock music all in one place at one time. Like there was an American commander in Afghanistan who famously wore a sheriff's badge and a ten-gallon hat and that is exactly the sort of behavior that makes Europeans think Americans have something wrong in the head parts I do not know what the Afghans thought about it but I am assuming it started with whatever is the word for fuck in Pashtun. A hat like that has swinging big dick energy and why would you ever show a bunch of snipers your dick energy that is just putting a target on your energetic dick.

But that is not to say there is no swinging dick energy in Europe there is so much dick here sometimes you would actually think there was no room for more dick but newsflash: there is always room for more dick and on that basis there is the Mercedes G-Wagen Service Edition. The original '70s model was a street-legal German military truck and the Service Edition is the modern cartel-grade road tank executive upgrade and this one has been additionally pimped with big lights on top like you would use to shoot squid from a boat if that was a thing anyone did. It is less a vehicle than an enormity with wheels and I see it before Agent Hannah or the driver because I happen to be looking out the right window. It is going to T-bone us like a bear taking a buffalo calf like that.

Huge.

Fucking.

Truck.

Do you know the Greek royal family have these, they bought like a baker's dozen in anthracite matte apparently so all the kids could have one.

Wow that is so big and I start to say LOOK OUT but I say: LO—

I am thinking: huge big thing big coming so fast I swear every fucker in this conversation has meaner tools than I have I am woefully under-tooled—

No not like—no I mean—
WHAM.

There is clarity in flight.

I do not mean in flying but in being in flight because the whole world stops and you see everything in the future and the past and you see it perfectly because you have stopped too. You don't have time for extraneous thoughts you just have one endlessly extended instant of frozen white light and knowing and I know:

We are upside down in midair.

Agent Hannah has her hands braced against the ceiling and her head is half turned to me to tell me something probably that I am an asshole. She probably thinks this is my team but I already know it's not because if it was my team they would have used Saul and Saul would have used a spike strip.

Out of the front window I can see the sky like an endless nighttime blanket over the mountains and the world.

And under me I can see—

I can see the road but not just the road I can see—

Metal—

And—

What the shit is that is that—

Like seething velvet: moonlit and cloudy and blue.

When we hit the water I bang my head so I do not get to feel the cold. At least I do not feel it as it happens. But my bones remember it and I think they always will.

The water comes into the car and I am upside down so first it is great I am hooked to the ceiling and FUCK MY FUCKING FEET ARE ON FIRE no that is water O SHIT COLD COLD and it is rising and the agents in the car are not looking so good and the car is fucking SINKING are you KIDDING ME—

Right now I would give anything to have Lucille's appalling sweet potato ballsack. I think my balls are not so much blue and frozen as retracted into my body as if I was a baby again and I think probably they will never come out again and I do not honestly blame them if I could go somewhere warm and hide I would also do that.

The water is rising up my chest up my back the car is O SHIT the car is TURNING OVER and so I will go down into the—

—ICE WATER—

Ice water white and blue and green and chalky and thick and I cannot tell you how cold how cold. Cold like another life like being hit like being—

At least—it's odd—at least in this cold I don't really feel the need to breathe. Or move.

In the water, I wonder if I should just die. After all that time I was scared of heights and burning and ash here I am cold and clean under a Swiss river with my hands hooked to the floor of an upside-down cop car and not—

My face breaks the water and we're like sideways so only half my face is drowning and I can breathe water if I just stay in this damned uncomfortable position forever and the car does not sink. Agent Hannah's cop friends are yelling but not screaming because they have serious intestinal fortitude I got to give them that they have integrity they have Swissness.

Heh. I'm pretty sure your boss hateboinked my fingers while she was arresting me and that let me tell you boys even I know that is motherfucking un-Swiss. But I love your integrity I do. And I love hers too because Agent Hannah is alive and awake and she looks at me and I see her see me seeing her and

I know what she's thinking because in the end we're not that different. She's a dedicated cop and I'm a professional criminal and there's all that but in the end—we're both people who do, and then there are people who don't, and that is all. And she is thinking that she cannot let me get offed here.

Someone gets shot in the face. It isn't me so I don't care.

Hannah lunges like a fucking eel from the front seat down into the back in her soaking sweatpants. Down between my knees and into the water and her fingers must be numb there's no way she can use a key there in the cold water and then the car is rolling again and she's standing on the roof and I am hanging by the cuffs and then real big I see the jawless man's residual head come toward me like a morning star from that awful TV show and I think there's some fucking karmic shit happening here and then WHUD.

Night night.

All the world is a gun and it is firing over and over and over and over and—

Ratatataata—yeah yeah that's just a waste of perfectly good projectiles none of you is—

Wait I'm alive that's good—

Fuck I'm cold FUCK—

Cold cold cold O JESUS so cold. Lying in the water faceup cold and all around this huge noise ratatatata. ZOING ZOING that's in the water that's not good that's where I am someone do something I pay taxes do I not? Under several names and in several countries actually so I ought to get at least some kind of fucking police presence for that.

Agent Hannah rattatatas and Agent Hannah's flunkies ratatatatatatat and then up on the bridge more people ratatatatata down at us and this is very fucking un-Swiss and it should not be allowed.

Things whizz by that are sharp and hard. Shrapnel and bullets and I fucking hate guns and how come everyone has one except me.

Ratatata.

Too cold to move like all my zing is gone into the—

I am Jack Price.

I am Banjo fucking Telemark.

There is not enough cold in the whole world to take my zing.

"In that case Jack is necessary you move fat bourgeois ass and not die am I right?"

"Yeah big guy I hear ya it's just cozy here."

"Yeah was cozy also in the snow machine where I threw myself to give you a chance so—"

"Fuck don't guilt me I hate that—"

"Yeah also as it happens I fell in by accident I actually was hijacking but did not go well. Now move Jack. Is bad manners to die with my red corpsicles still in your blood."

"I think that would be corpuscles—"

"Sure splain to the dead guy why not you got time—OH WAIT NO YOU DIE HERE UNLESS YOU MOVE ASS—"

"Shit all right all right—"

I drag myself up out of the water my hands are just white clubs on the end of my arms my feet are clumsy but I move until I am behind a little low wall on the waterside with the cops. Agent Hannah has found a crappy little boulder to hide behind all Butch and Sundance and we all know THAT turned out well.

Hannah says something and one of the guys ONLY TWO GUYS says something back: Chäschuechli Chäschuechli.

That is the Swiss word for cheesecake and they are not saying
cheesecake but if you are not Swiss and you are listening to
deep Swiss gunfight crisis lingo it really does not matter how
good your language skills may be some variation of that is
what you are hearing.

There are seven men from the G-Wagen up on the bridge
and they have some serious weapons and they are—

Ratatataat—RATATATAT—

And we are pinned down and I'm amazed I am even alive
because there is our car sinking in the Aare and Hannah must
have actually fucking unlocked me under the fucking water
and dragged me here that is super-duper responsible and law
enforcey and Swiss but she is not fucking Wonder Woman so
she cannot—

RATATATATA—

RATATATATAAATATATTTAA—

Ratatata SPLINCH.

That is Hannah's left-hand guy leaving his thinkparts on the
white stones by the side of the river and leaking into the cloudy
blue water.

White lights shining down on us like an eye. G-Wagen.

What the fuck is the response time here it cannot be anything
this is the fucking federal capital is everyone a-fucking-sleep?

There's Hannah now by herself and she's too exposed over
there she needs to be over here but she cannot get from there
to here and they will kill her and then they will come down
here and kill me.

Agent Hannah's right-hand guy says this and she says something and he says no and she says no and he pops up and gives
her covering fire and Agent Hannah says NEEEIIIII—

And that turns out to be a bad decision for him and so she
is alone and so am I. Which means— O for fuck's sake really

we're doing this? What the actual fuck Doc will—well she will not be happy whatever happens here.

I get my feet under me.

Ratatatatatata! Stay where you fucking are Jack Price or I shoot you myself—

I don't run toward her directly so I do not get shot at right off. I run the other way to the dead left-hand guy. By the time the G-Wagen guys wake to what's happening I get him on my back in his bullet vest and I run back to Hannah with him pushed up onto my head like a stupid hat and that is how I get to her alive. It feels as if dead man and I are together holding up an elephant because all the bullets in the world are hitting him FLOB FLOB PIZZIAAAOW ZIAAAOW ZNOING FLOB FLOBBBABLOB. Hannah looks at me like this is the worst thing that has ever happened in the world (FLOB FLOB) I grab her and drag her back and back to the little wall. It is like running with an umbrella under a meat shower. Then we get down behind the wall and the rain stops and she stares at me. She has some of her friend in her hair.

"What the fuck is WRONG with you?"

"Lady you are looking in fact for the words Danke schön or THANK YOU would also be fine—"

"LOOK WHAT YOU HAVE DONE—"

"What you think he still gave a shit his face is over there by the water—"

(Ratatatatatatata but whole meters away this time so I hardly notice.)

"You are a monster."

"I am not—"

"Get your damn head down criminal—"

"Much as I would love that now is hardly the time—"

She stares at me: "You would make that joke here and now?"

"Lady you inappropriately lovebuttoned my innocent finger and I am going to sue the fuck out of that later and I realize you do not believe this but my name is BANJO TELEMARK I am an ARTIST not a fucking—"

"O sure—"

Ratatatatata SPLUDDER.

And that is another man down and that is it. Now it's just us versus them and Agent Hannah's big gun is empty and she has a backup and—

I don't know where the fuck would I find out about little European popgun thingies but it is the first gun I have seen this trip that does not make me feel inferior and HOW THE FUCK IS IT THE GUN BETWEEN ME AND DEATH that is just fucking annoying.

It is a tiny fucking gun.

RATATATATATA ZING SCHWING ZING.

Agent Hannah's gun goes ponk.

RATATATATA. RATA ATTTATATATATATATA ZSCHWING FRISSSS ATATATA!

(ponk)

For actual fuck's sake.

I may die of just being fucking embarrassed. I'll sure as hell die if I try to run.

Except.

Something weird is happening right now.

In any other country on earth you would hear sirens right now and helicopters and sure you can hear those things.

But you can also hear something else. It is a really fucking weird sound. It sounds like geese.

Angry fucking geese.

Angry geese talking about cheesecake so—

Not geese. People.

And doors opening.

Because this is Switzerland.

Until a couple years ago every household had a service rifle in a case. Most every single guy here shoots off a mandated number of rounds per month. They've been cutting back. But not that much. There are still plenty of homes here that are armed. And the people in them are actually trained in the use of weapons and in group maneuvers. They have a rank system and assigned roles because they are the Swiss. Fucking. Army.

Ratatata.

(ponk)

RATATATA—

But now also:

"DURCHZÄHLEN!"

"MORGES!"

"KRIENS!"

"MORGES!"

"DREI MAL—"

"VIER—"

"OFFICIER, DÉTACHEMENT DE RECONNAISSANCE DE L'ARMÉE DIX—"

"À VOTRE COMMANDE—"

"À GAUCHE—"

Clickaclack and running feet crisscrossing. Tic tac tic tact: infantry advance, urban warfare style.

This.

Is.

Awesome.

Because this here is a gunfight in the heart of a nation's capital city. It might be a terror attack. It might be something else. But it is dangerous and criminal and not allowed and for whatever reason the people who should be dealing with it are not here yet and so it is continuing in despite of good order and public safety—

And that is not fucking Swiss.

BROKKA BROKKA BROKKA

Semiautomatic rifle fire.

From.

Everywhere.

BROKKA BROKKA BROKKA

BROKKA BROKKA BROKKA

BROKKA BROKKA BROKKA

BROKKA   BROKKA   BROKKA   BROKKA   BROKKA BROKKA BROKKA BROKKA BROKKA—

Seven guys from the G-Wagen are right now having a totally shitty night.

And I'm happy.

Because here I am freezing on the banks of a river and some cop lady who wants to arrest me who has this tiny gun is defending me from being deadified by men in a giant death car who are—going out on a limb here I'm gonna say Hans Eiger has made a call—and now the citizenry has risen up and taking a stand and at last at fucking last I understand what the shit is happening in the world.

Robbing a bank? Sure. Sure I get that. I see it but it's not actually my jam.

This though.

This is like when you've been away from your house and you get through the door and you're not really thinking about it and you've got something to do right away and you draw that first breath and the exact combination of smells and moisture and your life hits you in the brain and you know you're where you are meant to be.

Where I'm meant to be—

Ponk ratatatata ponk BROKKA BROKKA—

I take three steps and fall forward into the river as Agent Hannah turns and sees me and screams WAS SCHEIßEREI—

But she isn't going to shoot me now because she wants to arrest me and because although it was disgusting and appalling she knows I just saved her life and she saved mine and that is a thing.

Another thing.

Between us.

Agent Hannah lowers her gun and screams at me and I let the ice-cold water wash me away and away.

River flows fast. Don't know if Hannah came after me. Guessing not. Guessing the G-Wagen boys are more her priority right now.

Paramilitary operations in her capital city and all that.

So cold. How long do I have before I freeze like three minutes. Less because I was cold when I went in.

Doesn't matter. Hypothermic is fixable shot is not prison—

Well prison is negotiable except that once you're in everyone EVERYONE knows where to find you and for a man in my position that is not good.

Out in the main stream. Getting warmer.

Which means going under.

Behind me far away bokka bokka still and now sirens now helicopters. Not long before Hannah tasks one of them in my direction surely time to get out.

Just don't know if I have the energy.

Gravel under my feet. Huge bend in the river and here's the strand. Bathing spot with a wooden pontoon that's convenient if only I could—

"Ayaaaawuh that is correct come come—"

Help. Switzerland of course there is help.

Yes of course.

"I'm—"

"Here quickly we must dry you—there is an ambulance here—"

Heat packs all over agonizing agonizing pass out don't pass out—

"Sit still here you will be fine but you must get warm here are clothes who should we call for you—"

"I'm—"

Who am I? Who's safe to be—

Tired. I'm tired. "Need a drink is there something hot?"

"Yes there is soup goulasch soup from the café here—"

Of course it is.

"Sit there I will get some."

He goes.

I do not sit there.

"Sir I am afraid you cannot come in in that—"

"MY NAME IS BANJO TELEMARK I AM A GUEST HERE GET THE MANAGER IMMEDIATELY—"

"O Mr. TELEMARK I had no idea so sorry MY GOD what has happened—"

"I was ATTACKED yes ATTACKED by TERRORISTS I must have champagne immediately and my room my room and warmth and—"

"Yes yes of course come with me—"

Doc will find me. She'll know to look here.

Before they do.

But I'm so tired and the hotel was the first place I thought of.

Concierge takes me upstairs and opens the door.

"Welcome back Herr Telemark."

Stupid to be here. Stupid should take a different room tell the hotel—

Too tired to be clever. Call Doc. Fuck this shit just—

Sit down on the bed and sleep in my heat packs and my borrowed sweats and Egyptian cotton sheets the good kind not the bullshit kind they sell everywhere now.

All fine all fine sleep—wait what is that smell that is weird is that those nasty chocolates on my pillow or some kind of floor polish—

That is when Evil Hansel falls from the fake A-frame rafters like a giant bat and slams a plastic refuse sack over my head.

I fucking hate Switzerland.

It is a Swiss refuse sack and so it is paid for by taxation at point of sale and you have to use these sacks to get your refuse taken away although recycling is free but that is not the point the point is that it is tough and thick and industrial and Evil Hansel gets it tight over my face so that the lip of the sack is pulling up under my chin like the strap on a helmet. He is actually standing on my shoulders and lifting with his legs strongman-style. I struggle of course but he's a limber little shit heel and I cannot get rid of him. I smash myself against a wall but he shifts grip around to—I'm not sure. It's hard to say. It's hard to say anything.

Hypoxia is amazingly quick and faster when you're working hard. You have breathed every second every day of your life. Try not breathing and running at the same time and get back to me.

I try to breathe and the air in the sack tastes of solvent and hydrocarbons and a hint of antibacterial cleaner. At least the floor polish smell is gone now all I can smell is my own dying. I guess that is Swiss. Evil Hansel is killing me with a sterile murder weapon.

Sterile and gray. Battleship gray like the doors of the Festung which if I die here I will not rob. Gray plastic and gray steel. I cannot see the gray plastic because it is opaque and over my eyes. My face feels as if it will explode off the front of my skull.

Well I guess this is going to suck but at least Doc will have to shut up about it.

Doc would not give me a tracheal stent but she gave me a modified tactical pen. This is an ordinary pen but made of titanium dragon penis or something and it does not break and the edges, if you remove the rollerball cartridge, are really sharp. The front inch or so is detachable to make an emergency stent and Doc and Charlie gave it little tick arms so that once it's in it's in.

I flick the lid off and punch myself in the throat with it.

The sharp end of the pen cuts right through my skin like almost too far. It hurts like fucking hell and then I heave my chest and something goes SPLURT and that is the little plug of me flying out of the tube and then I am breathing through a surgical hole in my neck.

I am a fucking genius. I totally saw this coming and I planned for it and I am a fucking genius bleeding all over the sheets.

Evil Hansel says something that sounds like "ach, you minor goofy" and the grip slackens. I figure he is right now pretty fucking startled and maybe a little horrified even if he is a nine-year-old psychopath with impeccable Aryan hair. I buck and feel him rattle against my torso so I do it again and then I catch him in one hand and pull at the bag with the other and I pull them apart and—

The world is still there.

Bright and dizzy and I am alive and FUCK YOU AGAIN FUCKERS I am alive.

I look around and see Evil Hansel and his whole face is covered in red me-funk. I wait for him to pull the knife and come at me but—

But Evil Hansel is just completely still.

I realize he is listening to my breathing which is a weird fucking noise like a seal barking in a plastic box.

"Yeah you little Nazi I'm breathing through my neck hole! You try it and see how that goes! C'mere I'll show you ya little fucking Heydrich on a tricycle—"

I can say this because my special tactical trache pen is fenestrated to allow for speech it is not like that thing you see in movies where the guy sounds like a kazoo. Doc has all the best stuff.

Evil Hansel actually flinches.

I wonder for a second if he is afraid of blood but he can't be that's not it.

I wonder if he thinks I'm just going to kill him now with laser vision or something I mean in the end he is nine so—

Evil Hansel runs out of the room and I swear he is crying.

Well sure fine be a kid suddenly. Be a fucking kid and run away you little—

Fuck you anyway you murderous little bastard.

. . .

. . .

Fuck.

Fuck fuck FUCK IT.

I'm standing here with another fucking hole in me and breathing through a TUBE for the love of—

And HE'S the one crying that is just—

Fuuuuuck it FUCK it.

How the fuck do I feel like I'm the monster here?

———

Call Doc, Doc sends Saul. Saul comes and carries me down to the goods bay and we disappear. It's not the most sophisticated disappear not like we have actually vanished more like quietly left and not waved at anyone. There is blood everywhere in the hotel room so we may assume the management will be calling the cops on Banjo Telemark.

CATASTROPHE ARTIST MISSING AFTER TERRORIST SHOOTOUT

It's a headline, but it's one of those headlines. It's too obviously something from a movie to be actually true, especially in Bern. The truer it seems the more there is something else going on particularly when you throw in the presence of a noted asshat prankster like Banjo. The more it looks as if it must be fake, the more Agent Hannah's bosses will represent that it is the exact truth and no they are not even a little bit joking. The more they say it is the truth the more they invest in that the less they will believe her crazy theory that Banjo Telemark is Jack Price and the more she will know it is true.

And Hans Eiger will still hate every word of it.

Mr. Eiger.

O Mr. Eiger.

Gunmen in armored cars? In a civic space where there are homes and families? Where there are children sleeping? What if someone found out? People might say that it is inappropriate to a gentleman of your associations and position in society. They might say MY god that is NOT correct that is QUITE IRRESPONSIBLE it is anti-social really and scandalous there should be a criminal investigation serious consequences HERR GOTT NO'MAL.

Influential people. Sensible, right-thinking people. Mothers. Fathers. Train drivers and technologists and chocolatiers and ski teachers and scientists and—you know—

The Swiss.

Mr. Eiger.

For shame sir.

For shame.

Doc comes and I am a mess with blood and by now it's really uncomfortable having a pen in my breathing parts and every time my lungs work it's like well exactly like you would fucking imagine. Hashtag do not want.

"Price what the fuck—"

"Just glue it—"

"I am gluing it shut up for ten seconds—"

"Just OW—"

"Shut up ONE Thermopylae TWO Thermopylae . . ."

" . . ."

" . . ."

" . . ."

"TEN O thank God—"

"You PINCHED me in the TRACHE HOLE ow Doc enough with the needles already—"

"That is a drip full of good things you need at this time. Now hush. Our guest is here. At least you are authentically tousled and disreputably drug-seeking—"

"I am not drug-seeking you pronged me in the blood parts—wait what guest—"

"Remember last night before you started a war in the capital of a peaceful nation?"

"That was not me that was them but also too YOU SAID—"

"I said distraction—with an A not a U—"

"I see what you did there but Doc it truly it was not my fault also too Agent Hannah—"

"Hush Jack."

"Wait what?"

"Hush. Jack. It's fine."

". . . You called me Jack?"

"I did."

"Because of the future we have that we totally do have?"

"Because use of an injured person's first name is demonstrated to have an immediate calming effect and even there are studies showing increased healing."

"Or that."

"Jack."

"Yes?"

"Also because of the future."

"The future that we do have?"

"That future. Yes."

"Aw Doc."

"Always accepting that the future as we construct it is—"

"I have glandular feelings for you Doc such as would be observed in a brain releasing oxytocin and associated neuropeptides that are linked with the human experience of positive emotion but also with the urge a starfish has to evert its stomach and devour small crustacea as prey."

". . . Shut up or I will have sex with you now and it would hurt you."

"Ooooooh . . ."

In fact Doc does not have sex with me because somewhere between the moment when she leans down to kiss me and the moment I touch the skin of her stomach with my hand and I hear her chuckle in her throat and she captures my hand—the one which was inappropriately touched by a significantly excited federal clitoris but the one also which held the tactical pen—and slips it into her mouth—which I totally remember happening but she says never happened—I fall asleep.

Here then I guess is the scorecard apart from that we successfully kidnapped a nice lady from a seal sex establishment:

I have annoyed Hans Eiger enough that he called in Monsieur Leclerc the Franco-Belgian Nazi. Leclerc is not a drawing room guy he is not presentable not Swiss-friendly he is a tough guy. He has crossed the line and in fact metaphorically he has peed in the civic fondue and the whole of Swiss lawful goodness desires his balls in a bucket—though they are too lawful good to actually bucketize him—all the same the heat is on him and that is nice. It is not on Eiger so long as Leclerc does not squeal like a—

We do not discuss the squealings of pigs in that way anymore they are family now.

(The ones that are left.)

The heat is somewhat also on Jack Price the international criminal although not very much on actual me right now because Agent Hannah is drowning under legal challenges to her irresponsible and defamatory treatment of the artist Banjo Telemark. Banjo does not take kindly to being pushed around by the running dog lackeys of capitalism and unfreedom and he has unleashed upon her the firm of Jaeger Globus & Driskoll of Geneva. Why them well because obviously we murdered the only lawyer we knew in this town and plus also Banjo Telemark needs lawyers not in any way associated with this whole thing so far. In any case I have in my life been exposed to some vindictive motherfuckers but I had not until I spoke to Ms. Jacinta Globus encountered anyone so necrotizingly joyous at the idea of fucking up a federal agency. It seems to me that Ms. Globus takes an unholy pleasure in such work and what is weird about that is that she is herself as far as anyone can tell—and when I say anyone I mean me and Charlie and Mr. Friday's nephew in Hafnarfjörður who does odd information security jobs for him between fishing trips—she is totally without criminal history or activity of her own. It is just a thing with her but fuck me she is good at it and she has the knowing of every nook and cranny of habeus gofuckyourself.

For the next few days while all that is sorted out Agent Hannah can look at my corpus delicti but she can't touch any of this yes I do know that is not what that means.

Corpus delicti.

Cannot—in fact—touch this.

Tra la la tra.

Cannot touch—any—of my corpus delicti—with her federal agent lovebutton—or any other damn thing she brings to the yard—YES I have changed songs sue me O RIGHT YOU CANNOT because I have a Jacinta in my pocket and she is not pleased to see you.

And Doc's plan for the Kircheisen Festung . . . it is good. She has the necessary elephant tranquilizer and she has a vector for it. She has the physical body of Elena Riccardi the programmer, last seen passing out in FischFisch from a high dose of whatever, and soon she will have answers.

All security systems have dirty secrets. It just depends how dirty you are prepared to get yourself to uncover them. We went to FischFisch and I got clitorally assaulted so we are already quite dirty and I think my suffering should entirely count for something.

And it does because Elena Riccardi is waking up.

Charlie says: "Good morning sleepyhead YAWN."

Elena Riccardi says: "VASS?"

"Oooo Tiger steady it's a little bit early for shouting although I do like it when you yell—"

"VASS—WHAT WHAT O SHIIIIT—"

Fisahypnozerasol plus some high-grade opiates to trigger it will leave you with a sense memory of fairly humungous physical pleasure and no idea what happened to cause it. That is fine if you wake up next to your acknowledged sexual partner and less good if you walk into the breakfast room of a log cabin full of weirdo strangers wearing nothing but a borrowed XXXL tour shirt for a Euroskiffle PMV band called the Dover Bends.

If you do not know what PMV is do not Google it.

"Owwwww loud loud loud Elena fercrissakes not cool—"

"Oh hey Rita you here too?"

"Yes Banjo," Doc says, "me and Lulu and even Bad Man Adams from the band."

(That's Charlie and Lucille she's pointing at and of course I have a hole in my neck that has recently been superglued but even without that the idea that one might have done sex with Lucille is a troubling sort of a thing. Lucille looks like a hair puller.) "Aaacccch ne ne ne ne—where are we? Where is my husband—"

Charlie says: "Well this is our house and Oscar well he bailed after you guys got into it a little that guy cannot take his hooch I am afraid he was way grouchy and you told him to— well you were clear about who wears the pants in your house sexually speaking—but wow lady—you! You are THE dirtiest hunter in the ocean sweetheart that I gotta give you I have not been speared and flensed like that in—"

". . . o SHIT du meine Gute shit shit shit . . ."

Elena Riccardi is having a really bad morning right now and

Charlie is just grinning at her and bringing her coffee and that
is making it worse because she cannot remember anything at
all except being really really you know—

—satisfied—

—by person or persons unknown but if you're lucky maybe
you can piece it together and find them again and pin them to
a wall and—and she does not feel good about that but at the
same time she really does and—

And that is why you go to FischFisch in the first place.

This is the key to a professional drug amnesia play. In the after-
math the subject should feel incredibly uncomfortable with the
idea of asking questions about what they don't remember, but
not so uncomfortable that they want to call the police or alert
their employer to a potential security breach. You definitely
do not want a software engineer specializing in security wondering whether she might have given up the details of a massively secret project she worked on as an associate a dozen
years ago. You would not want her thinking that she had for
example given you back doors and exploits and vulnerabilities
and the Internet Protocol address of the system's only contact
with the regular interwebs or any of that shit. If she thought
that she might call in to work and tell them what has happened
and that would put a massive crimp in your robbery and you
would need to take steps but Mr. Friday was real clear about
the rules of engagement here so those steps would be prob-
lematic. No long-term harm he said and there will be none.
Just a few days of mild ethical discomfort and emotional woe
because she inexplicably forgot her husband somewhere along
the road to orgytown and that is not part of their Deal.

No sirreebob. That is a big fat no-no it is on their list of no-nos that they keep on the fridge door beside the little bright colored alphabet magnets and the school calendar. In truth probably her husband would be okay about it he is not a bad guy and he loves her. That slightly makes it worse and so now she has to deal with that fuckup and it is in the forefront of her mind and she wants it gone from there—

"(SCHEIßEREI!)"

—and she is definitely not asking awkward questions about whether she compromised Hans Eiger's impregnable fortress.

There is no such thing as ethical fair trade kidnapping but if there were it would be this and I am mostly fine with it. We have done a crime to her and a mean one which preys upon her emotional vulnerability and her lifestyle and that is a shitty thing to do. But on the other hand Elena Riccardi will eventually work out what really happened and she will be pissed as hell and she will be right, but in the long and even the medium and actually the short term Elena will be as okay as anyone ever is and unlike let us say Sharkey or Volodya she is alive. In this world you have to wake up every morning grateful about that or you will just blink and miss it.

Doc days: "Well that went well."

"It did?"

"It absolutely did. Charlie has everything she needs."

"Well that is good."

"You do not think that is good."

"I just think we are the bad guys."

"Well we are the bad guys. It's just we are against the guys who are also the bad guys."

"Yeah that's true."

"Do you have everything you need?"

"I am working out the kinks I am plotting I—"

"You aren't ready yet."

"Are you?"

"Charlie says some of the locks are isolated from the main system. She thinks we will need to get a security guy with an eyeball who is alive and hold his face to a scanner for the biometrics."

"Is that what you think?"

"I think that is the most straightforward way. The system does not confirm with voice or heartbeat so he can be unconscious just so long as he is alive."

"Taser?"

"Medication of course Tasers can be unpredictable."

"So can medication."

"Tcha."

"I guess."

"You're not happy."

"I have forebodings Doc I feel there is something I don't see."

"You will see it. That is what you do."

"I guess."

"You see universes of crime."

"Aw shucks."

"Call Friday and tell him the Riccardi woman is fine. It will make him happy plus you like him."

". . . I guess that I do."

"Call him. It is nice for boys to be friends."

"I don't know about friends exactly—"

"Price. It is okay to have friends."

"Yeah I suppose."

VoIP outgoing—

"Hey Friday."

"Mr. Price?"

"Yeah it me."

"You do not sound well."

"I have something in my throat."

"Oh do you wish to cough? It is important. Many people from countries where coughing is considered embarrassing die every year because they leave meals to cough in the corridor or the bathroom and they die by choking."

"They what now?"

"Jes. It is awful."

". . . Yeah it is about one of the most worst things I've ever heard."

"That cannot possibly be true."

". . . No I guess not."

". . ."

". . ."

"Are you injured?"

"No no I'm fine. Mostly fine I have a hole in me. Two holes actually that are not natural to my basic you know humanity there is one in my leg and one in my neck."

"That . . . does not sound fine."

"I just wanted you to know that—I mean yeah there was some stuff—but the programmer lady she is fine too."

"O God will she recover?"

"Jesus Friday no she is fine—she is FINE—like she is fine like perfectly okay. Embarrassed now and a little guilty and she will be really really pissed off when she figures it out but— fine. No injuries and all what you said. No lasting trauma."

". . . That is actually very good of you to tell me."

"Yeah man I'm just a guy trying to get along I keep saying."

"Thank you, then."

"You're welcome man."

"That is—all?"

"Yeah man that's all. I mean hug everyone for me."

". . . I will."

"You don't have to if it's weird. It's weird isn't it?"

"Jes. Very."

"Okay don't hug anyone but maybe tell them I said."

"What will you do now?"

"Now I gotta get this done. I'm buying a chair and we're running out of pigs."

". . . And inevitably I am sorry that I asked."

"Love you man bye."

". . ."

". . ."

"It is not like you to speak in this way."

"Yeah man Doc is helping me with my emotional well-being I guess. She says it is okay to be friends."

"With me?"

"Yeah I guess."

"Well that is—nice."

"Isn't it?"

"Jes?"

". . ."

". . ."

"Bye man I gotta go."

". . . Goodbye."

And then Charlie says:

"ROOT! ROOOOOOOOOT! I AM ROOOOOT!"

NINE

YOU HAVE NOT HEARD A MUPPET ORGASM VOICE until you have heard Charlie's Muppet orgasm voice. You might think that in a professional setting this is inappropriate but in fact with creative people you have to accept a certain amount of inappropriate. The Muppet orgasm voice is an important part of Charlie's oeuvre and you do not fuck with the oeuvre.

"MM MMM MMMMM! OOOOOOOOOHHHH YES! YES YES!"

And then:

"I AM ROOT I AM ROOT I AM ROOT!

"I.

"AM.

"ROOT!"

Charlie puts her head round the door.

"I am root," she says.

"Gotcha."

This is genuinely a very good thing it means Charlie has certain powers like total domination over the mere matter of the security system at Kircheisen and these powers are significant. We put I AM ROOT in the assets list on the board and Charlie says it like ten more times before Doc writes it in the NO column next to CRIME VAGINA.

So now Doc only needs my distraction to be ready and to kidnap a guy and she is all in.

I need to go to an arcade. With coin-op video games.

Yes they still have those.

Incoming call ring ring:

"Hi it is Banjo Telemark the great artist OR IS IT hello?"

"Mr. Telemark it is Jacinta Globus good morning you may now leave the house without concern for arrest."

"I may?"

"Yes. I have filed" blah blah law blah blah papers and also blah blah precedent in triplicate ingenuity blah Federal Government v. Go Fuck Yourself 1997 blah blah money power "so that is fine."

"O thank you."

"You should obviously take care to commit no infractions of any kind even for the sake of art or JONAS task force will almost certainly take full advantage of it."

"My art is all entirely legal I assure you."

"I am prepared to take that on faith you are a client."

"O good."

"But I should point out that even an ambiguous situation would afford them the opportunity to arrest you. In the normal run of things I find your approach to art hugely amusing. However in this context I must inform you it would be better if you did not indulge your need to epertay laborjwazay."

"I beg your pardon that would be teper zlaborjwa is that Polish?"

"No it is not Pig Latin Mr. Telemark it is French it means to outrage the straights."

"O yes I see."

"Do not outrage the straights for another week Mr. Telemark and then we will have all this sorted out permanently."

"Thank you Ms. Globus."

"You are welcome Mr. Telemark."

"Please send me an enormous bill."

"Of course."

I like arcades and this one is a classic. There is air hockey and there is actual *Pong* and actual *Space Invaders* and *Asteroids* alongside all the modern cabinet games which you sit in. There is that thing with the bubbles that you shoot with little harpoons which I have not seen since the '90s when it was in every airport departures hall on Earth. There are no tickets here and no tokens you just pay and play and the costs are high but honest. Even the claw machine which lets you win marmot toys is honest I win seven marmots in little red hats that yodel when you squeeze them. I also win a bag to put them in because Switzerland.

Finally I play the *Star Wars* machine for an hour.

It is a two-person game and the other position is empty for that whole hour and I spend like a hundred francs during that time because I am not completely great at this.

Which is a lot until you think about how that is really not expensive to arrange a meeting like this one.

I hear the scrape as a little plastic box step is dragged along the floor and then I have a copilot or more accurately he has me. He does not try to kill me and I do not try to kill him and that is an acceptable beginning.

We play without speaking for another hour. My dime of course. I lose track of how many times we win and in all that time he does not die once. He's like a little tiny *Star Wars* ninja in an ESA jacket and brown corduroys. If you had to describe him to police you would automatically call him a scamp. Then somehow it's time and we look at one another as the stuff on the screen just blows up and there's nothing left to do but talk or try to kill each other.

"Good game," Evil Hansel says.

When we have not tried to kill each other for a few minutes I tell him what I want and he says he cannot give it to me.

So I offer him his heart's desire because that is what I do.

It is not until we are done talking and he has gone away into the pinball and the claw machines with the little toys and out into the sunshine like an ordinary little kid that I realize what was bugging me. Whenever I got close enough to notice it, Evil Hansel smelled weird. Volodya always smelled like shoe boxes and bear grease and generic log cabin stinky and it was disturbing at a mammal level because I have read where bad diet like also possibly human ham will make you smell bad and this was not that. Evil Hansel smelled like walking through the hardware department and all the auto air fresheners are open in rows for your motoring cleanliness but that is not it because it is like—like a really bad chocolate box like rose water where there should be caramels and that really amazing praline thing and instead you get rose and orange creams and that disgusting purple one—

—he smelled—

—awful—

—but also familiar—

—and why am I thinking of sea urchins and the sound of a squeegee? Who washes sea urchins they are what they are—

And then I get it and I just stare at the air hockey for the longest time and watch the puck go back and forth and back and forth zip zap clack.

Quite a long time ago now in another country when I was young and foolish I did a good thing. I mean it was not a heroic thing but it was basically nice and I will tell you about it now and then we will not talk about it anymore.

I was getting a train from the city to my mama's house up along the coast where things were not good economically speaking and little by little the old farms were turning into derelicts and from time to time I guess some guy would buy an old place and make it into a lodge where he could snort coke off his secretaries and make 8 mm pornos and then project them onto his secretaries yes Mr. Farnham I SEE YOU—

Never mind that now.

I was getting the train and there was a guy with a backpack he went for the door just as another guy pulled it closed and there was somehow one of those perfect bad moments and the latch was very sharp and it cut off his finger like BLOOP.

I swear BLOOP or maybe SCHWIPP it is hard to say but there was a tonal quality.

And then there was the guy screaming and I could not get past him to get on the train and the train was leaving with a great long smear of red across the door panel.

A bunch of people came and helped the screaming guy and a woman from the local market puts her huge thumb on his artery at the biceps and I was just left there on the platform because I did not know field medicine or whatsoever. Then there were like seven hours to the next train and I had nothing to do so I went and looked for the finger.

I looked where you would expect like at the tail end of the blood drops and it was not there and I thought did someone get it already? But then I thought maybe the wind blew and it had and there in the hard by the rail was this finger and I picked it up.

This was the first time I ever picked up a severed human appendage by the way and yeah the first time stays with you.

I went over to the concession stand to get some ice because I had this idea which is true that you got to put a severed appendage in a cold place. Concession guy would not give me ice unless I paid for a drink and also too I was not to put my gnarly severed appendage on his countertop at any time that was a code violation.

So I put the finger in my breast pocket and THAT is what those fucking things are for and I put it nail down so that it would not drip gore on me and I bought a soda and a paper towel at like a one thousand percent markup and I left the soda on the countertop and fuck you very much and I went off to the hospital to do my good thing.

When I got to the hospital with the finger wrapped in ice in a blue towel I went to the main desk and I explained the situation and the nurse practitioner said okay and she called another nurse and he called someone and la la la la and then the cops who were present arrested the shit living shit out of me.

Because it was not the right finger.

I do not know why or how and I do not want to.

But this is the moment that I understood the depth of the world I guess for the first time. I sat in a green triage room on a gray office chair with worn patches on the lumbar support and a tiny wiry cop motherfucker told me that I was holding some other fucking finger and please to give it to him now and I saw the walls disappear and time unravel all the way back to the moment when I picked up.

The wrong.

Finger.

An old cold murder finger.

And I felt the whole world come back together exactly the same as it always was but I was new.

Then I spent forty eight hours in jail instead of at my momma's house and finally Uncle Teague came to get me and we rode all the way home in his truck and he did not say a word until a mile from my house and then he said:

"So now you know."

And I said:

"Yes sir."

Teague is a Scottish name it means poet and that was the only poem he ever said to me.

In the arcade on the Ahornweg the air hockey goes zip zap clack and it's sort of another poem I guess if you are inclined to the metaphysical it is a synesthetic poem about details and the world unfolding and exploding in your head and coming back exactly the same like the finger because Hans Eiger did not smell of rose water and nor does Evil Hansel. Not rose water and not chocolate and not air fresheners.

They have been in a room with Mrs. Van der Zee and her nasty signature perfume and that changes everything because in crime there are no coincidences.

So now it turns out there are things I have to do.

I sit in front of a computer and I lie to Charlie.

"Hey boss whatcha doin'?"

"I am looking at the golfs Charlie."

"Golf what?"

"I like the golfs they are happening in Dubai they have made a whole golf in the desert out of I do not know I assume space science and I am watching on the interwebs come watch too!"

"Uh no thank you boss I am robbing a bank over here with Doc."

"O good of course sorry my bad."

I am not watching the golfs I am murderizing people in futurity. The sort of murderizing this requires is not improvisational it is process-driven it is downstream complexity made simple by stages. Of course it helps that I had planned to do some serious murderizing and so I was already preparing for it infrastructurally speaking but still. But that is my modus: you break it into manageable tasks and you make sure that you assign—

Yeah.

Yeah fine it's how I do. I am doing it the way Karenina taught me to I am finding friendships and connections and names and place I am finding Mrs. Van der Zee and here she is, O and there is Jort also this is his website but now we are looking where are we looking we are looking at . . . O here is the launch of VDZ-Hatterstadt-Klemp's new housing project in Dresden how nice and the gang is all here that is to say this is Mrs. Van der Zee and who should be one of the contractors on that project but the young and thrusting firm of Schempp Kosterlitz AG and of course there is no Kosterlitz and only about ten percent of a Schempp they are a shell for another company and another and another all set up by a law firm in Bermuda for use by a firm run out of another shell in London which is owned out of an office in Martinique and la la la la and—

VoIP outgoing call ring ring.

"Hi this is Carla at Zebedee Bogotá Reception how may I help you today?"

"Hi Carla MY but that is quite some voice hello Carla gosh."

"Hello sir that is charming of you to say I am sure."

"Carla this is Jack Mahboubian I was there at the hotel a little while back it was a LOVELY stay."

"Why thank you again sir."

"Carla I have to ask you a question and I want a straight answer for which I will pay a great deal of money."

"Oh—"

"No Carla listen I am not even slightly kidding I will give you a million dollars American for usable information and it is not even particularly secret it is just gossip but I need to be sure."

". . . Are you fucking with me Mr. Mahboubian?"

"Carla right now I am sending an email to the reception account with a number put that number into your browser window and you will find an account with your name on it with money in it. I will give you the access details the moment you tell me what I want to know."

"I—"

"Carla are you aware of the existence of a rich old Dutch lady who smells like someone sexually molested a coffeepot with a violet cream?"

"O shit her yes sure she does not stay at the Zebedee but—"

"But she is so fucking rich every hotelier in Bogotá knows when she is in town."

"Yes sir."

"Million-dollar question Carla when was she last there?"

Carla tells me and of course it is the same time as Frankie Leclerc and his emeralds. That would not hold in a court of law but I am not one and I already know. If you join the dots in the money you find the same thing that is in the picture: the guy in the nice suit standing a little way off and behind Mrs. Van der Zee and totally not her date or her friend he just happens to be in proximity . . . why that is François Leclerc.

This is not about me at all.

(I know weird right?)

It is not about me at all.

And most specifically this whole thing—this whole thing is not about money or even politics. Volodya is dead and Reinhard and Sharkey and Agent Hannah's left-hand guy and her right-hand guy and some of the G-Wagen guys and a lot—really a lot—of other people are about to die because of one thing and that thing—

Tycho the saluki's questionable libido.

Tycho does not fuck Mrs. Van der Zee's dog and Mrs. Van der Zee takes offense and so obviously—OBVIOUSLY this is just what you do in that situation OF COURSE—she buys a shit ton of conflict emeralds and puts them in Eiger's bank and uses them to hire Frankie Leclerc to do horrible things to Doc's friends. She lets him see the stones and she lets him hold them but unless he wants to try and kill her right here in Bogotá against whatever precautions she has taken—I am guessing big sturdy Dutch security assholes—he cannot have them unless he does what she wants and even then she is going to keep him on retainer. A billion is a lot of money when you are trying to make your way in the world so Frankie swallows the hook and on her instruction he nudges up to Eiger to hire us and kill us off because that will solve his money problems. It's like stupidly complex but she is Mrs. Van der Zee and no one ever tells her no.

Mrs. Van der Zee set us up—she made all this happen—because Tycho did not bone her dog.

She did all this to hurt Doc. Just to be mean.

And if this is all about Doc . . .

. . . then they will be looking for the subtle move behind the loud stupid Banjo thing . . .

. . . and Doc's plan to rob Die Festung is probably about to get the same treatment as Mrs. Van der Zee's Semper Augustus. Which means we need a new plan and Doc cannot be a part of it. She cannot even know until after.

I do not know what she will think about that.

Apart from Mr. Friday and a guy in Japan who says he will have me killed if I go there most of my friends are dead. I do not have lots of people I can ask for advice and if I did I could not tell them about this.

I go out and see the little guy in the cigar store and once again we do not talk but this time he hangs a note on the door and we go and not talk in a café and it is a really great coffee place you can tell these guys are serious but impossibly the coffee is bad.

I see in the little guy's face that he is embarrassed but does not wish to say so to the team here. This is a legit thing they are his people but also it is a legit thing for a great coffee place to fuck up no one needs to be ashamed. I go and nudge the guy behind the laminated wood bar top and I say that the beans have gone over and he says that cannot possibly be true and I put my hand in the jar of the grinder and lift out one bean and rest it on the tip of my finger. Guy smells the bean and looks at me and just nods and a little while later we get amazing coffee and we sit. I kind of figured we would play chess or something but the little guy evidently does not like chess so we play backgammon. We play for wafers and for about twenty minutes I owe him something like 140 wafers and then the game shifts a bit and by the end we agree without speaking that we can eat the difference and we do.

TEN

RING RING "HI HELLO IS THAT THE COMMODORE HOTEL? I need to
speak to the concierge please—yes hi yes—yes it is Banjo
Telemark—very well I am fine I am totally alive and I have not
been assassinated in your establishment at all no sir all forgot-
ten of course—yes I need some things put on my bill—yes—
no no I would be delighted for the manager to send wine but
for the rest well you will see. Yes. Yes thank you yes. Yes you
have a pen? Okay. I will need a chair like a throne plus a rug
plus also some balik and fine white wine I will tell you where.
Also ten gallons of aniseed oil and a bunch of schoolkids for
a—what is it that you say a Geh-mineshaft-pro-yuckt?—for
one of those—o you have children in the local—that is ideal
how—a boy and a girl that is a full set I suppose—yes yes
indeed I am sure they are lovely. Please yes I have a credit card
here—"

RING RING—"O hello is that the Grand Kircheisen Palast?
Yes this is Søren Welk yes Welk—W E L K—yes. Yes I understand you have an excellent view of the—yes of the valley
and the mountain and the cable car station O it is that close?
That is wonderful you could walk that how lovely—well I am
organizing the—ah yes quite so you have already heard from
the school very good Mr. Telemark is quite emphatic—yes of
course we will keep the children away from the pool quite
so but—no I cannot tell you but I assure it is just aniseed oil
it will—it will—oh very well since you insist it will form an
olfactory imprint of a text Banjo has written it will be almost

impossible to distinguish although theoretically a person might follow all the trails and map it to read the text although as a practical matter no human really has a sufficiently astute sense of smell so it both exists and does not—yet of course you see quite so yes—no I appreciate that you run a very dignified hotel and that your present register includes a lady of some age who has taken the whole top floor yes quite so we will not trouble her—no no it is quite harmless to animals I assure you in fact I believe some even quite like the—yes quite so do not worry for one instant I am entirely cognizant there will be no harm to the dog I can assure you. No indeed I understand entirely leave it with me I will instruct the children to utmost respect—"

Loud Banjo Telemark playing the fool.

Quiet Doc in the background moving her chess pieces.

And Mrs. Van der Zee laughing at us both and thinking I do not see her.

And that is fine.

Big boots like a cavalry officer and jeans by Yamamoto and a midnight sou'wester coat borrowed from Bruno in the Black House, which still has Z-Vat and what I suspect is Charlie's lip gloss on the zip fastening. The coat is so much bigger than I am that it comes off my shoulders and I am basically wearing it like a cloak like a medieval tabard and I am on my way to steal the ducal hat of Burgundy—I love this country I honestly do ANYWAY anyway I am working now I am focused like a razor on the neck I am in the zone—I am in Bruno's coat and an aqua shirt that is mostly undone and I have a cane with a rat skull on the top which I am motherfucking TWIRLING yes twirling like music hall like Fred motherfucking Astaire.

The Banjo is IN.

Walk up glass stairs with everyone looking at me and don't know just throw that fucking door wide open on its expensive cantilevered modern art hinge and hear something pop in the mechanism so it hangs there—

"Hi Director Desirée baby it is BAAAAANJOOOOOO! Are you pleased to see me don't answer that I can already tell that you are."

"Oh goodness! Mr. TELEMARK what are you doing here?"

"O I am sorry you must be super busy I really came to say hi and let you know everything is shaping up supercoolio for the EVENT I am putting on at Kircheisen and I am of course not under arrest."

"I was sure that you were—"

"That is my art Madame Director and I am not the first and greatest of exponent of Ambiguitionism for no reason. In doubt and dismay and the sense of a world gone mad—that sense which touches the edges of our minds at all times in this runaway century—that is where I live. I am Banjo Telemark and that is my truth now show me yours."

"I—I am not sure I have one ready."

"Perfect! Please tell Hans the bulldozers will arrive tomorrow by helicopter he should be ready. And some other stuff. O do you know who I talk to at the Swiss Air Defense Force to let them know there will be fireworks?"

"Well yes but the Air Force they do not fly during the nighttime it is against noise regulations."

". . . I love this country Madame Director. I truly do. Ciao! Baci!"

". . . Yaawuhhh. Baci. Yaaawh. Absolutely. Quite."

———

Since I am out anyway this will be an opportunity to return Bruno's coat. It is not nice to keep things people have loaned you and if it rains he will need his enormous coat and Charlie would be cross with me. Plus I like Bruno I do not want him to be wet. I am an international villain bajillionaire murder kingpin bank robber that does not mean I have to be a prick.

Plus there is just something I would like to ask no big deal but I would quite like a few bags of Z-Vat and some user instructions maybe a little help practical assistance in exchange for an intro to Mr. Friday and a serious motherfucking upgrade to their revolution if they're serious about it.

So I go to the Black House to return the coat.

I open the door on a scene from a horror movie and not one of those nice black-and-white or early color ones where the horror is basically a woman in a nightdress shouting fuck but one of the modern ones which are a lesson in trauma anatomy and the audience is mostly medical students and snuff perverts.

Leclerc has been here.

Charlie will be—I don't know what this will do to her I honestly do not. It's on another order of things.

I don't know what it's doing to me.

There is Loob and he's just dead like mercifully if that makes any sense, which it does not. There is a hole in the middle of his face but no one tortured him. Rosa has been shot a bunch of times because obviously a woman who makes cakes really needs taking down hard. Thing and Thong are face-first on the sofa and someone walked a pistol up their spines from pretty close range so I'm guessing they surrendered and Leclerc's people thought that was hilarious. I'm not going to go on because you can make it up you won't get it wrong. The blood is like oil on water in the dark.

For a yawning moment I wonder if the farm house looks like this too and I will go there and find Doc dead and Charlie and Rex and even Saul and Lucille but no. You cannot just walk up on my Demons. They frighten me. They are strange and even quirky and bad things would happen in unpredictable ways: you would explode and pigs and doors would devour you. Strange diseases would melt you and then a walking knife collection would open your veins and a scary commando would blow you away and you would cease to exist across a whole range of media and your body would never be found. This— this is just—this is just to be unkind. François Leclerc is writing his name on the world. On Charlie.

Hell is other people they say and in this one instance it is exactly true.

I stare at hell for a while. I make myself look. Look Jack look. The world has this in it do you understand? The world has this man who did this. People pretend that it does not and they live and have children and if they are lucky they get old and die with their pretense intact but this is the truth right here. These are the rules. Anything you get that is not this was fought and won. A price was paid.

Someone puts a coffee cup against the back of my head and it goes phudd.

Phudd is the sound of the universe not coming to an end but for a moment there I really think I'm about to die and I just haven't felt it yet and the only reason I do not lose control of my bladder is that I don't have time before I realize it has not happened.

Phudd is the noise a shotgun-type weapon such as a Don-nerbüchse makes when you pull the trigger and it does not fire. The hammer comes down on an empty cartridge and it goes:

Phudd.

Again. And again and—

She keeps pulling the trigger and recocking it phudd click-clack phudd clickclack phudd and I really should stop her because if it's misfiring, sooner or later it'll go off but I already know that isn't going to happen and so does she. When I turn around there's nothing in the barrel except a grief that will never go away.

Flavia throws the Donnerbüchse on the ground and jumps on my back and starts to claw at me but honestly her heart isn't in it. She hates me about as much as she hates everyone else in the world but what she really wants right now is to book a flight yesterday to far away from here and to wake up and find this was a nightmare and she's in Hawaii in a stinking capitalist resort with waterslides and all her friends and she knows with a stark misery that that did not happen and here we are this is the world. The best she can hope for is just a hug and I so I hug her and she screams and screams and water stuff comes out of her face that is not tears and not snot and not vomit it's just horror.

This is the shape of the world and how it is and you believe it is not and that is nice for you.

I know better and now so does Flavia.

She gets in a few good ones and my ribs will feel those later but who the fuck cares about my ribs when Bruno's ribs are over there on that table about two meters from his head and yeah Flavia you beat the shit out of me you are totally right that this is my fault.

But honestly it's not me you want to kill and we'll come to that sweetheart I swear we will.

She pukes on my shoes and then she apologizes and I just hug her some more. I am a monster and I live in a world of bad things but that does not make me a monster and if you find that confusing, then I don't know what to tell you to make it make sense, but I wouldn't leave you to look after my kids. No obviously I do not have kids.

Flavia pukes some more and this time she gets the back of my legs:

"Sorry sorry I'm sorry—"

"There there honey. Jack's here now. There there."

"Did Charlie send you Jack?"

"Naw Flavia she doesn't know it's gonna wreck her. Like it'll break her apart I don't know what she'll do. I just came to give Bruno back his coat."

She looks. "I gave him that coat."

I put Flavia down for a minute and explain there is something I need to do and then I throw up into a vase. I don't clear up. Don't judge me it's not like the place doesn't smell awful already. Then I wrap her in Bruno's coat and I hide her somewhere safe.

But not so far away I can't use her when I need her.

I sit in a classic recliner chair in Agent Hannah's apartment and I wait for her to come home. Every so often I practice raising my hands so that she does not shoot me before I get the chance to say hi, and I wonder whether maybe just waiting in the hall would be better but it would not. People get shot outside their apartments just as often as they get shot inside and I have brought schnapps and pickles and salami and this weird little rye bread thing that smells of ginger, and these are all on the table, which I hope will also make the point that I did not come to be unpleasant.

I'm not shivering anymore.

I don't taste puke or blood when I swallow anymore.

But I can smell it when I breathe through my nose not all the time but sometimes.

Charlie I'm so sorry.

I put my hands in the air again: I surrender.

Keeping your hands in the air for even a little while is hard you have done it in gym class so you know.

Practice: up.

Feel the burn.

Down.

Sit around getting bored and wondering whether she's out with friends and this is a huge waste of time but I know that she is not because Agent Hannah has no friends not while this is happening in her city not now.

Up.

Keep 'em up.

Ow ow ow down.

Up.

Ow ow ow down.

Up . . .

Agent Hannah says:

"What the actual fuck are you doing?"

She is pointing a gun but everyone does that to me these days and her finger is quite a long way from the trigger.

"I am practicing putting my hands in the air so that you will not shoot me."

"You are terrible at it."

"Well I have been practicing a lot and my arms are tired."

"You're under arrest."

"I'll tell Jacinta she will love that."

"You broke into my . . . Shit just pour the schnapps you look ridiculous."

"Well that is a bit mean I am just trying to make you feel okay about me being here."

"You want me to feel okay about an international terrorist breaking into my apartment? Pour the schnapps and fuck off out of my country that will work fine."

I pour the schnapps and I say that I am not a terrorist and she snorts, which is rude.

"I am seriously not a terrorist."

"Please don't tell me you make art. Zum Wohl."

"Kampai."

Agent Hannah puts the whole shot down not fast but slowly and then she cuts some bread and pours another.

"What do you want?"

"Hannah Berlickon of the JONAS Einsatzgruppe. Hi. My name is Jacob Morgenstern Price of the international criminal organization known as the Seven Demons. I am here in your country to do crime. It was not intended that it should be loud annoying crime and I made—I made several bona fide efforts in the direction that it not even be obviously illegal. I am not—you have heard about the Seven Demons because they are known for tearing up the world in places that are unlike Switzerland and because under my predecessor they were a significant threat to the maintenance of international peace and security—but I am just a guy trying to get along in the world and honestly if we never did another thing that was insanely evil I would be fine with that. For years I was a dealer in locally sourced branded cocaine and there was not one death during that time not one. I specialized in victimless crime. In fact I specialized in the atomization of crime to the point where almost no one committed an actual offense under law. Do not misunderstand me I do not propose you believe I am a good guy and in fact I am here to suggest you be complicit in quite a lot of murders and you will hate this evening forever but I guess—I guess I want you to know I am not some guy who just lives to murderize people in outré ways. That is a response to my environment like there are some breeds of amphibian which are insanely toxic that is me. I am not venomous I am poisonous. I will now pause so you can say I'm under arrest again."

"You're under arrest."

"I turned off your recording system. I'm here to talk not hand you my ass in a bouquet and now I'm thinking of an ass bouquet, thank you so much by the way. Send someone to the Black House please."

"What?"

"Send a cop to the Black House."

"That is a territorial violation—"

"Hannah. They only have to look through a window."

I don't know what she sees in my face but she gets on the phone and says something and it's happening. We sit and eat salami and drink more schnapps. It is the kind that is made with plums. The Swiss word for it means small plum. The plum is not all that small and it has muscles.

A few minutes later she gets the pictures on her phone and I wait while she looks at them. I see the color go out of her face and her lips get very tight.

"Hannah," I say, "I am going to happen to the guys who did this. I am very, very going to happen to them indeed. I would like to talk to you about that. And then I will go away and whatever else I do I will not come here again."

She nods once, sharp, and pours the schnapps.

It is almost morning when I leave Hannah's apartment and no we do not have sex what is wrong with you? But all the same, I have been out late so it is just natural that I go and buy another cigar. I walk through the empty streets to the cigar shop and wait on the doorstep like a hobo, which they do not allow here, so I take care to stand like a rich party boy instead. Eventually the little guy comes and if he thinks it is weird that I am here before he opens he does not say so. If he can smell the schnapps he does not say that either. Instead he takes my money and he says is today the day. I ask him what I want to ask and I say that it is, and he does not say anything else.

The cigar has a weird orange tint woven into the paper and the tobacco smells almost like fresh water it is so pure. It is a vastly expensive cigar. I stand there and think for a while about tobacco and how strange it is that Switzerland is one of the last places in Europe where they still sort of go for it.

"You smell of death," the little guy says and I don't say anything because I do. He says: "More today even than before."

"I guess you would know. Caporal-Chef."

Little guy snorts and says yes, he would know.

Caporal-Chef in the legion back when and so they were all together and it was this little man's job to keep them alive and point them in the right direction. Hans Eiger and all his friends including Frankie Leclerc. Caporal-Chef Aaron from Addis, whose mother was Beta Israel, looking after the squad so white they gotta throw shade. Hashtag. Caporal-Chef Aaron who has a mezuzah on his door frame and family in Addis and Istanbul and Eilat and Eiger must walk past it without paying attention every single time he comes in.

He must know and yet he doesn't even consider it something that matters because he is an old white guy in an old white country and things have always been this way.

Little guy goes to the counter and into the baggie with the cigar he puts a single memory stick poking out the back half of a plastic cow. Figure there was at one time a front half also but it is gone now. I do not know because he does not supply any detail and he does not need to. It is a gift.

"Five minutes," he says.

I go down the street to a copier place like a business center and I use the computer there to do some very small mostly unimportant things to the file stored on the memory stick and then I take the little half a cow back to the tobacco shop and the little guy puts it back behind the counter.

Sometimes you don't have to pay a man or threaten him or anything at all he is just right there in life's window waiting for you to come and stand underneath, and when you know that, he can see that you know it, and then you are together in a kind of conspiracy forever that is deeper than friendship because it is about souls.

And usually it is what happens when a bad person or someone who is just flat out an asshole relies on the best person he knows to do something secret and important for him and little by little that good person who is his friend gets a sense of who he is friends with and then one day very quietly after a long long time, all he wants to do is punch that fucker in the head until you can see bone because good people are not weak people or even necessarily nice people they are just slower to get to where the rest of us are all the damn time and that is as good as souls get in this world.

I do not believe in those but even so I know this is true.

I know because Caporal-Chef Aaron—after all this time and coffee and not talking—just gave me Eiger's fail-safe code key and he knows that means Eiger is likely going to die. This is Eiger's super-secret system for designating an alternate if he is compromised. His death beeper in his watch or his pacemaker or whatever the shit it is sends a message to this little guy and the guy walks the memory stick to a lawyer's office and they put it into the system and authorize the new person and then and only then does anyone outside of Eiger and the little guy know who that is.

And this is the moment at which I kind of could just shut this all down because from now on the only thing between me and Eiger's bank is Eiger's heartbeat and if Volodya was here—

Well. He's not.

They say that in the end everyone dies alone but in pure mathematical terms I am bound to say I doubt that will be true in this case.

I go back to the pig farm and tell Charlie that Bruno is dead.

Charlie says "Oh."

I tell her to take a moment to appreciate the hugeness of the universe and all the many suns and the wide expanse of the mountains and the sky and the deep earth beneath us and she says yuh-huh she has done that.

I ask if she wants to kill a bunch of people and she says she is wondering what Giant Egg would do.

I tell her Giant Egg would appear and cause everyone to reassess their life choices.

Charlie says no that is Giant Egg and she is talking about the negative energy Giant Egg from the dimension of purest evil and I say I'm pretty sure that negative energy Giant Egg would do exactly the same thing because that is Giant Egg and she says yes that is quite true and then she says that she is not Giant Egg and she would very much like to murderize the shit out of a lot of bad guys now and I say that is fine and she says okay.

Lucille takes off his knife suit and sits there in his appalling undies and Charlie cries onto his chest hair until it is matted with snot and really I do not know what to say about that.

Rex makes comfort food. The comfort food is bad. It turns out Rex is great at eating and terrible at cooking and bad comfort food is not comforting at all.

Saul takes the bad food away and comes back with crispbreads and cheese. They are Swiss so they are amazing. Everyone eats rotted bovine lactation and compressed wheat.

Doc does not speak at all but I can feel her eyes the whole damn time and I look back and I tell her yes. On the HOMER board all the things in her page have little green ticks next to them except the security guy who has to be fresh. I go to the board and look at my page. I feel like a dick looking at Banjo Telemark's joke page while Charlie is weeping but there are jokes and there are jokes and this one has a great punchline. There are many many words on my page and little drawings and some helpful remarks from my people, which are not hugely helpful, and someone has drawn a forest of trees with male genitalia instead of fruit but even so it is possible to see that Banjo Telemark has bought or rented—

Two large bulldozers
Colored smoke (red green yellow blue brown)

Many tons of recyclable traditional copper cowbells
  (heavily oxidized)
Many tons of recyclable aluminum auto paneling from
  expensive consumer vehicles
Professional-grade pyrotechnics to a value of one
  hundred thousand francs (assorted pinks and
  purples, some gold scatter)
Ten 3,000-watt equivalent searchlights with generator
  systems for exciting nighttime displays
A concert sound system of epic loudness I do not even
  know how many zoinks or wallabies it emits and I
  do not care it is too loud.

And most of these have been delivered to the Kircheisen Festung although Hans Eiger has been in particular very grouchy
about the heavier items which he says cannot be transported
using his precious itty-bitty cable car they are too heavy so
they are waiting on the valley floor while Inge Desirée runs
around yelling. I am sure everyone is having a great old time
indeed.

Rex now is sitting alongside Charlie and Lucille, and he is
saying something that makes her laugh through the snot.

Good for Rex he is a good human.

I go to Doc and tell her she will not like what happens next
and she takes me into our room and pointedly has sex with me
and then says that she did in fact like what happened next. I
say obviously not that and she says if I do not control a given
outcome I should not make statements about it. I say okay and
bearing that in mind I go out again and I go to a phone booth
and call François Leclerc.

———

"We have nothing to talk about Mr. Price."

I tell him what we have to talk about and he says he will send a car. I say that I am not getting in his nasty Franco-Belgian ethnosupremacist automobile because number one I do not ride with the enemy and number two more important that is getting taken to a second location at which point he will ethno-supremely torture the shit out of me until I die and I am not at home to that idea. At. All.

"Then we cannot talk Mr. Price because certainly we cannot talk on the phone."

I could tell him that if he had proper VoIP secure calling from Poltergeist we could talk on the phone like FOR HOURS and all they would know in the many many rooms where such things are intercepted was that dot A and dot B were maybe sexting maybe plotting the end of human civilization. But he cannot have proper VoIP secure calling from Poltergeist because the anarchokobolds who make this happen think he is an asshole.

Instead I tell him where to meet me and I pretend I am bringing someone along to watch my back.

ELEVEN

USED TO BE THE BÄRENGRABEN WERE ACTUAL GRABEN, which is to say pits. There were three of them like circular stone holes in the ground each maybe fifteen meters across and dressed with sad little tree stumps and scratching posts. You went to a kiosk and you bought figs and threw them to the bears in the bottom of the pit and they would stand up and dance for you. You also could buy carrots and the bears would dance also for carrots but not with much enthusiasm because who wants a fucking carrot when you can have figs? I do not know what the interior accommodations looked like but I am guessing they were not the ursine Ritz either. The whole thing looked like medieval because it was medieval it was a reminder of the honored past but a few years back the cantonal government took a long look at itself and decided that actual bear pits were not how you honored your heraldic animal in the era of climate change and Miley Cyrus, so they built a garden for bears, which is like a terraced park with panoramic views on the far side of the river from the old site. It is wide and public and there is absolutely no way anyone can know they are not in the cross-hairs of a Dragunov. I am pretty sure I am in the crosshairs of one thing or another but I am used to that. Professional soldiers have rules about not getting into those situations so I am guessing Frankie Leclerc is not loving sitting in row three with a bucket of mineral-enriched bear kibble, which is what the bears get now instead of figs.

I guess some you win some you lose.

I can see some of the G-Wagen guys dotted around the viewing platform and they have little scratches and boo-boos from all the flying glass of their kidnap attempt the other day and I am guessing they are real sore that they got dinged up and a bunch of their buddies got arrested or shot to death by Swiss grocers with automatic weapons training. I guess they probably also do not love having to feed the bears instead of break me in half so I feed the bears a bit.

Then I sit down and say "hi" and Leclerc says we have nothing to talk about.

"Yeah we do."

"I think not."

"Then why are you here?"

"Perhaps I just like to see the dawning acknowledgment of death."

". . . Wow that is some fucking Gitanes black polo *Jules et Jim* gangsterism right there. Excuse me while I get my chessboard out."

"You are a tedious man Mr. Price. Offer me your deal."

I think about it. I think about the job and about Volodya and about my people.

The people who are mine.

And I do not tell him to shove it up his Arc de coq au vin. I give him what he wants as if I'm out of my depth. I let him see all my doubts.

Then I swallow the urge to puke or rip his face off and I make a deal—I make a solemnly binding vow—with François Leclerc.

After that I call Mozart and I tell her I'm sorry I haven't been in touch. Mozart says she's sorry too. I say why is she sorry and she says she has accidentally posted the security footage of me peeing on her plane on G-Bread so now all the low-to-mid-brow criminals in the world have seen my junk.

". . . Sure why not. Put me on speaker."

"You do not give me orders Jack. Plus your lady friend here is a drag she cries all the time and when she is not crying she yells bad words in Italian."

"You have fifteen million euros you can retire with that why are you still here?"

"I dunno asshat why are you still here?"

"To fuck some guys up who are assholes and make even more than that doing it plus also I'm gonna be faaaaamous. You wanna do that too?"

"Speaker on man."

"Flavia? Can you hear me?"

So here we are at last. Banjo's event is due and there's nothing left to do and when that happens you don't wait. You go. It all comes together now or it falls apart.

Incoming VoIP call Solidcrypt. Accept: y/n?

y

Doc says:

"I'm at the Nordwandhüs."

This is the name of the house where the security guard she has nominated to be her personal-entry key card lives. In Kircheisen, houses do not generally have numbers they just have names because it is small and totally picturesque. In fact, it is too much to say this guy will be her key card because although she considered bribing him, in fact, she assessed that way of doing things as being too high risk unless he was also unconscious, and in the end why would you pay a guy to be unconscious while you rob a bank? So he will not so much be a key card as he will be a key eyeball that she will carry around sedated because the machine can tell if the eyeball is not connected to a viable heart and if you have just ripped it out the doors will not open they are persnickety that way.

Doc says:

"It's time."

TWELVE

I AM HAPPY IN MY WORKING ENVIRONMENT and my professional role so I sing:

"Well I walked in / and she got up—I saw her draw / and I raised my cup—I looked right down that baaaaaarrel and I knewwwww—We'd be married and in bed / before that night was through—"

"Holy shinola boss what the crap is that appalling nu-country what—"

"It is my mojo song Charlie I am mojoing right now—"

"Who is the singer that is just shocking—"

"It is me singing Charlie me personally right this minute in the cable car I am singing my little song—"

"Well please do not anymore because it is very very awful—"

"MY SONG IS A GREAT SONG OF THE GREATEST SONGS—"

"Anyone gonna back me up here? I know you are all feeling it—"

"The song is horrible Charlie we all know that but he is making art it is his process."

". . ."

". . ."

"His process is horrible."

"Yes it is also flat but it is his process."

"Is it like a digestive process?"

". . ."

". . ."

"Everyone is mocking me Saul. Charlie is mocking me Doc is mocking me. Even Lucille is mocking me with his eyes I can tell. Even Rex et tu Rex. Saul . . . kill everyone. Save the last bullet for me."

"No sir."

". . . Well that is just dandy I am being mocked and no one will do anything about it not even my hireling minion."

"I'm not a minion."

"But—"

"Nope. Do not minion. Non miniono. Ne minionibus meum."

"You made those up."

"Yep. No minion, no language lessons."

". . ."

". . ."

"Fine then I am good with that cool cool onward and upward ahem ahem:

> I looked up and / all I saw was black—
> Her hair was long / her nails were red all
>   down my back—
> I felt the coldest metal onnnn my
>   brrrooooooowwwwww—
> I fell for her and how I fell oooooohhhh
>   hoooowwwww—"

"O God fuck boss lady I think I will die before we get there—"

"Silence I am making art—"

"SHUT UP—"

"BOTH OF YOU—"

"ROINK!"

"Whut—"

"What now—"

"Was that a—"

"Shush now please you are upsetting the pig."

". . ."

". . ."

". . ."

". . ."

". . ."

"Is there a pig in that bag?"

"Yes there was a slight issue in our final item for which obviously I had also prepared but still I do not wish to discuss it. It is all fine now."

"I think maybe we need to discuss it just a little—"

So the slight issue goes a bit like this I do not know I was not at the Nordwandhüs:

Doc: "Knock knock man in house on day off we are Girl Scouts selling cookies."

Target: "I am suspicious that is my job I am in security at a vaulty bank kindsa place."

Doc: "Knock knock we shall sing for you we are you know undangerous females of conceptual virginity we are from the church we do not wish to kidnap you for immoral robbing purposes AT ALL this is pastoral cookie vending."

Target: "You seem a little old for girl scouts also which church?"

Doc: "The totally religious one?"

Target: "Nope I am from the other one go away now strangers my suspicions are manly and erect."

Doc: "Charlie show him how pure and girlish you are—"

Charlie: "I am pure and girlish open the fucking door—"

Lucille: "LUCILLE!"

Target: "CODE RED!"

Doc: "What the fuck is Lucille doing here in a dirndl—"

Charlie: "Helping?"

Doc: "I do not think that is what that is—"

Target: "CODE RED CODE RED CODE—"

The Neighborhood: "AAAAOOOOOGAH! FOREIGN INVASION BY SAVAGE FOREIGNS!"

Doc: "I hate fucking Switzerland—"

Lucille: "LUCILLE!"

Charlie: "OPEN THE FUCKING DOOR OR I WILL BLOW YOUR FUCKING FOOT OFF—"

Target: "I FEAR NOTHING—"

Charlie: "Kewl pew pew pew—"

Doc: "Nooooooooooooo—"

Target: "O gosh"

Doc: —oooOOOooOOoooo—

Charlie: "Pew pew PEW oh wait unpew unpew OH ALAS that does not work entropy—"

Target: "I can see God now he is calling me—"

Charlie: "Oopla?"

Doc: "Ooooo that should have an exclamation point and yet now it feels inappropriately delayed to the point of otiosity DID I NOT express myself with perfect clarity?"

Target: "I am dying of death and also bullets—"

Doc: "CHARLIE WAS I NOT CLEAR?"

Charlie: "Uh no?"

Doc: ". . ."

Charlie: "Yeah okay busted sorry Doc."

Doc: "Shut up and get me the pig. And you Lucille—give me your sharpest fucking knife off that suit or you and I will have words and you will not like them I will make you cold sober and sane in half an hour and then I will fuck your shit up like Price cannot even imagine do you hear me?"

Lucille: "Knife for Doc lady yup yup yup sure."

Doc: "Damn straight knife and now where is my emergency kit we are doing this. And you assholes you GLOVE THE FUCK UP MOFOS THIS IS EVIL SCIENCE TIME YOU ARE NURSES NOW BWAHAHAHA."

Doc says that she is in no way that sort of outlaw scientist and she does not ever bwahahah but who are you going to believe here?

"Wait Doc so we do not have a guy to open the doors?"

"Were you not listening, of course not, Charlie shot him in the neck he is extinct—"

"I was AIMING for his foot I do not know how—"

"Well that is not good—"

"What we have is in many ways better we have a pig with a man's eyeball stitched in to its head whacked-up on veterinary painkillers so that she is high as a weather balloon. So long as you do not sing, the system will read her transplanted eye as a happy human, so long as we can get her to the reader. She is not ideally proportioned for retinal scans."

". . ."

". . ."

". . . Charlie is that how it went down for reals?"

"Boss I can still smell pig blood and hear the sound of the saw do not make me answer that."

". . ."

". . ."

". . ."

"All right let's rob this fucker."

"Amen."

And indeed it is time. Inge Desirée has sent a car and the Hermès lady to conduct me to the plateau this evening. I believe we will be the first bank robbers to be VIP chauffeured to their mark although this is hard to prove, as obviously we bank robbists do not much get to compare notes except in jail and I do not go there.

Also criminals, man, they lie all the time it is a thing with them.

Sit in the back of the limo with Doc and smell the leather. Lean over and smell Doc: her neck and her hair. This is a mammal thing and it is important. It is important when you do crimes that may kill you to remember that you are alive.

And it is important when you are going to kill people to remember the same thing so that you do not hesitate.

Driver's name is Pierre. Pierre has many opinions about art. Charlie talks to him about them.

In the truck behind, Rex brings our gear with Lucille and Saul. I cannot imagine what they are talking about but it is almost certainly country and western related. No one knows what the pig is thinking she is in the back. Rex made her a little seat belt.

Rex is a rock, man.

We get to the cable car station. There is not room for Hermès lady so we ride by ourselves in the bubble car. Little armored bubble going up into the evening. Look along the valley to the lights of the city. Look back and see the night coming.

I smell Doc's hair again.

Little cable car comes up over the rise and settles in the cradle. The Kircheisen plateau is very pretty in the almost dark and there are paper lanterns swinging in the breeze. It's cold of course but there are braziers and fires and wurst stands and people milling about with phones and so on about three hundred people it's a huge draw with plenty of press. There are artworks freestanding and board walls with pictures hanging on them sheltered under little awnings and a huge space in the middle for BANJO TELEMARK'S EVENT and—yes—there is a bulldozer right there in the middle and a throne like for bad guys. I have no idea how they got it up here maybe a helicopter that is just amazing I am SO flattered. I honestly have no idea what to do with it and that is fine that is everyone else's problem now. There is my playlist playing super-duper loud and people are dancing the very white dance of central European intelligentsia. It is somewhat like bad salsa and somewhat like a guy checking his shoes for gum. I have seen the Swiss dancing when they mean it and this is not it, but this is like a kind of exploratory thing where they make a note of who is prepared to really go for it and who is judging.

Next to the bulldozers there are steel plates from a train which I bought by accident when I was buying junk. They are heavy and enormous and I have had them stacked like playing cards and there are kids hiding and seeking underneath. This is totally safe because they are locked in place by their own vast mass. Inorite? I am the face of responsible crime. And that over there, that is some kind of bioplastic moss substrate that they use here to make helipads or something I got a bunch of it free with the bulldozer. There are a few cowbells and some door pancls but not a fraction of what I paid for in a little circle.

Look at all this glorious crap in a stack man it is INSPIR-ING what people will do to facilitate popular art and if you also give them money.

I mean I don't need it but it's definitely focusing the mind and you can bet Eiger's guys spent HOURS making sure there was no way to use it to crash the doors or whatever.

There isn't.

But that will have made it tougher for them and in the meantime everything Doc was doing just slid on by because I was right there

waving

my

junk.

Yeah I know I'm cheap.

Or maybe there actually was a way I could have done some-thing to the doors with all this I just didn't find it and they did or maybe they didn't and someone else will figure it out in the next twenty minutes and make it work. That would be hilarious.

But it won't happen because there will be other stuff hap-pening real soon now and it's gonna be hella distracting.

We get off the cable car and Saul waves and disappears like switching off a light. Guy steps into a shadow and he's just gone.

Mad skills is what he has and that is why I hired him.

We walk down to the plateau making nice all the way.

All the world is here very high very rich very society. Europe is here not just Switzerland and a few people from beyond it is that kind of party and somehow Banjo Telemark is at the center of it. There are other artists in little clumps and if I was really into this whole art thing it would bother me how much these guys hate me right now for coming out of nowhere and being the star of the show.

Not that a single one of them will admit to not having heard of me until last week. Hell no.

They cluster and wave. A meager little fuck in a robe thing puts out his hand Banjo hi hi it is Grover Linden we met in Auckland and of course of course Grover I love your work and now Grover is shiny and he will go back to his little clique to say I am a genius or maybe to laugh because I went for it and that does not matter at all.

None of it matters except the job. What happens next.

I'm going to change everything.

If it works.

In the meantime I am sophisti-fucking-qué up the wazoo.

I schmooze.

"Greetings!"

"Loved your Milan thing."

"Enchanté this is my manager Crianza Regatta enchanté."

"Saw your review you fuck I will cut you no I am joking of course hug me—"

Sophisti-fucking-qué. That is how I roll.

"I AM BANJO TELEMARK hallo hallo LOVE ME YES I AM YOUR GOD that is clearly a lie hello sir very nice to meet you THIS WORLD WILL END AND A NEW ONE WILL ARISE oh thank you no champagne just a juice of some sort would be—perfect—oh Madame Director such a pleasure is my equipment all in place—"

"Well some Banjo some I trust it will be acceptable we were not able to bring all of the scrap up to the plateau in time in fact I think perhaps half remains—"

"That is fine Madame Director that is perfect in fact the aspect of doubt the confusion PERFECT would you care to trigger the smoke?"

"What without announcing the EVENT Banjo people will—"

"Be confused? Miss the beginning?"

"Well—yes—"

"PRECISELY!"

"O o o yes the normal event parameters do not apply I see—"

"ROCK IT MADAME initiate this magnificence—"

And she does.

Purple smoke floods the plateau.

The fireworks start going off in all sorts of directions up above like a kind of air war and they are all pink and purple too and then the lanterns go dark as Rex trips the cutout, which means that the green clothes we are wearing all become remarkably hard to see.

All around, invisible, Saul has been dropping little doodads the size of croissants and all of these right now start hissing and letting off something Doc makes in a cauldron that she claims is an alembic but clearly that is a lie.

Ten seconds later people start to choke.

"OH BANJO THIS IS NOT GOOD AT ALL—"

"Trust me Madame Director you're gonna love it."

But I don't honestly think she will.

People are choking and now they are scared and they are looking at me and I am smiling. The smoke is harmless but Doc's brew is just a tiny bit caustic and right away everyone is assuming that the smoke is the issue because you can see

it. In fact the gas is not going to do anything worse than give
you a sore throat most especially on an open plateau but that
doesn't matter. The security team does not know that so they
will go with their existing protocol and they will put on their
gas masks. That is going to look absolutely motherfucking terrifying to the guests and they will assume it is either a terror
attack or part of Banjo Telemark's amazing art and that will
make them considerably less biddable. Half of them will want
to get the fuck out and half of them will want to find the best
place to sit or test the limits of the scenario because: assholes.
So someone will make nasty and get smacked down and the
other guests will see that and that will take the whole is it a
game or is it real thing up a notch and that will happen more
and more as three more events occur, which are that they will
stop coughing because there's basically nothing wrong with
the smoke, and then the next round of fireworks will start and
then finally the security guys will start to fall over unconscious
because—

"Charlie you can say it now."

"I can really?"

"Yes Charlie but only once. Here have a microphone it will
be really loud."

Charlie says:

"I am root!"

But the sound system makes it loud enough to cause ava-
lanches. Plural. It sounds like a jet landing.

"I AM ROOOOOOT!"

And she is. She is indeed.

She is root. And what that means is that when the security
system booted up this morning it ordered everyone to replace
the filters in their gas masks and the little hockey-puck things
they put in were not like the ones they took out. Nooooo

indeed. The new hockey pucks were sleepy pucks. Now if you put on a gas mask you will be asleep in two minutes. Less if you are doing exercise at altitude.

Of course that is just the guys out here. The rest of the security team guys are inside and now they know there is something happening and they have been waiting for it. They are even a little bit excited about it because Hans Eiger has been recruiting tough guys from around the world and you know everyone likes to do what they love.

The battleship doors are open because the rest of the fair is inside. There are lanterns in here too and more art including this thing that looks like a giant spoon. There's a lifeguard's chair and a row of canvases with nothing on them except white paint and a row of boards made entirely of paint from which the canvas has been removed and—

We walk through the hall in silence between the arts. Many many arts. One of them is a figure in a big coat and Lucille immediately hugs it and there is a sound like metal on glass and the art collapses in on itself like Obi-Wan. Lucille looks down at the rubble and I swear he does that dog thing and scuffs his heels back on it a couple of times like yeah you had that coming art.

At the back of the hall there is an ordinary door with a keypad lock and Charlie blows through it in a half a second. Behind that there is a really nice office with high-energy modern furniture in orange and blue and a great view of the mountains. There's still fireworks going off outside and a lot of people are just watching the show and drinking politely because although all the security guys have collapsed well yeah OF COURSE

because they were promised ambiguous stuff and challenges to
their sense of personal security THAT IS ART.

Art in the round I guess.

Behind the giant stripped pine desk which has been handmade and still has bark on the edges there is an expensive
office chair and behind that there is the first of the real doors.
The first X8.

We move toward the inner door.

Doc nods to Rex.

Rex gets the pig out of the bag.

She's a very happy pig. You can tell she's seeing things pigs in
the normal context do not see. Art exhibits and fireworks are
not the half of it that pig is way stoned. Which is a good thing
because there's a weird line stitched around her eye socket and
a blue human eye staring out at the world from what looks
to be an extensively adjusted skullhole possibly including a
rubberized Ping-Pong ball clip. If she was not way stoned, she
would almost certainly be screaming and that is not anything
you ever want to hear. She also weighs maybe fifty kilos, which
makes her in pig terms a tiddler, but it's also not nothing and
Rex grunts a bit as he lifts her face to the retinal scanner. The
X8 hisses a little as he steps into close proximity and a red light
comes on.

SYSTEM ARMED.

Rex lifts her face onto the scan plate.

The pig's eyes close very gently and she starts to snore.

RETINA NOT FOUND. SYSTEM ARMED.

Doc says: "O for shit's sake take the pig away for a second—"

She sticks a needle in the pig's ass.

ROINK!

PROXIMITY UNAUTHORIZED. SYSTEM ENGAGED. TEN. NINE.

"Doc this door is not a good door. It is a mean door."

"Put the pig back please Rex."

SCANNING . . . SCANNING . . .

ACCEPTED.

The X8 makes a disappointed noise and opens.

Good door.

Saul appears out of nowhere and the pig goggles at him like oooooooh magic. The rest of us jump a little because there just wasn't anyone in that corner there was not. He steps through the door without making any noise and everyone waits for sounds like kung fu in the movies and those sounds do not come.

Do not come.

Do not.

Saul waves us through the door.

Silence. And you have not heard silence until you have heard it in a vault on a mountain. There is silence here even with the crump crump of fireworks and the yada yada of all the people there is silence here like you cannot get in a town. There is no traffic, no infrastructure, no whisper of humans. Just room tone and something underneath like thunder that is the waterfall in the heart of the mountain going down most of a kilometer into places you do not ever want to see.

Down down in the deeps down and deeper into the wet black hell.

There are no guards in the corridor and none in the atrium. Maybe they were all out among the crowd. Maybe they are holed up waiting to ambush us. Maybe something else.

Maybe something bad.

Saul does not whisper and he does not really talk it is a special inside voice for commandos he says:

"Clear no contact."

But I can tell he is not real relaxed about that. Because according to Doc's plan there should be contact. If not now, then soon.

On to door number two.

Eiger's fortress is a maze of corridors which double back around U-bend corners and duck under and over one another so that you don't know where you are or which way you came in but Doc and Charlie have sucked the map right out of the system so they know that there are secret lines drawn on the floor in secret magic ink, apparently it is ultraviolet but that is magic. We follow the lines in and on and in and all the time hearing the thrumming from under us, which is the mountain singing to the deep deep hole in the earth and all the time waiting for soldiers to appear and they don't and they don't and that just makes it worse. The pig unlocks doors for us like she's getting into it now. Rex carries her and sometimes I carry her and then we get to a door and Charlie gives some kind of code response and then we have like a minute to do the scan before the X8 gets pissy and fires shotguns or electricity or whatever and the pig is like ooooooooooh shiny red dot oooh and she makes little pig sexy noises and opens the doors.

One.

Two.

Three layers in and now we are at the water room.

Charlie plugs a thing into the thing and says go and we go into the air lock. I think it is the worst thing I have ever had to do like going into a submarine knowing there is no submarine.

The pig and I are at one on this. She is not digging the water room.

The worst part of Doc's plan is the water room. It's com-

pletely dark and you go into it in this steel bubble thing and
you can hear the sound of the thing that is under you churning
and thrashing and there is a kind of vertigo that I have never
had before that happens when you know there is a current and
a stud wall and if you fall through it you will die of crushing.

It will be fine.

We get into the air lock and there are suits and they are
slightly awesome. Like they are plug-and-play suits. Like you
stand on the shoes and fall backward into them and the suit
closes over your tummy and then there is a helmet that you put
on and blam you are like an action figure.

The pig we have to kinda improvise. We feed her in and the
suit folds up around her and her head is in the helmet. Moving
in the suit in air is like lifting weights it is hard. The pig does
not approve of this situation she feels constrained and unpig
and she does not like that so she craps in the suit. The suit tells
Charlie the pig has crapped in it. The suit evidently does not
like the pig so now no one is happy.

This is hilarious so I laugh.

Inside my suit laughing sounds like a horror movie. It is
loud and close and nervous.

I do not laugh inside my suit anymore.

I turn on the comms channel and say: "Online."

Everyone else says online too so Charlie tags the machine
and the water starts to pour in.

Over.

My.

Head.

For some reason the protocol at this point means that all the
lights go out in the air lock. Now I am in the dark in a prison
suit with a million tons of mountain over my head and a bajil-

lion tons of water going down down to the black hell and it is dark and—

Charlie says: "Lights."

And the suits all have lights on them and they come on so now we are in a tiny room filling up with ice water robbing a bank and we have no guns because it is water. I mean Saul obviously has a water bag for guns to go in but they will not work until we are dry again.

Doc says: "Excellent."

I love her so much right now. Of course it is excellent. Everything is going perfectly. We are in the belly of the beast and that is where we belong. We did everything to get here this is the thing we are IN THE MOUNTAIN hallelujah.

The pig gets her snout on the chin switch and starts to scream and our comms are just all screaming pig.

EEEEEEEeeeeEEEEEEEEeeee . . .

The door opens into the water room and Charlie touches the door panel.

"Magnetic system is off," Charlie says.

(EEEeeeeEEEeeeeeEEEEEEAAAAA)

I lift my foot and it takes a long, long time and then I am almost falling forward because it is so heavy.

"SHIT—"

TLUNK CLUTTER TBONKLE

Strong hands on my arm—Saul and Charlie. She touches her faceplate against mine.

"You okay there boss?"

"I have never moonwalked before."

"Yeah it is not moonwalking it's like giant walking you got to think like you're a huge badly rheumatic elephant."

"And you know this because—"

"Because video games boss, virtual life is real life now."

". . ."

"Yeah okay Saul told me. Come on boss let's go."

So we walk out into the water room.

We are halfway across when the water starts to move.

The water room is like the size of a tennis court and it has rough-cut walls and a simple screed floor and lines that fluoresce in the suit lights to show you the way. You walk and you walk and you get to the other side.

We get halfway across when the water starts to move like to flow like a current like an undertow like a ghost in a movie is clawing at you clawing pulling grasping and getting stronger the more you are afraid.

In the water room there is no current because the stiff metal grilles at either end have basically only pinprick-size holes in but now that is changing. The grilles are opening.

Eiger's fucking mountain has a fucking sneaky fail-safe trap we did not find if you do not do something dance the fucking fandango tra la la la la then after the magnetic system is switched off the grilles come down and purge the room, which means us.

Us going down into the hole.

Everyone starts to move really fast. Like really really fast. But also really slowly because we are in huge moon suits weighing tons and the water is flowing across and if you fall you are going. Down. Down down.

Down.

Into the hole.

It is open behind me.

The darkest mouth I have ever seen.

I walk like heave stomp heave stomp like push push push and I am sweating inside the suit and I do not look to see who else is walking I do not look to make sure anyone else is walking at all perhaps they have all fallen and they are already gone.

If you slip if you fall you are going—

I am going—

Any of us is going down.

Into the hole.

Heave stomp heave stomp head down push. Push as hard as you can. Push or die is what.

I walk and I remember that I dreamed that the Demons would bury me in the ground and water would come up over my head and here I am I am a little bit psychic.

There's not enough air now in the suit. Or rather there is but it doesn't feel like there is because I am running against the flow of water that wants to wash me over on the left side and take me down the hole.

Silence and rushing water and the sound of the deep down there and the clank of my own feet on the screed and the sound of my own breathing.

One foot in front of the other. One foot—

Something hits me hard in the side. I am moving forwards so it bounces off and goes round me but I skid—I actually skid on the screed—and I realize it is a suit. A suit which has come unstuck and now is flying or I guess rolling towards the—

A suit which rolls past me picking up speed and—

Fuck I hope that is the pig.

Of course it's the pig the pig is an asshole there is no way it can do this no way anyone could hold on to it in this current and obviously that presents difficulties but one problem at a time so sure it's the pig and that's bad but—

God let it be the—

I almost turn and if I turn I'm going to slip and then you

know it won't really matter to me anymore whether it's the pig or not because it will also be me so I—

Don't look—

Just walk on. No point anyway you can't help. No time. If you go back the grilles will open completely and you will die.

I wonder if it's Doc. Or Saul that would be ironic that guy is super good at all the physical things.

I don't think about it.

I hear the tumbling suit scrape along the ground toward the grille and then I hear it reach the opening and stick and I do not look round.

The sound of the water is really loud so the suit must have been really heavy or maybe someone was trying to grip onto the floor.

Heave stomp heave stomp.

Heave stomp heave.

Stomp.

Stomp.

Stomp.

I am at the far door and it is open onto the air lock and I step through and I look round.

I see the suit hanging there on the edge of the drop and I see Charlie working at the console to close the grille and I see the grille start to move and I hear the sound of the suit scratching its way past the closing grille and I can actually watch it just—just—

—vanish—

and then I look back into the air lock and there are six suits and one of them one of them is on all fours on the floor and I know if I look though the faceplate and I see the pig that means someone someone one of my people—

I look through the faceplate and see Doc's face very pale but she is not a pig.

The door shuts.

Charlie cycles the air lock and we shed the suits.

Doc.

Charlie.

Saul.

Lucille.

Me.

And the pig.

One two three four five.

Once I caught a pig alive.

Six seven eight nine ten no there were only fiiiive then.

One two three four five.

One two three four five.

And a—

One.

Two.

Three.

Four.

FUCK.

Again and again but it doesn't matter how many times I count.

One of us is still the pig.

Rex's mother lives in a place called Gullit I do not know why it is called that. She is not that old because she had Rex and Billy real young and in fact likely someone oughta be in jail over that. She has a nice car and a big house in Gullit and her boys are the light of her life or they were right up until Fred killed

Billy for no good reason at all and now Rex is gone too and the common factor in these events is me.

People make choices you cannot stop them and you cannot take responsibility for those choices but likewise you got to recognize where your own momentum pushes someone along a new track and that is a thing that I do.

Rex was here because of me and now Rex is not here anymore.

Please do not get the idea that Rex will climb back out of the pit at a salient moment and save the day that happens in films sure but right now Rex has gone somewhere there is no coming back from. When you fuck up in the mountains there are not second chances and that goes double for water under the mountains just—

But we still have the pig so we can open the door and get to the vault section.

SCANNING—

Click.

The X8 swings back.

We're through.

We're alive.

And we're going to win this fucker.

There is a noise like really slow popcorn.

Hans Eiger is standing in the room beyond.

He is clapping.

It's a big room on two levels like an aircraft hangar and Eiger is on a kind of gantry in front of what can only be the final door. He has his guys around the place: lots of men in suits with him and they have many guns. You do not need many guns in this situation but they have them anyway. Eiger and his guys and some extras who are obviously G-Wagen men and yes, a little *Sound of Music*–looking motherfucker standing on a chair behind Eiger so he can get a decent view.

Clap clap clap.

Eiger is really loving this it matters to him. It is his win that he has always wanted. He has been tested and he has been found worthy by the bank robbery gods. He has beaten the Seven Demons.

Clap clap clap.

I wait for him to make a speech but he just keeps clapping until it is way past ironic or mocking he's just clapping like he does not know how to stop.

Clap clap clap.

Now everyone is looking at Eiger to see if he's okay and he is. He's fine. He's just—he's having too much fun now to stop. This is just the best moment of his adult life.

He beat us.

Legit.

Fair and square.

We beat his security system and we got into his head and onto his mountain but all the same, here, at the line, he won.

Fair and square.

Clap clap clap.

One of the G-Wagen guys says something fast in French: "You want us to kill them now?"

There is a version of this moment where we dialogue as dueling bad guys should and Eiger is totally up for that. I can see him shaping up to it like moohoohaha like so:

"I have raised the canton against you Mr. Price. You have done well to get this far into Die Festung and I am quite honestly impressed, but here it ends. Even if you should overcome these men, which you will not, you cannot escape. Your exit would be a running gun battle from here to—"

And Doc could maybe tell him she is wearing a phial of modified respiratory transmission hantavirus or I could say something about something but—

But none of that happens because Hans Eiger has crossed a line. Volodya told me that Swissness was a thing but I did not get it until I came here. You cannot get it from outside. Now I do and the thing is that sometimes it's easier to see the landscape when you don't have a house there. Hans Eiger does not realize it because as far as he is concerned people like him are the fountain, or wellspring, his national identity, but Swissness is a way of being, not something you just are. He has crossed a line in the Swiss. He brought anti-social Nazis into the federal capital and in the end—despite all this country's bad moments and sometimes regrettable choices, which let us be honest it shares with every other country in the world—there is nothing anywhere that is more fundamentally un-Swiss than a fucking Nazi. If you're going to Nazi about the place in a serious way, well, you may as well get your chicken out and fuck it right there on the Junkerngasse.

Eiger stops clapping and looks at us like he's fixing this moment in his head forever.

He says: "Ja."

Or he tries to.

But he can't because a wide, fat metal blade has just gone into the space between two of the vertebrae in his neck and severed his spine.

Eiger folds downward, taking the oyster knife with him. Behind him in the silence Evil Hansel looks pale and tiny.

Doc says:

"Price, you total fuck."

I say:

"The Demons have a new client Doc."

The sound of the first gunshot is really loud.

In a very real sense Hans Eiger was killed in 1976 by a guy called Joe Johnston. His boss came and asked him to design the thing that ultimately did the job and gave him four weeks and he sweated blood and got it done and finally it just dropped in my lap and I sent it where it was meant to go. That is one way of looking at it.

The other is that once upon a time there was a little kid whose grandfather was secretly an evil wizard. The little kid was totally in love with his grandfather and he wanted to be an evil wizard too when he grew up. He spent his young life copying his grandfather in every way he possibly could and developing his evil wizard powers so that one day he would be able to just become that old guy. Completely become him.

But a bunch of things happened along the way as things will do. The first thing that happened was that the kid became enamored of a sort of a romantic idea in a movie that he saw and when he compared that movie with the real world he came to certain conclusions about who was cool and who was not and Nazis very specifically were not. Furthermore the old man taught him to be Swiss, and while Switzerland is a long way from perfect and the banking community didn't one hundred percent or indeed really even fifty percent cover itself in glory in the twentieth century, in terms of right now this moment today there is very little that is less Swiss than a Nazi. Among many other flaws and failings such as being Nazis generally, Nazis are exactly the kinds of people who will fuck a chicken in public. And that is what Hans Eiger did when he started a gun fight in the capital of his own country for financial reasons. And when I called Evil Hansel a Nazi, the little psycho experienced what I guess is an epiphany or whatever that is one of those things kids go through.

Love turned to hate all at once and no one—no one—hates like a nine-year-old betrayed.

No one.

The second thing that happened was that Joe Johnstone and Ole Kirk Christiansen got together, at least spiritually. Joe was the designer on a popular movie you may have heard of named *Star Wars* and Ole was the guy who invented Lego, and in these great modern days it is possible to make a 1:1 model of the *Millennium Falcon* out of tiny plastic bricks. The schematic was created by a team of Danish enthusiasts who inevitably know Mr. Friday, and the model requires a total of thirteen million seven hundred and eighty-nine thousand eight hundred and twenty-one Lego pieces and costs a little over three million Swiss francs because there's no bulk discount although delivery on orders over seventy-five francs is free so there's that. There is a great deal of debate in the giant construction nerd community (which is global and very large) about the precise Pantone for the seat covers but by and large the end product is thought to be acceptable and the kid whom we have hereto known as Evil Hansel asked his grandfather for one and Hans Eiger said: Are you out of your tiny homicidal mind, and junior said no I am not this is a thing that I must do to become a man, and senior said work on your knife throwing and then we shall see, and then Hans Eiger went away and told all his man friends of this hilarious request and Evil Hansel was shamed.

People I tell you do not shame the pre-tween assassin you

have made it is a bad plan because then when it turns out you fucked a chicken in a public place . . . Why then su Hansel mi Hansel, if you get my drift.

So a little while back I went to the arcade and we blew up the Death Star together I said to Evil Hansel given all that I had made him cry by calling him a Nazi and given his grandfather was right now up to his ballsack in French Nazis and that must be causing some nine-year-old cognitive dissonance and from that trap there is really only one way out: how about he would kill his grandfather in the back of the head with an oyster knife and he said:

"I cannot give you what you want."

And I said that is fine because I do not want you to give it to me, I wish to pay for it or if you find that mercenary you will give it to me as a present and I will give you a present of equal scale just name your present.

And when I said present like that I saw it in his eyes.

So Evil Hansel named his price and I did not laugh because I am not a motherfucking snob I am a professional I said yes I will get you one of those and we will call that a down payment and then I will also put much money into an offshore account and all that shit. Evil Hansel said why? And I said because one day kid you're gonna be doing my job that is fucking inevitable and I would very much like for that day to be a happy one for both of us. There has been too much of that shit where we have to assassinate our forefathers to get on up and he said obviously excepting my grandfather obviously and I said yeah obviously that.

Hans Eiger falls to the floor and I can see that he knows what has happened and some kind of why and it hurts more than dying.

So that's one down and two to go.

As like a contractual rider on my deal with Evil Hansel I had to tell him I was going to cut a deal with François Leclerc too or I could not depend on his reaction in the moment. He didn't like it much but he said his emotional distress was covered under the original deal and I said that was real professional and threw in a trip to the studio experience as an ex gratia.

So then later I go meet Frankie Leclerc in the Bear Gardens and I say:

"You want that billion in emeralds without a leash, François? Because I will give you that."

"You cannot."

"That is not a no."

So we have lunch.

Yeah we have lunch in a little place down by the river. Me and the modern-day Nazi.

I eat Galgenspieß with Frankie Leclerc. Frankie is not a good man. He hurts people for ideological reasons and his ideology is a bunch of racist puke. This is what it means to be first of the Seven Demons. You eat mixed grilled meats on a spiked gibbet that looks like a gallows with a guy like that.

With rice and spiced fruit, which is double crap because it's really better with frites.

We eat lunch and we come to a deal. I take out Eiger, Leclerc will handle the guard team and then walk. He gets the emeralds. We get whatever. That is the extent of our deal.

See, if you're a contractor you need a client, and after all Frankie was always Mr. Client. There's optics in this situation, I tell him, matters of perception. You do not want to be creating a perceptual issue not at all.

Demon makes a deal with the devil. Film at eleven.

It doesn't take very long for Leclerc's men to finish off Eiger's security men and they are not tender about it there is some splat and some splash. Evil Hansel watches the whole thing like it doesn't really mean very much and perhaps it doesn't. He looks at me for a while and I give him the nod: yes I remember the rest of the deal yes I will deliver. Yes there has been enough assassinating our forefathers now that is enough enough.

Because I mean really haven't enough people died today already?

Eiger's wristwatch glows in the dark as the system finally acknowledges what Eiger knew some minutes ago: he dead.

Message sent. Green light.

Back in Bern in the cigar shop the little guy gets the message. He gets up out of bed and he plugs the memory stick into his computer and sends the text file to the place he's supposed to send it and then he goes back to bed.

I wait a minute longer.

Then I put my hand on the final door and I say:

"Open sesame."

The door opens.

Doc says: "You fucked up my plan and you made your own plan for the fucking robbery."

"I did."

"You made a deal with fucking Leclerc."

"He was Mr. Client. He was always Mr. Client."

"You stepped on my work with this bullshit."

"I did. For reasons."

"When we are out of here I am going to fucking kill you Jack."

"You're going to be pissed with me but you will understand."

"Will I."

"Yeah."

"Do you think that will make it better or worse?"

And that is that for the bank. It is only a bank after all, the hard part is always people.

I mean, that is not all, that obviously we have to bring lots of watertight cases out of the vault and drive them in little golf buggies along the corridors back to the main entrance and then we get them down the mountain using the cable car just like Doc said we would. We bring a bunch of boxes for ourselves also with much diamonds and bonds and monies. More than three quarters of what is there we just cannot goddamn carry.

All the same we have robbed the bank just like we were contracted to do by Eiger and then when Eiger turned out to have betrayed us we found a new client and now we will split the take with the new client and that is the end of that job. It was not quiet I guess I mean people will know we were here, but since the quiet thing was Eiger's stipulation—

This is what winning looks like I guess.

Four Demons and a reserve go down the mountain in silence.

We don't talk about Rex, and Doc stands at the far end of the cable car and looks out at the night and does not speak.

Leclerc is waiting down in the valley and he is very polite. Very professional and content he has everything he wanted from this hire. He gets revenge and he gets to polish his bastard medals and be associated with a loud, splashy situation where he was wronged and the wronger is gone and he looks cool. His oh-so-modern Fascist cred will go up and he will no doubt recruit many disenfranchised European youths to his righteous cause that is bullshit but bullshit is the soul of politics. I read where he has strong support as a political hero in some parts of Hungary and Poland. He is like a Fascist Carlos the Jackal I guess and do not tell me that Carlos was okay really because he was not. There are assholes across politics sometimes you do deals with them.

Very sensible François does not try to betray us. Profile like this, moment like this, no telling how people would read that. Maverick behavior, unreliable behavior. Kind of thing gets you enemies you never even know about.

I tell him we will go and get our transport and that I trust him to look after our share. He says my trust is well placed. I say I know our trust is well placed. We do googly trust eyes of death at one another for a moment and then I go. My Demons come with me. There are two little bulldozers next to the cable car station and some earth-moving gear but all the recyclable junk is gone.

We go and get our great big container truck for moving stolen goods. It is parked in a container truck park.

We get to the truck.

Doc punches me in the face.

I go down because it is a good hit and Doc keeps going in on me and I realize she may not stop. She maybe just doesn't have limits like a normal person and she may just kill me. She's using her boots now and not like to make me sad. She is hurting me.

WHUD.

And then she picks the next angle like a surgeon if surgeons used blunt objects.

WHUD.

I guess.

WHUD.

This is the thing.

WHUD WHUD WHUD.

Evil medical science.

Evil medic.

Doesn't have human limits.

WHUD WHUD WHUDWHUDWHUDWHUD.

"Khhhfffshit Doc! DOC! KAhhffshit shit—"

WHUD

"GODDAMMIT JACK YOU ARE A FUCKING ASSHOLE—"

"I—"

WHUD WHUD WHUD

"REX IS DEAD AND YOU MADE A DEAL WITH LECLERC AND YOU DID NOT TELL ME"

WHUD WHUD

"YOU—"

WHUD

"DID NOT—"

WHUD

"TRUST ME TO DO MY JOB—"

WHUD

"Docc cc I cck—Doc?"

"YES BY ALL MEANS EXPLAIN IT TO ME"

"Yes ma'am can't"

WHUD

And then I know I am really in trouble when she stops.

Doc says:

"Explain. Yourself. Now. Because Jack I liked Rex and he trusted you and so did I so do you see where his fate and your decision not to tell me things I needed to know might affect our relationship going forward?"

This time she does not kick me or hit me. She just puts her hand on me. Just that. Like just the gentlest touch in this particular place on my skin. She puts—

Her fingers

All the way around my windpipe

So that they meet without breaking my skin.

I can feel the hole in my trachea pushing against the glue.

But most of all I can feel her fingers in a place they absolutely should not be and I know she can keep me still like this forever. I will do anything she says.

And then I realize I can't breathe.

"Doc—"

(Disgust.)

"Can't breathe—"

"Shit fuck fine."

I can't because I am bleeding into a lung somewhere. It has gone wrong and I wonder if she meant that. Did she mean that? I cannot talk. What am I if I can't talk? I'm just meat.

Doc looks at me and at the strange shape of my chest where her boot went and she spits and drives an empty hypo into my lower ribs like WHAM and I feel the lung reinflate and I start to say—

But by then I do not have to because there is a dog barking.

Doc says:

"Tycho?"

But it is not Tycho. Tycho is back home safe and that is not his bark. That bark belongs to Marta, who belongs to Mrs. Van der Zee.

She is just over there like a hundred meters back down the road maybe a bit more.

Because that is where the trail of aniseed leads. I had the kids from the Kircheisen school create a very distinct track from the Kircheisen Palast hotel.

So that is where she came to when she went out for her walk.

Because a dog like that will walk through fire for aniseed. It is like cocaine for them.

Doc says:

"O shit Price—"

Mrs. Van der Zee says:

"MARTA! MARTA WHERE ARE YOU?"

I look at Doc and I say it again:

"I got a new client Doc and she told me to make a horrible plan and I did. Eiger's gone down Doc there's just two left. The dog—I'm real sorry about the dog Doc."

"MARTA!" yells Mrs. Van der Zee. "MARTA WHERE ARE YOU O YOU ARE HERE YOU BAD GIRL WHAT ARE YOU DOING ALL THE WAY OVER HERE—"

She's so fast, the Doctor. So fast. I see her mind working and she's so amazingly fast. She's putting it all together because what else can Mrs. Van der Zee be doing here? In crime there are no coincidences and if Mrs. Van der Zee is here I have put her here and why would I do that? And she remembers emeralds and the smell on Evil Hansel at the art party and I see her get there without ever being told and I see her know what I have done.

But no one is fast enough to stop this now. Not even Doc. Not even if she wanted to, and deep down you know she does not. She wants to want to. But she's a Demon. There are matters pertaining. There is old business.

You cannot go around shooting our friends with long guns.

Volodya is dead.

And this is how that goes.

The ground is shaking.

The ground is shaking. Doc looks at me and even the fury is gone now, just resignation like she should have known this.

And she should. This is what she asked for.

"What have you done Price?"

I look up at the mountains. From the far side of the valley, a line of burning white lights ignites. Searchlights. Spotlights. Picking out the Kircheisen Festung so that it shines in the dark like a radiant heavenly city. Between the lights you can just make out a flat patch of early snow and Ottavio Leopold Calvanese sitting on a very expensive chair as if to watch his favorite TV show. It looks like Rex went with the balik and it's going down very well.

Ah shit Rex.

Shit.

"What have you done Price?"

"I took your contract Doc and delivery is due."

The ground is shaking like vibrating and up on the plateau I guess there's still a couple hundred people and the really smart ones right now are heading for the tree line and right now I guess Agent Hannah is telling the dumb ones to do the same and both of those groups are almost certainly going to live. The only fairly smart ones think Agent Hannah is wrong or evil and they are heading into the bank and those guys . . . yeah they're likely not gonna make it. Figure there's about thirty or forty of those.

Someone somewhere is calling in his helicopter to get him

the fuck out and what the outcome is for him largely depends on the timing and I got no control over that now.

This is going down.

I can't see it—in fact no one can see it except maybe Rex if he's lasted this long in his suit, and I like to think that he has, so let's say that's what's happening.

Rex fell down over the ledge into the dark and the suit kept him alive exactly this long and he knows—he knows, down there under all that water—that he is no way getting out and the only question is whether the suit fails or he runs out of air and that is a shitty way to go either way.

But he's not alone down there.

Down there under a bajillion tons of water at a squidzillion atmospheres there is a pile of boxes with a coffin on the top.

Volodya's coffin of course.

And under him well under Volodya there is a bunch of boxes of Swiss junk ground up really small to powder. And I mean really a lot.

About a hundred tons of it.

And I threw in some magnesium from the fireworks Rex bought, and Flavia—yeah that Flavia who was hanging with Mozart—Flavia gave me some Z-Vat so that whole thing is kinda stuffed up together in a giant spiderball.

Copper oxide.

Aluminum.

Magnesium.

That is a mixture I have mentioned at certain times in other contexts. It is volatile and it is not your friend unless you like having dangerous and exothermic friends.

Which I do.

So here is what Rex sees in this last moment:

He sees a burst of light like a white basketball made of fire is eating into a tea crate. And then the greedy aluminum starts ripping oxygen away from the copper and the copper is not giving it up easy no sir. Not at all. That copper is stubborn Swiss cow copper it has seen life and it has done its military service and it will not be fucked with but in the end well there are laws and it has to comply.

In the dark heart of the mountain there is a miniature sun.

That is the moment at which Rex unquestionably dies and you know he was a Demon and he dies in a literal blaze of glory so there is that.

Now I am absolutely an amateur at this explosives stuff and if I still had an explosives guy on my team, I'd have known not to do it with a hundred tons of the mixture but you know, man, that's what happens in the world, people just aren't there when you need them, right, I mean they just wander off or marry a stripper with neck-down volitional alopecia or they get swept away by a death trap in a bank robbery. I mean that is just how things are and when those things happen there are echoes in the world and sometimes the echoes are small and sad and sometimes they are really loud and that is just the butterfly effect is what.

Tragic onward consequences here is what I'm saying.

Motherfucking tragic.

Here is a given amount of water occupying a given amount of space and it has no easy exits. And here now in the heart of that tense yet balanced natural relationship of pressure, cold and stone is a ball of superhot exploding steam which is expanding really fast and really hard. Some of that pressure goes outward in a wave and bounces off the walls of the lake— that is to say basically off the European continental plate, which is big enough to take it—and rebounds inward to the point of origin. Above that point there is now a column of rising steam and bubbles frothing like extreme cappuccino-style up into the vertical pipe leading to the Kircheisen vaults. Up above it there is a great plug of cold water and that water falls downward through the steam, which loses heat and energy and compresses rapidly so that the whole load falls down hard in time with the compression wave. Everything arrives in the same place at the same time.

This time, pretty much all the force of the explosion goes up the pipe looking for a way out.

Which isn't there.

Because Hans Eiger's vault is fixed over the top.

It's the weakest point in the mountain so—

The Kircheisen Festung explodes.

We can see what happens perfectly because of the spotlights. The mountain crinkles like cooking foil and then a piece slips and slides off to the side. The rumble in the ground becomes a howl like the biggest bottle in the world being filled from a spigot. I can see people running and being blown clear off the edge of the mountain and then—

The metal frame of the vault rips out like a spaceship launching on a pillar of steam and screaming white fire.

For a moment it just hangs there in the air at the top of a shallow arc.

Present moment perfect moment: I have made a bank fly.

Some parts of the mountain come too although not a whole lot percentage wise and I would say not very many people from the plateau but that's kinda ballpark.

Agent Hannah will probably be fine.

The vault turns through ninety degrees in place just like a diver coming off the high board.

And then it falls.

Down.

Down.

Down the way you always imagine God will come when you're a kid and someone's shitty to you and he never does come.

Until now.

Down.

Down.

Down.

Onto the cable car station.

And two dozen French Nazis in a fleet of four-wheel-drive cars.

And an old Dutch lady who was very rich and smelled like cheap chocolates.

And a saluki called Marta who really did not deserve any of this.

Say one thing for German auto design say this: the vault does not actually crush them completely flat. There's like a five-inch gap between the metal base and the soil.

I do not imagine the same thing can be said for Mrs. Van der Zee's hat.

I look up across the valley at the man on his chair with his wine and I think I can see Ottavio Leopold Calvanese applauding in the empty night.

One less person in the world who wants to kill us, I guess that's good.

A moment later we hear the noise of the impact and that's all we hear for a while because it is very loud.

"I've done my job Doc."

Doctor Client I guess.

Now it's done.

Sorry Rex.

Sorry Volodya.

Sorry Evil Hansel because I put you somewhere you likely never wanted to be.

Sorry Marta I'm sure you were a good dog.

Sorry but I am not Banjo Telemark.

My name is Jack Price and I am the First of the Demons.

This is my art.

EPILOGUE

THE VAULT WAS REALLY WELL MADE I GUESS so most of the stuff in it was A-OK. We used one of the little bulldozers to load it up onto a freight container and Doc was all ready with the truck but Mozart landed her butt-ugly plane on the road right there with its vertical doohickey and we just loaded that up instead.

It's true that the Swiss Air Force doesn't fly at night.

The Italian one does, though, and they got the call to come fuck our shit up.

But by some chance that no one's really got to the bottom of, they were given the wrong coordinates by the dispatching officer, who definitely does not work even occasionally for Ottavio Leopold Calvanese that is slander.

So we just flew away and we left Fred's horrible enormous porno jet right there in the hangar and sold it later to a movie star.

I hear he was real freaked-out about the guy in the crate, we completely forgot about Sean, there was just so much going on but when you keep pets you have responsibilities, and that is my bad.

Agent Hannah got kicked out of Einsatzgruppe JONAS and she left the Swiss police.

I don't feel like that is entirely my bad but I am reasonably sure she does, so I think it is best if I don't call her.

We had a memorial for Rex and Volodya. We sang songs and ate ham. Doc did a genetic assay on it first and she promises there was absolutely no human content at all.

Elena Riccardi figured out what happened and she and her husband went on a cruise. She also left a very rude message on our answering service that is just uncalled for but I guess she has cause.

I asked Barton if he would like to be Banjo Telemark and he said yes. So now there really is a mega-rich insane modern artist running around the world doing fucked-up shit to people to remind them that nothing is real. I didn't want the job but I'm glad someone has it.

We have a subscription purchase of cigars from the little guy in Bern. One a week delivered to a standing address. I don't know why and nor does he and that is as it should be.

Life goes on.

Life does indeed go on but even so Doc was extremely pissed with me about the whole thing and she absolutely did punish me for it.

For weeks.

Which I do not remember at all.

And then when she was through with that I was not dead although now I have a tattoo of my own skeleton in black-light ink on my skin to remind me what will happen if I do it again.

But then we had a kind of a problem because now there were too many Demons.

Doc

Charlie

Saul

Lucille

Mozart

Flavia

Me

And a head on a stick.

I mean the Eight Demons that is nowhere. And Evil Hansel is kind of an intern or some shit and you cannot—Eight Demons And The Kid—I mean no.

And in fact I kind of fucked up our business model because between Sharkey and Eiger and Leclerc and blowing up a mountain, there is some doubt about whether anyone will ever hire us again. I mean it's not like we need the money or like anyone is gonna think we're a soft target after this. But still that is my bad.

And it is also fine because when you get hired you have to do deals with guys like Leclerc and really honestly: fuck those guys.

Headline:

OUTRAGE AT KIRCHEISEN

Criminal gangs target world's most secure bank . . . many casualties . . . Most Wanted . . .

"Seven Demons" believed to have been working with neo-Nazis and Italian Mob . . .

Respected community members flattened in explosion horror . . .

Dog survives owner—inherits fortune.

"Wait Charlie read that last bit again? You're fucking kidding me GO MARTA! Well now I totally feel like less of a monster I mean that's practically philanthropy."